MW01611952

DEPUTY

DATE DUE		
JUN 0 5 2019		
JUN 1 5 2019		
JUN 1 5 2019		
JUL 1 5 2019		
SEP 2 6 2019		
NOV 0 4 2019		

WITHDRAWN

Copyright © 2019 by Fickle Dragon Publishing

All rights reserved.

No part of this book may be reproduced in any form or by any electronic or mechanical means, including information storage and retrieval systems, without written permission from the author, except for the use of brief quotations in a book review.

❀ Created with Vellum

PREFACE

FREE DOWNLOAD

Sign up for my newsletter and receive a free Jamie McFarlane starter library.

To get started, please visit:

http://www.fickledragon.com

1 / STUCK

COLD RAIN PELTED the side of my face as I stared at the numbered door. The Sunshine Motel was a seedy affair with rooms that opened to the parking lot. The building provided little shelter as a gusty north wind attempted to knock me from my feet.

I raised my hand to knock. A profound sense of déjà vu filled me as my eyes fell on the corroded brass letters — 1C. Ever since leaving the Army, I'd felt adrift. I'd tried on more than a few different jobs and couldn't find one that fit. After chasing down skips for my uncle's bail bond business, I'd fallen into a job as a special investigator for Sutherland's District Attorney, which required me to enroll in and graduate from the police academy.

In the beginning, the job of special investigator sounded promising. For the last six months, I'd played my part as a rookie, dutifully following my training officer's instructions, issuing summons, talking to drunks, searching vehicles and intervening in domestic situations. Once trained, however, I was returned to the D.A. who rarely needed my services and I'd taken to supplementing my income with private investigator jobs.

The resignation letter in my back pocket seemed to burn against my butt. I wasn't a quitter – at least I didn't *want* to be one. The day I graduated from the academy had been one of the proudest of my grandfather's life and I hated disappointing him. I was grateful he wasn't here to see what I was giving up a cop's life for.

"Who is it?" a man asked from the other side of the door.

I held the stack of folded towels I'd pulled from a cart earlier in the day in front of the peep hole, obscuring his view. "Someone called for towels."

"We don't need any," he answered.

The curtains next to the door moved, spilling light onto the concrete walk. It was too dark for him to make out any details.

"Look, I'm getting soaked. The office said bring these down. Do you want 'em or not?" I asked.

"They going to cost me anything?" he asked. I heard a muffled woman's voice but couldn't make out what she said.

"No," I answered.

I heard a chain move and the door handle turned. A thickset man wearing a wife-beater and boxers opened the door. "Thanks," he said, taking the stack from me. "Now, beat it."

I tried to get a look into the room, but he filled the door nicely. I'd have to go with Plan B. "Are you driving a white 2012 Civic? There were a couple of kids messing with it a few minutes ago. I must have spooked 'em."

"Fuck! Ellen, give me your keys," he said, turning away from the door and setting down the towels.

Ellen Kreps, forty-two years old, mother of two, part-owner of a chain of car washes, stepped into view wearing a black nightgown. Her purse sat on the dresser opposite the bed. "I think I locked it," she said, panicking. "Did they break in?"

"I thought I saw some broken glass, but the kids are gone now," I said. I felt awkward seeing the woman in her night clothes which thankfully hid the important parts of her mom bod.

"Dammit. Where?" the man asked, sliding his shoes on but not bothering with pants. He pulled a gun from a drawer next to the bed.

A plastic baggie of what looked like crystal meth spilled out onto the floor. Alarms bells went off in my head. The night had just taken a sinister turn.

"Hey man, I don't want to get involved," I said, backing out of the door. The concealed camera, supplied by my best friend, Alan Snerdly, or Snert as friends called him, had captured everything. Ellen Kreps wasn't just stepping out on her husband. She was hooking up to feed a drug habit.

"You're in it now, buddy," the man growled, turning his gun toward me. "I don't believe in coincidences."

"Jeff, let him go," Ellen said.

"We didn't ask for towels and now someone's messing with your car. How do I know he isn't going to jump me when I get out there?" he said, his eyes coming to rest on my chest where the lens of Snert's camera poked out of my shirt. "What's that?"

"Look man, I gotta go," I said, raising my hands defensively and backpedaling into the rain.

"He's wearing a wire, Ellen," Jeff growled.

Menace filled the man's eyes as he swung the gun toward me. I probably should have played it differently. He wasn't likely to shoot me for taking pictures. Unfortunately, that kind of thinking was contrary to all of my training. In the field, the difference between living and dying came down to a willingness to take bold action.

I stepped forward, spun into Jeff, brought my right hand across and jammed it into his wrist, grabbing hold. While turning, I brought my elbow around in an attempt to smash his face. He moved just enough that I made contact with his neck instead. Joined in an awkward dance, we stumbled back into the motel room.

Ellen screamed as Jeff wrapped a beefy arm around me, going for a bear hug. I had exactly one thing in mind, however, and that was to gain control of his weapon. He twisted his gun arm, trying to break my grip, but I wasn't letting go. With my free hand, I seized the gun's barrel.

A second scream from Ellen came as the deafening report from his gun kicked me into high gear. I bucked and slammed my head into Jeff's face. Momentarily stunned, his grip slackened and I stripped the gun from his hand.

"Fuck!" he grunted, bringing his hands up to his nose, which now bled profusely.

I jammed my fist into Jeff's stomach, pushing him onto the bed. Fumbling for a moment, I slid his gun into my coat pocket and then twisted his arm until he was face down on the bed. With the gun in my possession, all the fight had left him and he lay still, groaning under my weight.

"You okay?" I asked, turning to Ellen.

Her eyes were glazed with shock as she held a bloody hand in front of her face. She was clearly not okay.

"Don't you fucking move, Jeff," I ordered, jumping off.

"He shot me," she said. Her legs wobbled as she leaned heavily against the dresser. I managed to catch her before she toppled and gently lowered her to the floor.

"Where?" I asked.

Glassy-eyed, she looked up and then touched her hip.

Taking advantage of my distraction, Jeff nearly bowled me over as he bounded off the bed, reaching to grab his pants from the ratty chair. I prepared for a second fight, but that wasn't his purpose. With pants in hand, he ran out into the rainy night.

"Dammit." I rolled a towel and pressed it onto Ellen's hip. She looked up at me, eyes pleading for reassurance. "You're going to be okay, Ellen. Bullet passed through flesh. It hurts a lot worse than it is."

"My husband. He can't know," she said. "I can't go to the hospital. He'll leave me. I have kids. Please."

Her offer was tempting. This whole shit-show was my fault, at least that's the way my sergeant would see it. My resignation wouldn't matter. If I made the call, I'd be fired. Worse yet, I couldn't imagine how my grandfather, the man who'd raised me, was going to feel. Disappointment would only be the start.

"He already knows, Ellen," I said. "I'm a private investigator. He sent me to take pictures."

"You fucking asshole," she said, trying to kick me. The movement jostled her wound and she let out a chirp of agony. With a groan, her eyes rolled up into her head.

I pulled a comforter from the bed and draped it over her. "I can't argue with that," I said and dialed 911.

———

"How bad is it?" I asked as Sergeant Gus Williams, my old TO, entered the interrogation room where I'd been stashed.

"Bad enough, kid," he said. "You need to walk me through it."

"Do I need a union rep?" I asked.

"Maybe. Did you pull the trigger like Kreps says?"

That got my attention. She was blaming me for the shooting. Fantastic.

"She said that?"

"Said you were trying to roll her and her boyfriend," he said. "That how it went down?"

"Can I show you something?" I asked. Since I hadn't been charged with anything, I still had the recorder. I reached for the inside pocket of my jacket, which made Williams a little jumpy.

"Easy there," he said.

I looked back at him skeptically. "Seriously? You think I'd pull on you?"

"No. But I didn't take you for breaking and entering or robbery, either," he said.

I grimaced. They'd sent my TO in because they wanted to trade on my trust. I was being kept on the outside, which made me wonder what had been said in the hours I'd been sitting in the interrogation room. My guess was that the scene at the motel had been cleared and the detectives had finally made it back to the station. They were most likely looking to finish up and get back to their warm beds.

I pulled the recorder from my pocket and set it on the table. Long wires connected a solid-state device to a small lens. "I have the whole thing on video," I said. "I was hired by Kreps' husband to catch her diddling the guy who *did* shoot her."

"You got the whole thing on video?" he asked, reaching for the device.

I put my hand on top of it before he could grab it. "Last time I turned one of these over, someone erased it," I said. "You mind if I talk to the detective?"

Williams tipped his head, sizing me up. The thing was, I did trust him, but then I'd trusted his previous trainee and that hadn't worked out so well for me. "Look kid, I've got your back on this. You say you weren't the shooter, I don't need a recording."

The door opened and Lieutenant Sandy Chessen stepped in. Mid-forties and perpetually annoyed, she shook her head as we made eye contact. "Dammit, Biggston. I haven't had a night off this entire month and now I get called down here because you tried to catch our vic playing hide the sausage?"

I nodded. She'd nailed it in one. "I didn't shoot Ellen Kreps. Jeff, the guy who was with her, pulled a gun and I disarmed him. In the process he pulled the trigger."

"This Jeff have a last name? Mrs. Kreps failed to mention him, although there's some evidence of a second man. I'm assuming you don't wear an XXL mechanics shirt with a nametag that says Jeff?"

"His prints should be all over the gun," I said.

"So are yours," she said, flatly. "Tell me again how you got into the motel room? Sergeant Williams, you're dismissed."

"Yes, ma'am," he said, glaring at her. Rumor was, Gus had tried and failed to make detective several times. I didn't know if it was just Chessen or if he hated all detectives as a result.

Once the door closed, I recounted the events at the motel, skipping the part where I'd swiped dirty towels.

"And that video backs you up?" she asked, pointing at the device on the table.

"I was going to show it to Kreps' husband," I said. "He's the one who hired me."

"You might be the luckiest fuck-up in the entire world," she said. Her words stung, but I didn't necessarily disagree. She reached for the recorder, watching to see if I'd try to stop her. I didn't. Chessen was a good cop, albeit in need of anger management classes.

Chessen disappeared through the door and I sat back in the chair. The situation was a poignant reminder of just how little progress I'd made in my life. The last time I'd been interviewed by Detective Chessen had been in this same room. I'd handed over video from a recording device and that video had mysteriously been erased. Fortunately, Chessen was immanently aware of that having happened and I was certain she wouldn't let the evidence out of her sight before she viewed it.

An hour later, there was a knock at the door.

"Come in," I said, surprised at the sudden courtesy.

"Henry, you okay?" My grandfather, Lester Ploughman, entered the room. I sighed. Probably the last person I wanted to see under the circumstances.

"Heya, Pappi." I stood and gave him a hug. "They shouldn't have called you."

"Williams owed me one," he said, avoiding my eyes.

"I guess you know I got myself jammed up," I said. "Not sure it matters anyway." I took the letter out of my back pocket and handed it to him.

He frowned and pulled out a pair of reading glasses. "What's this?"

"I don't know if I can do this," I said.

He read quietly for a few minutes and then set the letter down. "Which part?"

"Working for the D.A. mostly. I haven't had a real case for months. I'm not even covering rent," I said. "You know the worst thing? I'm not even a real cop."

"That's not true, Henry," Pappi said. "I'm proud of you getting through the academy. You could transfer to patrol if you wanted. Williams said as much on the phone tonight."

"I probably screwed that up tonight," I said. "Even if they took me, I'd be stuck directing traffic for the next five years."

"Everybody has to pay their dues," he said.

It was an old conversation. The problem was, the Army had trained me for violent confrontation and I'd spent most of the last six years doing exactly that. When Kreps' boyfriend jumped me, I was suddenly back in the thick of it and felt truly alive for the first time in months.

"I know," I said, not wanting to get into it.

The door opened and Chessen walked in. She looked disapprovingly at Pappi. "Video checks out," she said, setting a piece of paper and the recording device on the table. "Motel could probably get trespassing to stick if they wanted. We made a copy. You need to sign a release."

I shrugged and signed. Chessen left the room, this time leaving the door open behind her.

"You need a ride somewhere?" Pappi asked.

I wanted to say no, that I'd handle it. The fact was, my Bronco was still sitting in the motel parking lot if it hadn't been towed.

We rode in silence to the motel. It was three in the morning when Pappi pulled to a stop in front of my truck. "Perfect world – what would you be doing right now? Aside from sleeping?" he asked.

It was a question I'd asked myself a million times. "I don't really know."

"Let me try a different direction," he said. "In the last five years, when have you been the happiest? Felt the most alive?"

"You're not going to like it," I said.

"Not mine to like, but I think I know the answer," he said. "Look, we have to hit this thing head on. I don't believe for a minute you enjoy stalking cheating spouses."

I thought about it and decided to give the honest answer.

"Hunting Richard Manning," I said. "When I knew he had those girls and it was up to me to find them. That was everything."

He nodded. "That's what I thought you'd say. Did you read the paper today?"

I smiled. I wasn't sure I even knew Sutherland had a newspaper. "Hasn't everything gone electronic?"

"No, some of us still like to hold something in our hands when we read. Gives us a sense of stability. And don't be a smart ass."

I laughed despite my bad mood. "Okay, I'll bite. No, I haven't read the paper today."

"Butte County has a deputy position open. I know the sheriff, Cal Leonard. Works out of the town of Wood Creek."

"Butte County? Do they even have crime out there?" I asked. "Isn't that the largest county in the state?"

"Three thousand square miles," Pappi answered. "And Cal has exactly four deputies to handle an area more than twice the size of the state of Rhode Island."

"Where's this coming from?" I asked.

"You probably remember a deputy being killed a couple of months ago," he said.

"That was in Butte?" I asked.

"That's right. What I didn't tell you was that Cal gave me a call. He'd heard about you taking down Manning and wanted to know if you might be interested in heading up his way," he said. "Pearl made me promise I wouldn't tell you about it. That never sat right with me. Sorry it took so long."

I felt a flash of irritation. I didn't like people speaking for me or holding back information. I stared out the window as I tamped down my frustration. Even in my weariness, I realized I was missing something. The conversation wasn't adding up.

"If that happened a couple of months ago, why'd you ask if I'd read today's newspaper?" I asked.

He raised an eyebrow and gave an approving nod. "Good question," he said. "Two weeks ago, another of his deputies was shot while on patrol."

"He okay?" I asked.

"She's alive," he said. "Vest saved her life. Multiple high caliber rounds were fired from a distance. They're not sure if she'll walk again."

"That's rough," I said.

"It gets worse," he said. "She has a kid and the husband's not in the picture."

"Any idea who the shooter is?" I asked, hoping to change the subject. Mom and I had been abandoned by my father before I was old enough to remember him. She hadn't been much better as a parent, coming and going from my life so much that I saw her more as a crazy aunt than a mother. The whole conversation brought up unresolved angst for me.

"Wasn't in the paper."

⊏⊐

I pulled into the driveway of my small rented bungalow. There was a light on in the living room and my buddy Snert's Lexus was parked out front behind Melinda Garcia's blue F-150. Mel had just returned from deployment, and I was hopeful we'd have a chance to get to know each other better now that she was back. I counted the fact that she was at my house as a good sign.

I was met at the door by Diva, my German Shepard. She wiggled around me like a puppy. I leaned down, gave her butt a good scratching and followed up with her neck. She'd nearly made a full recovery from being shot in the back several months ago. She was still stiff in the mornings, but even with that she insisted on running with me.

"What in the heck?" I asked as I entered the house and found Mel planted atop Snert.

Embarrassed at being caught, Mel scooched off and tugged at her shirt. "Biggs. We didn't see you pull in."

The lipstick on Snert's face was a clear message that I had things wrong about my future with Mel.

"Henry," Snert said, trying to get off the couch, not sure how to handle the awkward situation and navigate the overstuffed cushions all at the same time. "Um. Sorry. We were just talking."

I raised an eyebrow. I could count on one hand the number of women who'd given Snert the time of day. In that group, he'd missed every cue. As far as I knew, Snert had never so much as held hands with a woman. In that moment, I realized I'd blown it with Mel and needed to be happy for my best friend.

"You dirty dog," I said. "I had no idea you two were a thing. How'd I miss that?"

"Mostly just happened online." Mel stood and drew me into a hug. She was five-foot-nothing and curvier than average. "Alan was so sweet, calling me every chance he could while I was deployed."

"Where have you been?" Snert asked. "I thought you were going to be back before ten."

"Seems like you found something to do with your time," I said.

He considered my statement and couldn't stop the smile that burst onto his face.

"Tell me about Iraq," I said, sitting in a chair as Mel and Snert sat back on the couch with less than an inch between them.

"Actually, I visited your old stomping grounds in Bagram," she said. I mentally kicked myself. Too late, I remembered Snert saying Mel was in Afghanistan.

"Why are you so late?" Snert asked.

"I had a tough night," I said, dumping the video recorder on the end table. "Guy pulled a gun on me." I continued with the story until I'd told them everything, including my conversation with Pappi.

"You'd consider Butte County?" Snert asked.

I looked from him to Mel and back. I'd been looking forward to

Melinda's return and even considered trying to start something up with her. In that moment, I realized that was just a fantasy. I hadn't talked to her once while she'd been deployed.

"Can't hurt to take a look, can it?" I asked.

2 / GOOD IMPRESSIONS

"HENRY, YOU NEED TO RECONSIDER." Pearl might as well have been my mother, having raised me when my own mother couldn't. To say she wasn't happy about my interest in taking a job in Butte was an understatement.

I frowned in protest. "Butte County is only two hundred miles northwest."

"Nice try," she said. "Try two-hundred-eighty to the eastern edge of the county. There isn't a decent airport for a hundred miles in any direction."

"I'm not looking for a permanent job," I replied. "Sounds like they're in a pinch. If I can help, I'd like to."

"How about Alan? Have you told him? I can't believe he wants to see you leave," she said.

"Right now, the only thing Alan's thinking about is Melinda. I've never seen anyone fall quite so hard," I said. She smiled momentarily and then frowned again, a slight tremble in her jaw giving away her emotions. I stepped forward and pulled her into a hug. "Hey, I always come back."

She wrapped her arms around my back and held onto me, sniffling. "You never could run away from a fight. You're just like Lester."

"Sheriff Leonard might not even be interested," I said. "It's just a phone call."

"Well, I don't like it."

"I know," I said, letting her go.

For privacy, I went upstairs to the room I'd slept in growing up. It was like visiting a shrine dedicated to my younger self. Every trophy or ribbon earned in the various sports I'd played were still on proud display. Pearl had even updated it by hanging a shadow-box that commemorated my time in the Army as a Ranger. Unlike the sports awards, I was proud of the patches and medals in the box, just as I was proud to have served my country.

I sat on the edge of the bed and looked at the phone number Pappi had written on a piece of paper for me. The rhythmic thumping of Diva's feet on the carpeted stairs as she raced to join me preceded her bursting into the room, her tail banging into the door-frame and then the wooden dresser.

While rubbing her head absent-mindedly, I hit my phone's send button. She settled down next to me, her head in my lap.

"Butte County Sheriff's Department," a woman's voice answered.

"This is Henry Biggston. I'm calling for Sheriff Leonard."

"Sheriff Leonard has no further statements for the press," the woman said. "Please don't call back."

"Uh, no, I'm not with the press," I said, or at least I tried to say as I realized she'd ended the call. Diva looked up at me expectantly and I stared at the phone in disbelief. "I can't believe she hung up on me."

I dialed the number again and it rang six times. On the seventh ring a machine picked up. "This is Sheriff Cal Leonard. There's no one in the office right now. If you're having an emergency, please dial 911 and a dispatcher will locate the officer on call. If you need to leave a message, you probably understand that you have to wait for the beep. Have a pleasant day."

"Sheriff Leonard, this is Henry Biggston calling. My grandfather, Lester Ploughman, recommended I give you a call about a position in your office. I'll have my phone on me all day. Feel free to call back when convenient or I'll try you again tomorrow morning," I said and hung up.

"Feel like working on the truck?" I asked, patting Diva's head. She gave me the look most dogs have mastered, indicating she'd happily follow me just about anywhere.

"What'd he say?" Pappi asked, when I got back downstairs.

"Had to leave a message," I said. "A lady screening calls thought I was press."

"You have a Sutherland phone number. They've probably been getting a lot of those calls," he explained, nonplussed. "Small department like that have their own personalities. You going somewhere?"

"Thought I'd finish those brakes on the Bronco," I said. "Maybe see about that rattle in the exhaust."

"I'll tag along," he said. "We should check your timing. I feel like you've got a bit of a knock."

My last truck had been a classic Ford F-250. Pappi and I had spent hundreds of hours in the barn restoring it before I'd joined the Army. Earlier that spring, the F-250 had been blown up by a would-be assassin. All I had left of the truck was a fifteen-thousand-dollar insurance payout. I'd used eight thousand of that to buy a rusty old 1979 full-size Ford Bronco and burned through half of what remained replacing the engine and transmission. The rest of the money went to new tires, shocks, brake assemblies and a long list of aftermarket parts.

"We'll have the wheels off, we could put those shocks on too," I said.

He clapped his hands together and rubbed them vigorously. "How about that new brush-guard front bumper you got laying in there?" On a whim, I'd bought a bumper to replace the old original rusted chrome. Instead of just getting an equivalent piece, I'd found one with tow hooks and a winch compartment. Complete overkill, but it was every bit as rugged as it looked.

"I was kind of hoping to have her painted first," I said. "But I'm about out of money. So yeah. Let's do that."

By four o'clock, truck parts were strewn everywhere. As expected, the new bumper's *perfectly matched* bolt patterns were close, but not close enough. We'd tried heating the metal with a torch but ended up re-tapping the holes instead. The good news was, the bumper was now in place. The bad news was we'd spent the entire day and only installed eight bolts.

My phone rang while I was deep beneath the beast torqueing the last bolt. I knew from experience that I had no hope of getting to my phone before it popped over to record a message. I slid out anyway, so I could return the call.

"Three-o-eight area code. That's western side of the state," Pappi said, waving the phone under the Bronco. "Want me to pick it up?"

"Sure," I grunted as I continued to work my way out.

"Henry's phone. This is Lester Ploughman," he said and paused for a moment, listening to whoever was on the other end. "Right. Cal, good to hear from you. Nope, no snow yet. We had freeze warnings last night. Pearl had me out covering her flowers."

I stood and squirted a bit of goop onto my hands, rubbing it in to release the oily grime. With a paper towel, I wiped them down as much as I could.

"No. We're just out working in the barn. He's right here. Want to talk to him?" Pappi asked, smiling as he spoke with his old friend.

I accepted the phone and placed it to my ear. "Hello, Sheriff Leonard, this is Henry Biggston," I said.

"Call me Cal," Leonard said, his voice booming into the phone. "I was just talking to Lester. Said you might be interested in coming to Wood Creek and checking things out. That sound about right?"

"I don't have much experience," I said. "I just got off my training rotation with SPD."

"Humble too. I like that," he said. "Way I hear it, you did two tours knocking down doors in towel-head country and then took down a mob boss. Around here, that's not exactly what we call rookie material."

I winced at his derogatory reference to the Afghans. I'd heard worse, but it seemed odd on an introductory phone call. "Well, I'm just saying, I don't have a lot of law enforcement background. As you say, kicking down doors I have some experience with."

"Well you see, Henry ... the thing is, with George and now Char out, we're stretched mighty thin up here," he said. George Lynch was the officer who'd been killed in the line of duty a couple months ago. I didn't know the deputy's name who'd been shot, but it stood to reason her name was Char. "Finding qualified candidates who are willing to work in this part of the state isn't all that easy. I'd love for you to come out for a visit so I could give you a first-class tour of the place. We'll even reimburse you for mileage."

"I'd like that," I said.

"You still have that dog your grandpa keeps going on about?" he asked. "I heard she got shot in that mobster deal."

I glanced at Pappi. He'd obviously been talking me up to Sheriff Leonard, which took me off guard. I never really felt like I measured up to his standards, even though he never suggested otherwise. "Diva. Yes, sir," I said. "She's almost back to full health."

"Sheriff or Cal," he said. "Don't call me sir."

"Copy that, si... Sheriff," I answered.

"When do you think you could make it out here? They say we're in for some weather this weekend. Might make travel rough," he said.

"If I can get my Bronco back together, I was thinking about driving out tomorrow afternoon." I'd seen the weather for the northwest part of the state and he was right. It was Wednesday and there was a chance for three to four inches of snow late Friday afternoon. As the system traveled across the state it would turn from rain to sleet and finally to snow, making for icy roads. Delay wasn't my best option.

"A man of action," he said. "I'll tell Mortimer to put a room aside for you at the Sage and Rosemary Inn. See you first thing Friday morning?"

"Sure thing, Sheriff," I said.

"Looking forward to it, Henry," he said and the phone went dead.

"That sounded promising," Pappi said, pushing off from the workbench he'd been leaning against while listening to my side of the conversation.

"How well do you know Sheriff Leonard?" I asked.

"I was his TO back when," Pappi answered. "Full of himself back then. Still is, best I can tell. Good man, though."

"Why'd he leave SPD?" I asked.

"His family is from the Wood Creek area," Pappi said. "There was an opening in the department. Five years later, he's running for office and wins."

"Isn't Pearl from around there? Did she know him?" I asked.

A momentary frown crossed Pappi's face. "They dated in high school. I don't know much more because she won't talk about it."

"Do we have family out there?" I asked.

"Distant relatives, maybe a couple of second cousins," Pappi answered, still uncomfortable. "Think we can get those brakes back on before Pearl has dinner ready?"

I'd hit a sore subject and knew better than to keep pushing. "Sure," I said and accepted the rachet he held out to me. "Should be able to get the front shocks on too."

———

I spent the night at my grandparent's house since, as usual, I'd been overly optimistic on my timing for completing the repairs to the Bronco. There were two rules I'd learned while working with older vehicles. First, no bolt on an old vehicle will turn without excessive force, the application of which often caused some sort of injury. Second, the last step of any project will take three times as long as the first step, no matter how similar or simple that last step is.

"Would you like breakfast, Henry?" Pearl asked as I came downstairs. At nine-thirty, they'd both been up for at least three hours. "I made muffins this morning."

"A muffin would be great," I said.

"Snow already made it to Butte County," Pappi called from his easy chair, setting the newspaper in his lap.

Pearl shot him a hopeful look and jumped in. "Henry, you should really consider driving out next week. I don't like the idea of you on those icy roads,"

"Coffee," I said and turned into the kitchen. I filled a cup, grabbed what looked like a cranberry muffin and returned to the living room.

"Did you hear me?" Pearl asked. "The weather is bad, you shouldn't be driving."

"That's kind of the point of the Bronco," I said, taking a bite of the muffin and swiping open my weather app. "I already called in and let the office know I'd be unavailable."

"Does it make sense that the D.A. never has work for him, Lester?" Pearl asked.

"Not every case requires an investigator," he answered.

"Then why'd Turner bother hiring you? Seems like he should pay a retainer or something," she pushed back.

Pappi and I both knew she was looking for a way to keep me in town and that she'd decided to go on the offensive. There was no winning this conversation, not when Pearl got wound up. Weathering the storm that brewed inside this house would absolutely be more difficult than whatever Mother Nature might throw at me out on the road.

"Williams thought he could get Henry into a patrol position on SPD," Pappi said. I looked over at him, eyebrow raised. He'd just thrown me under the bus and the twinkle in his eye told me he knew it.

Pearl's head swiveled so fast I thought it possible she was possessed. I decided I'd be better off to deflect before things got out of control. "Pappi said you and Cal Leonard knew each other in high school. I didn't know you were from up there."

"That was a long time ago," she said. I could tell from the way she was standing that she hadn't been diverted and intended to get back to her original purpose.

"Leonard said we still might have family?"

"My older sister lived there until she passed," Pearl said. "Near Crawford, though. Not Wood Creek."

"She have kids?" I asked.

Pearl smiled. She knew what I was doing but was too nice not to answer. "Actually, yes. Her daughter Hannah has two boys and I believe they still live in the same house I grew up in."

"You don't talk about that much," I said.

"No. I don't," she said flatly.

"What time are you thinking about taking off?" Pappi asked, changing the subject.

"I need to run by the house first, but I'll be headed out soon," I said.

"How will you swing two places if you take a job in Wood Creek?" Pearl asked.

"I'm month to month at the house," I said. "I can pack everything I own in the truck."

"At some point you need to stop living out of a suitcase," she pushed. "Put down some roots. I'd like to see that happen in Sutherland."

There it was. She'd finally said what was on her mind.

"I know and I love you for it." I crumpled the muffin wrapper, tossed it into the waste can and finished the last of my coffee, before turning to Pappi. "I'll probably get going in an hour or so. Think I should bring a weapon along?"

"Do you have a service piece from the D.A.'s office?" he asked.

"No."

"I'd pack your .243 and both of your handguns," he said. "Make sure to take your social security card and passport too. They'll need to run their own background check."

"Right."

———

I didn't run into rain until I was more than halfway to Wood Creek, putting me in the small town of Thedford. The town had exactly two gas stations and a bar that looked to double as a restaurant. For a Thursday night, the bar was a hopping place and I considered stopping in, but with another two hours of driving in front of me, it was smarter to keep moving.

I fought to stay awake as I drove down Highway 2, which was icing up as the temperature dropped and the wind picked up. When there'd been light, I'd enjoyed the rolling grass-covered hills. The prairies stretched for miles without anything more than a fence to suggest humans had ever lived there. For the last forty miles, I'd been driving by a man-made national forest, which in the dark seemed rather sparsely treed to be considered forest.

I'd just turned up Highway 385, the final stretch toward Wood Creek, and was taking a pull on the thermos I'd filled with fabulously wretched gas station coffee, when I got lit up by a police car. I looked down at my speedometer. I was doing sixty-eight and thought back to the last sign I'd seen. It was either sixty or sixty-five, but with no other traffic around I hadn't been too concerned. Especially once I'd hit snow instead of icing rain.

I slowed and pulled to a stop, Diva stirring next to me. "It's okay, girl," I said, trying to keep her calm.

The cruiser pulled in behind me. The officer left a reasonable gap between us and was sticking out into the road, which would give a safe buffer from traffic. A textbook stop. I waited several minutes until I saw the silhouette of a man about five-foot-eight and at least two hundred twenty pounds approach the vehicle. I stiffened as he unsnapped the buckle atop his pistol.

I rolled the window down and he shined his flashlight through my back windows as he got close to the driver's side door. Diva growled, not appreciating the light in her face. I turned on the truck's dome light and put my hands on the steering wheel, hoping to set him at ease.

"You have any idea how fast you were going?" he asked, holding his light so the beam shone directly into my face, blinding me.

"You want to get that out of my face?" I said.

"I asked you a question," he pushed.

I closed my eyes. "Sixty-eight," I answered.

"Bennet plates," he said. "What's in the truck?"

"I'm an officer with SPD," I said. "I have weapons in the car, although they're cased."

"Step out of the vehicle, sir," he snapped, stepping back into the road and clumsily pulling his revolver. Diva barked, not appreciating his attitude. "If you don't restrain your dog. I'll have to do it for you."

"Diva. Setzen," I ordered. She gave a final bark and then sat on her haunches, ready to respond in an instant. "Will you let me leash her?" I asked.

"Stay in the vehicle, sir," he ordered. "Take your keys and throw them to me."

I pulled the keys from the ignition and threw them out to him. It was an unusual way to detain me, but he was alone on a very dark stretch of highway and I had him outnumbered. I missed the toss by a couple of feet and watched as he bent uncomfortably and plucked my keys from the snow. He then walked to his car and got back in.

I waited, using the time to snap a leash on Diva. Forty-five minutes later, flashing lights appeared through the snowy gloom and raced toward us. It was then I realized he'd called for backup and it had taken almost an hour for the second vehicle to arrive. A newer SUV pulled off the road and parked facing the wrong direction, directly in front of me with its lights illuminating my Bronco. I appreciated that he doused his headlights before exiting the vehicle. That said, his protocol was wrong. If I was armed, presumably the reason for backup, he was now in the line of fire.

The first officer came back over to my truck, approaching carefully and standing just back of the driver's door, once again raising his weapon. "Sir, you're ordered to exit the vehicle. Will you comply?"

"I've leashed my dog," I said. "Do you want her in or out?"

"Leave the animal in the vehicle," he ordered.

I slid out the door, keeping my hands raised. From the corner of my eye, I saw the second officer working his way over to the passenger side of my truck. I sincerely hoped he wouldn't open that door, although I seemed to remember it was locked. Once I closed the truck door, he continued. "Hands against the side of the truck, spread your legs."

I complied. It seemed excessive for a traffic stop. "Gene, pat him down. I've got him covered."

"What's going on, Raff?" the second officer asked, coming around the back of the truck. "Did you see something?"

"He wouldn't get out of the truck," Raff lied.

"That right? You wouldn't obey a lawful instruction?" the second officer asked, running his hands professionally across my body in search of weapons.

"I asked if I could leash my dog," I said. "I'm an officer with SPD. Diva is a service animal. He pulled on me and she got nervous."

"Identification?" he asked.

"Right coat pocket," I said.

He located the wallet that held my shield and pulled it out. "Badge number, Mr. Biggston?"

I recited it to him.

"Aww, for fuck sake, Raff! This guy's a cop. Did you even call it in?" I put Raff in his late twenties and Gene in his late forties. Gene handed my badge back and turned to Raff. "Put the goddamn gun away."

"I didn't know," Raff argued. "He could have been lying. He said he had guns in the truck."

Gene shook his head. "You can relax, Mr. Biggston. On behalf of the Butte County Sheriff's department, I'd like to apologize. We're all a little jumpy due to recent events."

"Just doing your jobs," I said. "No harm done."

"I'd take it as a favor if this could stay between us," he said, shaking his head in disbelief.

I held out my hand. "Never happened," I said. "Mind if I get those keys back?"

Red-faced and still annoyed, Raff handed over my keys.

"At least apologize, Raff," Gene pushed.

"No, seriously," I said, looking at Raff. "I get it. Gnarly night like this. Appreciate you guys keeping things safe. Any idea how far we are from Wood Creek?"

"You need to slow it down," Raff pushed. "Speed limit is sixty-five, but conditions don't warrant. Keep it under fifty-five."

I nodded, working to keep my irritation from showing.

3 / KIN

A LITTLE AFTER MIDNIGHT, I pulled into the sleepy town of Wood Creek. With only five thousand inhabitants, the town was bigger than I'd expected, especially given all the unincorporated hamlets that I'd been driving through proudly boasting double-digit populations. I pulled into a park on the edge of town and got out, allowing Diva to stretch her legs.

Wood Creek had been cold enough when the storm hit that they hadn't seen rain, but instead received six inches of heavy snow. Like with most early-season snows, my boot prints crushed the snow sufficiently to leave a wet track, meaning the ground had been warmer than the evening suggested.

I took a few minutes to orient myself and was pleased to discover my cell phone had good coverage, unlike what I'd experienced during most of the trip. I fired off a quick text message to Pearl's phone, letting her know I'd arrived and was safe. Almost immediately, I saw three dots jumping at the bottom of the screen, showing she was forming a response. She'd been worried and was glad I'd arrived safely. I pushed the phone into my pocket and loaded Diva into the truck.

The Sage and Rosemary Inn was located downtown on Wood

Creek's main strip, two blocks west of Highway 385. I cruised past and located the courthouse in the center of a large, open square. The brick two-story sheriff's office shared space with other businesses in a row of interconnected buildings directly across from the courthouse's large front doors. Dim lights behind the large plate glass windows illuminated a law enforcement logo on a mint green wall inside.

Now that I knew where I'd be going in the morning, I continued through the deserted town square. Movement caught my eye as, two blocks away, a white truck careened onto main street, fishtailing and swerving into the opposite lane. Moments later a second vehicle, an ancient lime green Subaru, swung through the same intersection and followed. Its engine was revving hard, but the car wasn't moving nearly as fast as the sound would lead one to believe.

I punched the gas pedal and followed. I wasn't looking to intercept as much as I was interested in finding out what was happening. I chuckled as, a block further down, I found the Subaru sitting against the curb. The vehicle's front wheel had popped when the driver had taken an uncontrolled skid and slammed into the curb. I pulled over and jumped out. A teenager with a thick head of curly hair looked ruefully at the damage.

"Doesn't look too bad," I said.

"Dad's gonna be pissed," he said, sizing me up, his eyes traveling back to the Bronco.

"Need any help?" I asked.

"I've got a spare," he said. "Thanks, though."

I could just hear the thumping sound of music in the distance. "What's that noise?" I asked.

"Music?" I nodded, so he continued. "Press Box. They're open 'til two."

"On a Thursday?"

"College town. Only two bars," he said as if that was the only explanation I needed. It probably was.

"You sure you got this?" I asked.

"Not my first rodeo."

I chuckled. He didn't look at all like a cowboy. My guess was, he was one of those college students, probably into computers or something like that. I hopped back into the car and was greeted by Diva's wet tongue. She hadn't liked having guns pointed at us earlier tonight and was being a little over-protective. I turned the truck around and headed back to the Sage and Rosemary. The row-style buildings continued down Main Street to where the Inn was located. I parked in front and told Diva to settle, but left the truck running.

Broad sandstone steps led up to an ornate glass door. I was glad when the knob turned easily in my hand, although when I entered, the old hotel's lobby was completely devoid of people. I walked to the front counter and was about to ring the bell when I found an envelope with my name on it. Inside were keys to a room on the second floor and instructions to park in back.

"Find everything you need?" an older man's voice asked from behind the counter, startling me. It sounded like he'd been asleep.

"Sorry to wake you," I said, holding up the envelope. "Henry Biggston."

"I don't sleep like I used to," he complained. "Mortimer Cook." He walked out from behind the counter and offered his hand. He smelled of booze.

"You always leave your front door open?" I asked, shaking his hand. "Nice to meet you."

"Only when we're expecting late guests," he replied with a smile. The man was well into his sixties, if not seventies, and wore a well-trimmed white Fu Manchu mustache and beard. "Cal said you had a dog. I'm okay with that as long as it won't make a mess and isn't a bother to the guests."

"Diva won't be a problem," I said.

The name made him smile. "Diva. Now that's a proper name for a bitch." I searched his face to see if he was trying to elicit a reaction with that term. He seemed completely unaware that he'd said anything even slightly off-color.

A second man came out from behind the counter. "You'll have to ignore him. I know I do." He might have been a few years younger than Mortimer. He was heavier and his skin wasn't quite as wrinkled. "Denholm Campbell."

I shook Denholm's hand.

"What?" Mortimer demanded.

"Polite people don't use the word *bitch* in casual conversation," Denholm chastised. "It makes you sound like a queen."

Mortimer widened his eyes and shook his head. "And I care about this because?"

"Young Mr. Biggston here is an Army Ranger. If you piss him off, he'll break your arms."

Mortimer smiled. "Interesting. *That's* why you were talking to Sheriff Leonard. Will that be ready to go tomorrow?"

I'd become lost in the conversation and shrugged in confusion as Mortimer looked at me.

"He's asking if my interview with the sheriff about his search for a new deputy will be ready for the newspaper tomorrow." Denholm explained. "And the answer is no. I wanted a chance to talk with Mr. Biggston here to add some flavor."

"Hmm," I said, not really looking to extend the conversation. One of the courses we'd taken in the academy was about how to keep our names out of the newspaper, local or otherwise. "Mind if I get things put away? Big day tomorrow and all."

"See! You went and scared him off," Denholm chastised and turned to me. "You go by Henry?"

"Most people call me Biggs."

"Oh, I like it," Mortimer said. "Gives him an approachable feel. Headlines just write themselves. Grisly vet with a heart for the bitches." His high laugh continued past the point of being uncomfortable.

Denholm sighed. "I prefer Denholm but he goes by Morty. We're either here or at the newspaper across the street. I think I need to get Morty back to bed."

I nodded and smiled to myself as I wondered what I'd gotten myself into.

There were only two other cars in the lot behind the hotel and I parked in the front row. I led Diva up to the second level, walking up a creaky narrow wooden staircase. The building was ancient. I placed the décor as Victorian, but with a serious slant toward bawdy, given the nude paintings on the walls.

My room was spacious; a queen bed centered on a wood-paneled wall, two chairs, a credenza with a television and an old trunk under the window to set a suitcase on. A tiny bathroom without a shower opened into the room, which was certainly enough for my needs. By the time I'd set my toiletries in the bathroom, Diva was fast asleep on the bed, taking up most of it. It was a fight I'd deal with later. I stroked her head and quietly ordered her to stay. She wasn't about to argue and settled back to sleep.

I arrived at the Press Box Bar at twelve-thirty. I could hear the music from the parking lot and wondered if I'd be sticking around very long. I didn't love loud music, but could definitely use a drink after the long drive and the bullshit with Deputy Raff, who I would no doubt get to meet tomorrow. Thanks for bringing the awkward, Raff.

Scanning the room as I entered, I tried to get a feel for the place. As expected, it was filled with college students. When had these kids gotten so young? I wasn't thirty yet, but there didn't seem to be anyone in the room over the age of twenty-five.

At the bar, I leaned against the end next to an empty chair, trying to decide if I was staying. "What are yah drinking, cowboy?" The woman behind the bar was mid-thirties and nice looking, probably the worst thing you could be in a bar full of drunk twenty-something men. The look on my face must have conveyed my indecision and she laughed. "One mile north on 385," she said. "Hootskill. Might be more to your taste."

"Bar?" I asked, surprised she'd send me to a competitor. She nodded. "Thanks." I pulled a five from my pocket and reached out to put it in the tip jar.

"Save your money, cowboy," she said, tugging at the leather vest she wore with no blouse underneath, exposing a little more of her cleavage. "If you can stand the noise, this place is a gold mine."

I smiled and dropped the tip anyway.

Fifteen minutes later, I pulled into a parking lot packed with pickup trucks. The building was nothing more than a barn with a well-lit billboard sign reading *Hootskill*. The music was just as loud as the last bar, but at least it was country music.

With only an hour left before closing, people were well past the point of no return and I was jostled several times as I worked my way to the bar. Cowboy hats, blue jeans and western style dress shirts were the obvious dress code. A live band played on the stage and the people who stood closest to the front moved in unison, dancing in lock-step precision, most of them singing along.

Four women worked behind the bar. I'd no sooner put my arm on the woodwork when one of them appeared. "Damn, that's pretty good," I said, leaning in.

"You're not from around here. What'll it be?"

"Anything light and on tap," I said. "Are they line dancing?"

"That's right. Four bucks. You want to start a tab?"

I handed her a ten. "No thanks."

She drew my beer into a glass and slid it and six dollars pulled from her apron over to me. I sat on an empty stool and turned back toward the band. The dancers were having a good time, although it was clear that drinking had a detrimental effect on the skill of many on the edges. The beer disappeared and I wasn't a bit surprised when the same bartender showed back up.

"You should try it," she said, smiling but not flirting.

"Maybe," I said. "Not tonight. Mind if I get another?"

"Wouldn't be in business if I did," she answered, refilling my glass.

I slid the remainder of the ten in her direction. "Keep it. My limit's two."

I'd just picked up my beer when angry sounds erupted and a giant of a man wearing a white cowboy hat crashed into me. His body slammed me forward, crushing my ribs into the hard wood of the bar top and jostling my beer so that it splashed over the counter and onto the bartender. My ribs hurt like the devil, but I hadn't heard a crack so I hoped nothing had been broken.

"Fuck!" the bartender yelled. "Get Jimmy!"

I grabbed the bar with both hands and pushed back against the hulk who was pinning me in place. Someone was pushing him into me and I could hear fists on flesh. I finally gained enough leverage to shift the guy off me and twist away. The man had to be six-foot-six and weighed well over three hundred fifty pounds. He was so wide, I couldn't see around him enough to figure out who was tuning him up. Apparently, he'd had enough though, because he roared angrily and started forward.

From the corner of my eye, I saw a tall, lanky man approach carrying a baseball bat. Jimmy, no doubt. I read concern in his face as he watched the hulk pick up a much smaller man and toss him clean over a pool table several feet away.

"Luca! Knock it the fuck off," Jimmy shouted, circling into the big man's peripheral vision, menacingly holding his bat.

"This is bullshit!" Luca roared, cocking back his giant arm and smashing someone in front of him to the ground.

Jimmy used the distraction and swept his bat for a perfect strike on Luca's back. The meaty *thwack* sounded like it should have broken something, but Luca's only response was to rear back, catch Jimmy with the back of his ham-sized fist, and send him sprawling.

"Call 911," the bartender said, looking at me. She swung herself over the bar in a single move, a pink baseball bat in her hand. I stepped in front of her and handed her my phone. "Get out of my way, asshole. Jimmy can't take Luca by himself."

"I'm a cop," I said. She pushed my phone into her pocket and shook her head, giving me a bewildered look. "Not like you're taking him down either."

During our short conversation, Luca had grabbed one of his attackers, holding the man up by the neck with one hand and using his free hand to pummel him. The fight was quickly getting out of control, as the raw strength of the man would soon cause serious damage.

"Luca, stop!" the bartender said, hitting Luca's arm as he drew it back. She caught his elbow which either intentionally or not must have stung because he spun on her, dropping his victim, murder in his eyes.

"Oh, damn." I leapt in front of her, unloading my best open-handed slap to Luca's ear. The strike didn't stop him, but it did end up having the intended effect. Luca forgot all about the bartender and his stinging arm.

For a giant drunk, Luca was surprisingly fast on his feet. I suspected he was a football player and that I should know his name since he clearly could have gone pro – maybe straight from junior high. His shoulder caught me in the ribs and he drove me backward into the side of the barn, unwary patrons in our path careening off my backside. I felt contact with barnboards and heard the crack as we made it through to the parking lot.

"Freeze." I heard the order, but before I could respond, my body went rigid as electrodes attached themselves to my back and electricity coursed through me. I convulsed, howling uncontrollably at the pain. After several seconds, the pain was gone, leaving me twitching and completely disoriented. "I said freeze, dammit!" The second jolt lasted longer than the first and this time, I didn't move when it stopped.

"SPD, huh? Think your shit doesn't stink out here?" Deputy Raff roughly pulled my arms back and cuffed me.

"I was helping," I said, careful not to move, which I was sure would bring back the juice.

"Shut up and stay down," he ordered. I couldn't fathom what I'd done to piss the fat little midget off, but he had a big hate on for me. The arrival of an ambulance told me that things had indeed gotten serious. A few minutes later, he returned and helped me up. "You can sleep this off in a cell."

"I'm not drunk," I protested.

"I can smell it all over you," he said. I looked around. The bartender was standing next to Jimmy, who was sitting on the edge of a gurney next to the ambulance. Raff pushed me over to his cruiser and ordered me into the back seat where he'd already loaded Luca the giant.

"You're putting me in with him?" I asked. "He nearly killed me."

"Better luck next time," Raff said, pushing my head down and forcing me next to the man who took up more than half of the back seat.

"We're cool, man," Luca said, his head resting against the side of the cruiser.

I shook my head as the second sheriff's vehicle arrived and Gene jumped out. He looked over to me and back to Raff. The two argued for a few minutes and then separated, Raff coming over to the car. If I'd thought Raff was going to let me out, I was sadly mistaken.

"You shouldn't have come to Wood Creek looking for trouble, because buddy, you found it right here," Raff said as he slid into his seat, shining his flashlight into my face and holding it on my eyes. I turned to look out the window.

"You got a big mouth, Raff," Luca said.

"Shut up, Quinn. You finally did it this time. You'll be spending some real time," he said.

I looked over at the big man. Luca Quinn. It was the last name of my second cousin, Hannah. How many Quinns could there be? Right now didn't seem like the time to ask.

When we arrived downtown, Raff pulled through a paved alley behind the sheriff's station and waited for an automatic garage door to open. Onto the back of the two-story brick building, the city had built a squat steel garage. At the front of the garage, stairs led up into the building.

"You first, Mr. Biggston," Raff said. "And please, resist. I'd like to add a second count to your sheet."

Fortunately, Raff wasn't in the mood to cause further trouble. He led me to a room, where he searched me, removing the few items I had in my pockets and dumping them into a plastic bag. My cell phone was missing, and I remembered handing it to the bartender just before Luca ran me through the side of the bar.

Raff loaded me into an old freight elevator that took us up to the second floor. Just off the elevator, he pushed me into a cell with iron bars on two sides. The rest of the room consisted of a few feet of walkway around the iron cage in both directions, with windows toward the front, starting at waist level and soaring up to the tall ceiling.

"When I get back with Luca, make sure you're sitting on one of those bunks," Raff ordered, removing the cuffs and pushing me into the cell. Even though I was the prisoner, his sloppiness bothered me. If I'd wanted to take him at that moment, I easily could have. He should have put me in the cell and had me back to the bars, so he could remove the cuffs safely.

Hanging by chains on the back wall were two bunks. I wasn't sure the top bunk would hold Luca, so I climbed up and sat on the soiled cushion with my back to the wall. Rays of moonlight streamed in, shining on the elevator door. Apparently, the storm was over. From my perch, I could see the courthouse, still covered with fresh snow. I worried about Diva. She'd be okay for a few hours, but I didn't want her getting hurt if someone who wasn't good with animals was sent to my room.

My thoughts were interrupted by Raff bringing Luca up. There was arguing in the elevator, but the sounds stopped when they exited.

"Now, you boys play nice," Raff said, pushing Luca into the cell. It wasn't lost on me that Luca's handcuffs had already been removed.

At first, Luca sat heavily on the bunk below me. I thought he'd probably go to sleep, but he stood back up once Raff got back in the elevator.

"I'm really sorry about this," he said, looking across at me.

I shrugged. "I'm okay. It was the heat of the moment," I said. Luca Quinn was currently the least of my problems.

He shook his head. "Not what I'm talking about."

His beefy arms shot out and he grabbed for me. His hot/cold behavior was confusing. In the back of the sheriff's vehicle, he'd been calm, almost friendly. Now, it appeared he was ready to start things up again. I barely rolled out of his way in time to miss his big fists. Like before, at the bar, he was fast and adjusted, grabbing my clothing, pulling me off the bunk and throwing me to the floor.

"Wait," I said, rolling to my feet. "We don't have to do this."

LUCA'S EYES WERE CLEAR, apologetic even, holding none of the rage he'd had in the bar. He'd adopted a wrestler's stance and was clearly intent on grappling with me. I looked for anything that could give me an advantage. The cell wasn't tiny but at that moment, he seemed to fill most of the space.

"Hold on," I said, jumping past him as he lunged and we traded corners. "Can't we talk about this?"

"Nothing personal," he said. "Just take your beating. I won't break anything."

At six and a half feet tall, I gave up four inches. That wasn't so much the problem. I only weighed in at a hundred ninety. While I'd always been strong, Luca had proven that his additional hundred and fifty pounds hadn't all gone to fat.

He lunged again and I slapped away his hand, slipping past him. I kicked off the side wall, jumping upward and onto his back. He stumbled forward as I added my weight to his and brought my arm around his neck for an arm bar. For a moment, he was stunned and spun in place, trying to throw me off. His motions were ineffective and more about surprise than any great fighting instinct.

Unfortunately, Luca quickly figured out that my move had been deliberate and that my arm around his neck was a serious threat. Identifying the problem, he brought his meaty hands up to pull my arm down. The force he exerted was tremendous, but I'd locked in and was holding on for dear life.

With a deep growl, he tried to escape by stumbling back and slamming me into the prison bars. Pain spread through my body at the impact, but I knew better than to let go. I redoubled my efforts, barely able to keep my arm from being ripped free. Recognizing that I hadn't been knocked off, Luca spun and pushed back toward the bunks. The two-inch wide metal edge of the top bunk caught me in the back and I yowled but held on.

The big man's strength gave way even as he pawed at my arm. In a final, desperate move, he lurched backward. I caught much of the force of our combined weight on my hip as we hit the floor. I fought through the pain, still holding on, until finally the fight drained from Luca Quinn.

I struggled for a moment, awkwardly working to push the unconscious man off. My eye caught a red light I hadn't seen before in the corner of the room, outside the cell. A video camera had caught the entire altercation. Luca's words – *nothing personal* – rang in my ears. Was that what he'd been arguing with Raff about in the elevator? Did Raff threaten him with something so that he'd give me a beating? It didn't make sense. Until a few hours ago, I'd never in my life even heard of Rafferty Butler.

I checked Luca's pulse and verified he was still breathing. I'd never been choked out before, but I understood it left the recipient with a massive headache. With the excitement over, I checked myself for damage. I couldn't see my back, but didn't feel like anything was broken, although no doubt I'd have a few bruises. My hip still stung from impact with the floor, but it was the same story. I'd be bruised but would otherwise survive.

From my position, I could just see the clock atop the courthouse. Three-thirty. Still spun up from the fight, I decided to move Luca over to the bottom cot. I could have left him on the floor, but it didn't seem right. Once I had him in bed. I removed his belt and shoe laces and used them to bind his hands and feet together behind his back. I wasn't sure I'd be able to sleep with him in the room, but if I did doze, the restraints might help – that is, *if* he didn't just snap them.

Sunlight streamed through the tall windows and I brought my hand up to shade my eyes. Sitting up, I realized I had fallen asleep and the harsh beam of light was a reflection off the clock on the courthouse. My eyes fell on the hills that rose up behind the town to the west, thick with pine trees covered with a fresh blanket of snow. We were still a hundred miles from the Rockies, so I was surprised at how mountainous the terrain looked.

"Hey, buddy, you mind untying me?" Luca Quinn asked.

"Depends," I answered. "Are you coming at me again?"

"Nah," he said. "That was a pretty good trick, getting on my back like that. I don't think you'd last too long in a fair fight."

I chuckled. I wasn't sure what part of a fight with Luca Quinn would ever be fair. I hopped off the bunk and stood in front of the man. He had a boy's face, with wisps of black hair where a beard should be. "You happen to be related to Hannah Quinn?" I asked, untying the laces around his ankles.

"Who's she to you?" he asked, suspiciously.

"Somebody my grandmother used to know," I said.

"That's my mom," he said. "She's sick."

"Sick?" I asked, loosening the belt from around his wrists. If he was going to come at me, this would be his moment.

"She has the cancer. Made her terrible sick," he said.

I patted his knee as I stood up. "Sorry to hear that, Luca."

"You gonna press charges for our fight last night?" he asked, soberly.

"I feel like we got things worked out," I said.

He smiled, showing a mouthful of crooked teeth that hadn't seen the business end of a toothbrush in a good long while. I turned and checked the courthouse clock. Seven-thirty. Morning had finally arrived. Angry voices filled the adjacent room on the other side of a solid-looking door.

"Mama's here," he said. "She sounds mad."

"What's out there?" I asked, nodding at the steel security door that separated us from the shouting.

"That's the station," he said. "She's mad because I gotta see a judge."

The steel door slammed open and a harried looking woman in dirty jeans, worn brown leather coat and a cowboy hat entered. "What the fuck, Luca?" she asked. "What were you even doing at Hootskill last night? You know how you get when you're drinking."

"I'm sorry, Mama." His voice was high pitched as he jumped up and crossed the room to stand next to the bars.

"Goddamn deputy says you busted the place up good last night. Put Jimmy in the hospital. You do that?" she asked.

"Yes, Mama," he answered, looking at the ground. "They were making fun of me. I couldn't just let them. I didn't mean to hurt Jimmy."

"Call you a big retard, did they? They're right. You're a good-for-nothing fuckup," she said. "Enjoy your vacation while I do all the goddamn work."

"I'm sorry, Mama," he said. "I just got mad."

"Well, that's just great," she said, her eyes full of fire as she turned on me. "What are you looking at fuck-tard?"

My eyes grew wide under her withering stare. I fought to keep a surprised smile from my face. Fortunately, she turned and stalked out before the smile reached my face.

"Oh man, she's intense," I said when Luca finally turned around.

"That's Mama," he said, apologetically.

"What do you mean he's in the cell?" I recognized Sheriff Cal Leonard's voice as it filtered in from the other room.

"Raff locked him up last night," a woman said. "Big fight down at Hootskill. Faith Hudson is on her way down."

"Is she pressing charges?" Leonard asked.

I'd moved so I could see through the doorway and was rewarded when a heavyset middle-aged woman in stretchy black slacks and a cream-colored sweater crossed my field of vision and looked out the windows in the next room. "You can ask her yourself. She just pulled up."

Sheriff Leonard appeared in the doorway. He was a big-framed man and was dressed in blue jeans, a uniform shirt, cowboy boots and a gun belt. "Henry Biggston?" he asked, looking across at me.

"Sheriff," I said, giving him a small wave of my hand. I was pretty sure that whatever interview I was to have had started poorly.

"Where's that good-for-nothing Butler?" I heard a new woman ask, catching Leonard's attention.

A look of resignation crossed the sheriff's face as he turned back to face what sounded like the second angry customer of the day.

"Faith," he said. "Thanks for coming down. Hollie will be happy to take your statement."

"I'm not here to give a damn statement," she fired back. "I just heard that Raff locked up the only man with any balls in this goddamn county."

"Settle down, Faith. We'll get all this sorted out," he said. " Why don't you tell me what you're talking about."

"Luca Quinn got out of control last night and busted Jimmy up," she said. "Some guy, said he was a cop, got between Luca and me. Probably saved me from a good whooping. And when I'm not looking, Raff fucking takes him away like a common criminal. You got him locked up in here?"

I heard a scuffle and imagined the same woman who'd hopped across the bar, pink bat in hand pushing Leonard out of the way.

"You can't go in there, Faith," Leonard said.

The bartender from the night before stepped into the doorway. I hadn't remembered her as quite so tall, putting her at a lean five-ten.

She had naturally sandy-blonde hair and a tanned angular face. I'd been leaning against the opposite wall and waved at her as she looked me up and down appraisingly.

"That's him," she said. "Get him out of there. I saw the whole thing. That turd Raff tased him before he even hit the ground."

"You sure about that?" Leonard asked.

"I have security video," she said. "Watch it yourself if you don't believe me."

I could hear a long sigh and the jingle of keys as Cal Leonard appeared behind Faith Hudson. She hadn't taken her eyes off me and gave me a crooked grin as she stepped into the open space next to the cell.

"Hollie, call Raff and get him in here," Leonard said, separating the keys and finding the one that unlocked the cell. "We need to talk."

"You really a cop?" Faith asked. She had a predatory look on her face, like she was deciding if she wanted to try finishing what Luca had started.

"I've got a badge," I said, walking out of the cell and shaking Sheriff Leonard's hand.

"Mr. Biggston is from Sutherland PD," Leonard said.

"Mr. Biggston have a first name?" she asked, still looking at me. She pushed off from where she'd been resting against the wall and walked over to me, holding my cell phone in one hand. I caught a hint of expensive perfume.

"Henry," I said accepting the phone. She held on to her end for a minute. "Most people call me Biggs."

"Well, Biggs. I put my phone number in your phone," she said, releasing it. "Call me if you want to cash in on that drink I owe you." I raised my eyebrows. I started to wonder if I had a type, because this girl was definitely trouble and I was definitely going to call.

"Careful with that one," Leonard said once she'd left the room.

"Yeah, those Hudson girls are bat-shit crazy," Luca added. It made me wonder what a person would have to do to get Luca Quinn to think they were crazy.

"Sorry we're off to a rough start," I said, taking in the station as Leonard lead me into the main room.

The room was long and narrow, sparsely appointed with furniture, including a few narrow desks that sat back to back. In the corner, along the back wall, was a larger desk that obviously belonged to the sheriff. Opposite his desk, on the same wall, were double glass doors flanked by another desk where the middle-aged woman in civilian clothes sat. It was probably the same woman who'd hung up on me when I'd called the first time.

"Deputy Butler is a work in progress," he said. "Sorry if he roughed you up. Do you want to press charges?"

I shook my head. "He was just trying to do his job," I said.

"I heard about the traffic stop on 385 last night, too," he said. "We've all been on edge since Char got shot. It's not an excuse, but I appreciate you not making a thing out of it."

"You mind if I go over to Sage and Rosemary to let my dog out?" I asked.

"Hollie, we'll be back in a couple of hours," Leonard said, grabbing a wide-brimmed cowboy hat from a coat tree.

"What about Raff?" she asked. "He's on his way in."

"I imagine he has some reports to write after his busy night," Leonard said. "I'll see him when we get back."

Handing me my coat and baggie of personal items, Leonard gave me the onceover. "You have a hat?" he asked.

"Got one in my truck," I said. "Oh, right, that's probably still over at Hootskill."

Through the glass doors, we turned to our right and caught wooden stairs leading down to the first level. By my reckoning, we were just behind the large sheriff's logo that I'd seen lit up the night before. Reaching the first level, we had a choice to go back to the garage area and processing, or to go forward out the front door.

"Got some good snow yesterday. Tough drive?" he asked, making small talk.

"Not once I got past the sleet. There weren't a lot of people out on Highway 2," I said.

His rig was a new GMC Yukon, painted white with gold-trimmed stars on each door. The vehicle smelled new and lacked the electronics package I'd become used to while on SPD patrols. His equipment was minimal, with a radio that hung from the dash and a shotgun locked in place between the front seats. Wire mesh separated the front seats from the middle bench and even more wire separated the rear cargo area. He caught me looking over the vehicle.

"Quite a change from patrol. Am I right?" he asked.

"Not sure what I think about it," I said. "Good information on the terminals, but they can be a pain too."

He laughed. "There are eight thousand souls who call Butte County home. Most of those folks abide by the rules. We're here to deal with the rest. Our best computer sits between our ears. I'd rather have a man with his head up and eyes on the terrain."

He backed out from the angle parking that ran the entire block in front of the sheriff's station. A plow had been by in the middle of the night and the snow on the road was already melting under the bright sun.

"Pretty country," I said. "I didn't realize this area of the state was so nice."

"Most people don't," he said, turning down the street behind the hotel. Across the parking lot, I saw Mortimer Cook standing in a silky bathrobe, wearing a fur-lined hat and throwing snow at Diva, who pranced around him excitedly. "What the heck is he doing?" the sheriff wondered idly.

"That's my dog," I said, hopping out as we pulled to a stop.

"Out of jail so soon?" Morty called.

"Is everything okay?" I asked, worried that Diva had gotten into trouble.

"Sure. What's it look like?" he asked.

Diva, seeing me, raced over, tongue hanging from her mouth, pure joy on her face.

"Hey, girl," I said, scratching behind her ears.

"I got a tip that you'd been locked up after a fight at Hootskill. Figured I'd save my wood floors from any accidents. She's a good girl, she is," he fawned over her. Diva was picky about people and I had no idea what her rules were, but Morty was clearly good people by her estimation.

"Appreciate it if you didn't run that story," Sheriff Leonard said. "More of a mix-up than anything. I'd owe you one."

"Still protecting that Butler kid?" he asked.

"You'll do it?"

"Ah, wasn't much of a story either way, seeing that you've decided young Mr. Biggston here isn't a bad egg," Morty said. "Word is, he was protecting the virtue of Miss Faith Hudson. Of course, that path only leads to madness."

"Be nice, Morty," Leonard warned.

"Just saying. She's chewed up and spit out more than her share," Morty said and stomped back toward the hotel entrance. Diva ran after him, thinking it was still play-time.

"Heel," I ordered, raising my voice only slightly. Diva flipped her head back and perked her ears. It was unusual for me to have to give a second order and I clucked my tongue for a light reinforcement. That was all she needed. She ran back to my side, brushing her right shoulder into my leg.

"Impressive," Leonard said. "You need anything from your room?"

"Don't think so, although I'm not sure what you have on tap for the day," I said.

"Thought we'd get some breakfast, then take a drive," he said, swinging his bulk up into his truck.

I walked around and opened the door behind mine on the passenger side. "Kennel," I ordered. Diva complied and jumped onto the seat, her paws crusted with snow.

"She's smaller than I'd expect for a K-9 unit," Cal Leonard said when I jumped in beside him.

"Her primary mission was explosives and narcotic detection," I said. "She's trained in apprehension too, but size isn't required for takedowns."

"Some K-9s are big," he said. "I remember some of those beasts from back in the day."

"More likely guard dogs, where size is a deterrent. Trust me, she'll knock down any perp on the run."

"Even Luca Quinn?" he asked, grinning.

"I don't think you could knock down Luca Quinn with a tractor," I said.

"Did he really run you through that barn wall out at Hootskill?"

"I thought he was going to murder Faith," I said. "I've never seen a big man move that fast. Did he ever play ball?"

"Full-ride scholarship to the university but never played a single game," he said, turning north on Highway 385 toward the bar. "Got caught selling weed during training camp."

"That's a shame," I said.

"He's your kin, you know," he said, pulling up behind my truck. "Grab your carry piece. I don't want anyone riding in a marked car empty-handed."

I opened the truck and grabbed Diva's go-bag that had everything from leashes to water. I unlocked my gun-safe and extracted my Kimber 1911 forty-five with the inside waistband holster and the ankle-strapped 9mm Walther. I also grabbed a camo stocking hat and tight gloves I could shoot with if necessary.

"Hannah Quinn's a piece of work," I said, picking up the conversation we'd been having before we'd stopped. "If I have it right, she's my second cousin."

"That's the way I figure it."

"Pappi says you and Pearl dated in high school," I said, changing subjects. "What was she like back then?"

He pulled out of the parking lot and headed back to town. "Surprised he brought that up. I always believed he held that against me," Leonard said. "Pearl Quinn was the prettiest girl ever to go to school in these parts. Biggest regret of my life, letting her slip away. That Lester, he's a lucky man."

It was interesting to hear about Nanna from another man's perspective. I'd always thought of her as pretty and valued the special bond I had with her. Part of me felt jealousy at hearing his wistful memories of her.

"He's only had good things to say about you," I said. "You must have made a good impression. Pearl, too."

"Less complicated time back then," he said, pulling into the parking lot of Boone's Diner. It was like a page out of the fifties with faux stone walls and angled glass windows looking over cushioned booths. Porcelain gas station signs and rusty farm tools hung on the walls as decoration. "Will the dog be okay in the vehicle?"

"She's a registered service dog," I said, pulling out the harness I used in crowded areas.

"Does she alert on weed?" he asked.

"She might," I said. "Most of the time I have to tell her to search."

He smiled. "Could be interesting."

We were met at the front register by an older black gentleman, wearing a collared shirt and an apron. "Sheriff, can't have dogs in the restaurant. Health code violation," the man said.

"Boone, she's a registered, drug-sniffing service dog," he said.

"That so?" Boone asked. "Look, Sheriff, you know I smoke some for my glaucoma. Why you looking to make trouble today?"

"No trouble, Boone. Just looking for breakfast," the sheriff said.

Diva whined as Boone passed in front of her. He gave Diva a baleful glance but grabbed menus and hastily led us to a table at the front of the restaurant where we could look out at the highway.

"What can I tell you about the position?" Leonard asked, turning over a white coffee mug and sliding it to the edge of the table. I settled Diva onto the floor next to me and sat, doing the same with another mug.

"I'm more interested in why you think your deputy got shot and if you think that shooting is linked to the deputy who was killed in the line of duty," I said.

He sighed. "Geez kid, you remind me so damn much of your grandfather. Don't you want to know about money? Hours? If you're going to report to Raff? Those sorts of things? I've got this whole sales pitch worked up."

I held up my hand and counted off on my fingers. "More than I make now. I don't have a life. You'll find Raff in a trunk somewhere if you do. And I don't think we'll know if I'm a good match until we give it a try."

He grinned as Boone returned with a coffee carafe, which he dropped on the table and looked at us expectantly.

"Trust me on breakfast?" Leonard asked, looking at me. When I nodded, he turned back to Boone. "Two hot strippers. Eggs over easy, extra bacon."

"Any juice?" Boone asked, looking at me.

I shook my head. I was already tired. If I had too much sugar, I'd crash and fall asleep.

"The only thing we know for sure about George Lynch's death was that it didn't happen where we found his vehicle," he said.

"Somebody moved him?"

"He took a fifty-caliber round to the chest while he was sitting in the vehicle. Right through his vest," he said. "Whoever shot him then went to all the trouble of driving the truck back to the highway and putting George back in the driver's seat."

"You sound pretty sure of that," I said. "How is it you know that, but not where he was shot?"

"He'd gotten a call that night. Fish and Game requesting backup. He never showed up. We have GPS units in the rigs. When they get into cell range, they upload data. Whoever shot George knew that detail, because at eleven-twenty-two we got the last update from his unit," Leonard said. "He was shot at twelve-thirty, nearly an hour and a half later."

"And you know he was moved because the highway is within cell phone range," I said, filling in the blanks. "If contact was made there, GPS would have kept updating."

"That's what I figure. Plus, there was no glass from the windshield anywhere on the road where we found the car."

"What about Officer Shephard? She got away," I said. "Paper's account wasn't anything like what happened to Deputy Lynch."

"I'm not even sure it's the same group," he said.

"Heads-up," Boone said, pushing two steaming plates of food onto the table. Diva didn't even bother raising her head as he reached across her.

"Best breakfast in the county, right here," Leonard said grandly. "Thank you, Boone."

"Dog like some bacon?" Boone asked.

I chuckled absently. Bribery wouldn't work with Diva. Alerting on drugs was a game for her and she could care less whose it was. That said, she was probably hungry. "Sure," I said.

Atop a waffle sat three strips of fried chicken drenched in white sausage gravy. As if that weren't enough, three strips of bacon lay atop the gravy, acting as a shelf for three eggs, over easy. I cut into the end of the waffle and took a bite. I was hungry, but the talk of George Lynch being murdered made the food taste like ash. I set my fork aside, poured coffee into my cup and sat back in the booth, trying to work through the problem.

"What was the call from Fish and Game?" I asked.

"That's right where I get to every time," the sheriff said, enthusiastically cutting into his own stack of food before jamming a big bite home.

AT CAL LEONARD'S INSISTENCE, I made an attempt at the meal in front of me, but I just didn't have the heart for it.

"I'd planned to take you out to the range this morning and qualify you on weapons," he said. "It's department policy. After that, I thought we'd run over to Crawford, then down 71 and bring county roads back. That'll put us to midafternoon."

"My time is yours," I said.

"You boys finished here?" Boone asked, picking up Leonard's plate. Diva raised her head, thumping her tail at his presence.

Cal Leonard caught the interaction and gave me a questioning look. "You sure she can't be bought?"

"Oh, she can definitely be bought," I said. "She's ruined for apprehension with Mr. Boone here." My statement caused Boone's face to light up with a broad smile. "I'm just saying that if we took her back into the kitchen, she'd alert on that first refrigerator and it wouldn't be for the bacon." Boone's smile disappeared and he turned away, hurrying back to the kitchen.

"Boone's good people," Leonard said. "I don't come down too hard on personal use."

I nodded. In the academy, I'd learned that every officer was responsible for enforcing the law. No superior officer could direct another officer who reported to them to do otherwise. If I'd gone in fresh from high school, I might have bristled at Leonard's conflicting statement, but my time in the Rangers had taught me to pick my battles. The fact was, Leonard was running the show and as long as his grey areas didn't run up against what I felt was reasonable, I wouldn't buck him.

"Imagine you'd feel differently if you thought he was dealing," I said.

Leonard gave me a sharp look. I held his gaze impassively as he looked for hidden meaning in my words. I'd learned long ago that veteran cops had the capacity to read minds as long as they could look a person in the eyes. "You're tough to read," he finally said.

"I wouldn't have had a social life in high school otherwise," I said, allowing a slow grin on my face. "Any chance we could stop by the hospital and talk with Char Shephard when we get back in town?"

He shrugged and pushed his bulk out from the cushioned booth. "Staties have interviewed her pretty thoroughly." I was pretty sure he was referring to the State Patrol Investigative Services Division.

"This is an ISD case?"

"They're treating her shooting and Lynch's death as separate incidents," he said.

"Heel," I ordered, pulling my wallet out. I hadn't seen a bill but figured a twenty ought to cover my side of things.

Leonard waved me off. "You're a guest of Butte County," he said.

"So ISD's running both investigations?" I asked, following him through the front door. The job suddenly lost much of its appeal.

"If you can call it that." He swung up into his truck with an audible grunt. "Working theory is that Deputy Lynch was killed by a hunter who covered it up by moving the car."

I loaded Diva and climbed into the passenger side. "Fifty caliber is too big of a round for hunting."

"They know that," he said, pulling out of the parking lot, throwing gravel out behind his wheels. "They still haven't located the crime scene. Even if they had, we've had two snows since then. Unless they get a tip or a confession, the case isn't going anywhere."

"That can't sit too well with you," I said.

He slammed a meaty hand against the steering wheel in obvious frustration. "George Lynch was a friend of mine. He'd been a deputy for twelve years. Left behind a wife and a daughter who goes to high school here in Wood Creek. State says my department is too close to this and that *they* need to own the investigation. Amy Lynch is going to graduate high school without her father. She's going to walk down the aisle without her father. She's going to raise kids who won't know their grandfather. I sure as hell *am* too close to this! I'm also the law around here and the people of Butte County voted for me because I told them I'd keep them safe. How safe do you think they feel with my deputies ending up in the crosshairs?"

"Can you get copies of the evidence ISD gathered?" I asked.

Cal Leonard's thick jowls and cheeks were bright red and he stared straight ahead. "You know what we were doing the day after Char got shot?" he asked.

I shook my head, certain he wasn't looking for an answer.

"We were walking the hillside next to where she was shot, looking for casings or trash or anything that would give us a clue as to who'd shot her and why," he said. "We had twenty men out. Fish and Game, ISD, hell, we even had three local hunting guides join us. You know what we found?"

"I hope you found brass," I said.

"Nope. Eight hours. We covered five square miles and found five beer cans, two old shotgun shells and an empty tin of Red Man snuff. And before you ask, the cans were at least ten days old. What I'm telling you is there is no evidence from either scene. ISD has nothing and I've got eight thousand citizens who believe it's open season on the sheriff's department."

"Deputy Shephard is conscious," I said. "Why was your search area so big? Even if her memory wasn't that great, her GPS should have pinpointed where she got turned around."

"Turns out her GPS unit wasn't sending that day. ISD tech says there was corrosion on the connections. No foul play suspected," he said.

I sighed. No eye witnesses. No crime scenes. I understood his frustration. "What's Deputy Shephard say?"

"She doesn't remember a thing," he said.

"You believe her?"

"Char's new to the force, only been here three years," he said. "Came over from Wyoming. Single mom with no family in the area. I get a sense that she's scared, but Doc says short-term memory loss isn't uncommon in traumatic events. You ever been shot, Biggs?"

"Yes."

"You remember it?"

I nodded. "More than I'd like."

"Me too."

⸻

"You need a score of eighty-two percent," he said. "I'll run targets out to five, ten, and twenty yards. While we're on range, you need to show control of your weapon at all times." A shorter safety brief I'd never received.

The shooting range was little more than a locked wooden shed opposite a dirt embankment in a wide-open grassy field. Dirt had been piled up, flanking the shooting lanes. Idly, I wondered if the weapons check was a new interviewing requirement, given the state of things in Butte County.

"Any time limit?" I accepted a basket he'd filled from the shed with two boxes of fifty-round 45 ACP ammo and a single box for my 357 magnum. He ignored my question and peeled off several paper targets from a giant stack in a bin on the shed floor, handing them to me. "Clips are on the posts."

Bright sunshine reflected off the frozen crust of snow that crunched under my feet. The post at five-yards had seen much better days and fell over when I tried to attach a target. I picked it up and pushed it back into its hole only to get the same result once I let go. Looking around, I found a rock and wedged it next to the post. The design of the l-shaped holder was such that a good shot wouldn't hit the post, but rather sail through the paper and into the earthen backstop. If I hit this post just once, I'd be back setting it up again.

"Every deputy has to qualify with their sidearm each year. Deputy Lynch was my senior deputy and it was his responsibility to see to making sure everyone qualified," Leonard said.

"Who's senior now?" I asked, pushing squishy ear protection into my ears.

Before placing the targets, I'd left both my 1911 and Walther CCP on the bench that made up the firing line.

"Haven't identified one yet," he said. "Most likely be Gene Ellis. He's been here the longest. You any good with that little CCP?"

"At close range. The three-inch barrel makes it unpredictable at long range," I said as he picked it up.

"You mind?" he asked, nodding at the small weapon.

"Not at all."

He aimed at the twenty-yard target and squeezed off a shot. It was down and to the left by six inches. It wasn't a bad shot, but the position suggested he was anticipating the recoil. Cursing under his breath, he settled into a boxer stance and fired a second shot. This time the shot was up two inches but still well left of the target.

"Nice shots," I said.

"You mean not bad for an old guy, don't you?"

I grinned. I didn't want to insult him. "Not really. It's an unfamiliar gun at twenty yards. If you're aiming for center mass, that's a hit."

He unclipped the holster on his 357 magnum and handed it to me. The nickel-plated barrel was scratched from being holstered and drawn repeatedly. I pushed the extractor rod back and flipped open the cylinder. It spun slowly, obviously in need of a thorough cleaning.

"You put four out of six closer than I did at twenty yards and I'll check you off personally," he said.

I looked down the barrel. It was a nice weapon that hadn't been fired in a long time. I tilted my wrist, dropping the cylinder back in place. "Hardly a fair contest," I said. "This thing has a five-inch barrel."

"Humor me," he said.

I straightened my arm and slapped my left hand beneath, dropping into a weaver stance. Range shooting and returning fire were completely different things in my universe. The calm of hours of practice settled over me as I sighted down the barrel. And just as I squeezed off my first shot. I heard a gunshot right next to me. I flinched, sending my shot wild, hitting the edge of the paper.

"I'll give you that one," I said, not bothering to look over at him. I set his gun on the table in front of me.

"What are you doing? You've got five more to go," he said, chuckling.

"Resetting," I said.

I've always been a better shot when under pressure. For some reason, the tension focuses my senses and I can just feel when I'm perfectly lined up. With as little warning as I could give the sheriff, I reached for the gun and raised it, firing almost immediately. His old gun kicked like a mule and I was impatient at the extra effort required to push it back on target. I fired a second round. This time, I was aware of Leonard firing my CCP, but I didn't care or let it distract me. I fired twice more, only pausing long enough to regain my sight picture. After four shots, I set the gun down.

"You have one more," he said, setting the CCP down.

"What are we doing out here, Sheriff?" I asked. "I don't believe for a minute you interview other deputies by testing their firing accuracy."

He walked around the bench and headed out across the field toward the targets. He had long legs and I had to hustle to catch him.

"In the last two months, I've lost two friends. A good friend is trusting his grandson to my care. I need to know you're a shooter."

He pulled the target from the clips and the post fell over. My shots were closely grouped high and to the right, two inches from center.

"Damn son, that's some mighty nice shooting," he said, looking at me for a reaction. "By the way, I don't flinch. My gun shoots high and to the right. About two inches."

I nodded.

"Thirty-six thousand a year and five hundred a month in housing allowance," he said.

"Housing allowance?" I asked.

"You have to live in the county. Probably best somewhere close to Wood Creek," he said. "Other deputies are in county-provided homes. Technically, I should have kicked Mary and her daughter out, but I just don't have the heart to do it."

"Mary?" I asked. "Deputy Lynch's family?"

"That's right," he said. "Back in the sixties, things were a lot like they are today. We were having trouble attracting young deputies. Four houses were built, two here in Wood Creek, one in Crawford and another in Hay Springs. They're not much, but the price is right."

"What about Diva coming along on patrol?" I asked.

"She's welcome until she's a problem," he said. "First two weeks, you ride with Gene. After that, you're on your own."

"Patrol? Speed enforcement?" I asked.

"That's right," he answered. "We serve the occasional warrant. Judge Benz shows up twice a month, second and fourth Tuesdays, so we need someone to stand in while he's in session. Haven't had an eviction for a while, but we do that too. We get all DB calls. It varies. You'll be on five ten-hour shifts each week. Don't be surprised if most of those are nights and weekends. You'll also be on call. If you work past fifty hours, you can put in for overtime, but I need to approve it first."

While he'd been talking, we'd pulled the unused targets and

returned them and ammo to the shed. He handed me the partial box of 9mm. The sheriff had only used four bullets from my CCP's magazine, so I started to open the box to put the ammo back when he shook his head, stopping me.

"Keep it," he said, locking the door behind us. "Do you have any questions?"

"Will you or ISD get in my way if I look into the shootings of Deputy Lynch and Deputy Shephard?" I asked. "I'll do it on my own time, but you gotta know, that's why I'm here."

"You remind me of Lester," he said, jumping back into his vehicle. "Any chance we'll keep you after this mess gets figured out?"

"Honestly, I have no idea," I said, climbing in. Diva was sleeping in a ray of sunshine that had warmed up her seat. I had intended to get her out for a quick walk, but she looked comfortable. I looked around and worked to recall the Butte County map I'd studied before taking the trip out. South Dakota was to the north and I hadn't realized that the black hills extended so far south.

The sheriff had gotten us back onto the highway, but we headed away from town. The further we drove, the more we sank to the southwest and the far end of the county. It was mostly snow-covered grassland north of Wood Creek. To the south, however, a dark ridge of trees and tall hills rose to intersect with the highway.

"I never get tired of the open country," Cal Leonard mused as he sped down the highway. I was surprised to see we were doing eighty-five. "Those trees are the National Forest," he said. "You came through the eastern side of it when you came into Wood Creek last night. Hills are steeper out this way. Wyoming is only twenty miles west."

"Antelope season is about over. Do you get a lot of hunters up here?" I asked.

"That and deer," he said. "Busy season for our buddies over at Fish and Game."

"We get along okay with them?"

"You mean rivalry between departments?" he asked, to which I nodded. "Nah, nothing like that. They're more short-handed than we are. There's a lot of country out here to cover and not enough good people to cover it. That means most of the time we're running solo. Credit is a game we don't need to play."

"Is ISD part of that group?" I asked.

He laughed. "You got me there. No. ISD doesn't play nice. When they take over an investigation, they like to keep everyone else locked out."

The sheriff slowed as we crossed into the forest. The transition was like night and day. One minute we were in wide open plains with nothing but coyotes between us and the next state, and a second later, we were surrounded by giant pines. He picked the handset from the radio and depressed the lever.

"Butte Base, this is one," he called.

"Butte-1, go ahead," a woman answered.

"Hollie, give Jasper White a call for me," he said into the microphone. "We're fifteen minutes out from Crawford station. I'd like to introduce him to Henry Biggston."

"Copy that, Cal," she answered. "Butte Base out."

"Is White the ranger who asked for Lynch's help the day he was shot?" I asked.

Abruptly, Cal Leonard slowed the truck and pulled off to the side. Diva slid forward and almost fell off her seat, catching herself at the last moment. Pulled from her nap, she sniffed the air, wary of trouble. The truck listed to the right toward a deep ditch on my side of the highway.

"Right there is where we found him," he said, pointing across the road. "Just pulled off to the side."

"Can we take a look?" I asked, pulling out my phone.

"Won't be much left after two months," he said, pushing his door open. A car sped past, swinging wide but not slowing.

I didn't like Diva being this close to a highway without positive control, so I clipped a leash to her harness and got her out. The three of us walked across the road to a wide portion of the shoulder. The sun hadn't made it to this section of the road much and snow covered the shoulder, the nearby slope and the forest floor. A plow had been along at some point and pushed the snow from the road onto the shoulder in heavy clumps. Leonard was right, there wasn't much to see.

"Which way was the car facing?" I asked. We'd been traveling south, gaining elevation.

"With traffic. Downhill," Leonard said, raising an eyebrow.

"What kind of vehicle?" I asked.

"George had our new F150 Interceptor," he said. "Only twenty thousand miles on it."

I walked back into the road and, with my phone, took a picture of the spot where the truck had been found. I turned, taking more pictures of the highway and surrounding terrain in both directions.

"What are you thinking?" he asked.

I looked down the hill to the closest patch of legally huntable land. It was six thousand yards if it was foot.

"That's a helluva shot. Did anyone walk the area down there and find brass? And who hunts with a fifty-cal?"

"Don't know what ISD did, and that theory is bullshit," Leonard said, spitting snuff onto the ground. "You see what you wanted?"

I nodded and walked back to his vehicle.

"You're not a big talker, are you?" Leonard asked, after a few minutes of driving.

"A lot to take in," I said. "You have a lot of geographic diversity in the county: mountains, grassy plains, farmland, forests. About the only thing you don't have are cities."

"And?"

"Things are so spread out, there's a lot of privacy," I said.

"True," Leonard said, obviously trying to keep me talking.

"Seems like Deputy Lynch ran into someone doing something they didn't want him to see. I know that's obvious. It just changes how you think about it. He got moved because they didn't want to bring attention to where he was killed. I feel like if we find the crime scene, we might find the crime."

"Unless they've packed up and moved on," Leonard said.

"Doesn't it seem odd to you that Deputy Shepard can't remember where she was and that her GPS failed?"

"You think she's in on it?"

"No idea," I said. "How many of your rigs don't have operational GPS units?"

"You're going to need to dial that back, son," he said. "Char Shephard is a good woman."

"No one is going to like me asking questions," I said.

He laughed out loud. "You're kinda full of piss and vinegar, aren't you? It's the quiet ones that always surprise me."

"The Army used to say I had issues letting things go," I said.

We'd just passed the small town of Crawford when Cal slowed and turned west onto Highway 20. There was a sign that indicated a state park a few miles ahead.

"I need you to understand some things," he said.

I nodded, still looking out the window, my head moving perhaps half an inch. He needed me to acknowledge his comment, not necessarily to agree with him.

"I've been protecting the citizens of Butte County for thirty-two years. First as a deputy and then as sheriff. I take that responsibility seriously," he said.

I nodded again.

"On my watch, two of my officers have been gunned down in the line of duty. Do you have any idea how that makes me feel?"

I closed my eyes. My best friend in the Army had been Angel Lopez. He'd originally been Diva's handler and had taken a grenade for me. In the early morning hours when I was between sleep and wakefulness, I could hear Angel's shout for us to get down. The explosion always came and Angel always died. I knew what it was to lose a friend to combat.

"There are criminals in my county who have murdered once and gotten too close to committing a second one. I want to find out what happened to Deputies Lynch and Shepard more than you can possibly know. I want the people who did this brought to justice. And if I'm honest, I want to see them swing from the end of a rope."

Sheriff Leonard was getting riled up, steeling himself for the fight he knew would come.

"When I contacted your grandfather about this job, he told me he didn't want me talking to you about it. He's my friend and mentor, so I let it go. I figured he thought the job was too dangerous. I could respect that; he was protecting his own."

I looked out the window. He was wrong about Pappi. Pappi didn't fear the job. He feared my inability to back down.

"Imagine my surprise when I got his call two days ago, shortly after Deputy Shepard came under fire."

I nodded.

"Thing is, I've known men like you, Biggs," he said. "Men who know what it's like to stand between the darkness and the light. You see, I used to be like you, Biggs. But now I'm old and fat."

I decided that this time nodding was a bad idea so I continued staring out the window. He chuckled at my politic reaction to his self-assessment.

"I asked Lester why he had a change of heart. You have any idea what he said?" he said.

"I don't," I admitted.

"Not a damn thing. He just asked if I wanted to find my deputy's murderer. I told him I did."

"FORT ROBINSON IS one of two state parks in Butte County," Leonard said, his mood lightening as he switched to tour guide mode. "We'll get a trickle of visitors throughout the winter, but the parks really get hopping in the summer."

"I had no idea this was here," I admitted. The natural beauty of the entire drive hadn't been lost on me, nor had the scant number of vehicles we'd seen since leaving Wood Creek. "A person could get lost out here."

"Pearl never brought you out here?" he asked.

"Not that I remember," I said. "But she wasn't much into camping."

He frowned and I could tell he was carefully considering his next words. "Best of my knowledge, she still has property out here."

"I guess I didn't know that," I said.

"Surprised she didn't say anything before you came out," he said. "Yeah, her and her sister inherited the family ranch. I seem to recall it was split right down the middle when old man Quinn passed. Susie got the house and the farm, Pearl got the ranch land. Terrible what happened to Susie. I've always believed that's why Pearl never came back this way."

I shrugged. "I'm not sure."

"You don't know, do you?" he asked. When I didn't answer, he continued, "Pearl's sister, Susie, was murdered by her daughter Hannah's boyfriend, Joey Fritz. I was just a deputy back then. Fritz was bad news – a biker. Ran drugs, guns – anything to make a quick buck. Died in prison a few years back."

"I saw Hannah at the station," I said. "She's pretty rough. Was she involved?"

"Not as far as we could find," he said, pulling into a gravel parking lot at the back of a large, brick two-story building. Two official-looking pickups sat in the drive, one substantially older than the other. "Looks like Hollie got ahold of Ranger White. That's his green truck."

Diva stretched in the back seat and ducked her head. She'd been sitting long enough that she really wanted out. I opened the door and turned to grab her bowl and a water bottle from the go-bag. She was quick about her business and so I whistled her back to the truck.

"How many rangers in Butte County?" I asked.

"A dozen or so," he answered. "Maybe a few more. They keep mostly to the parks. Jasper's the senior ranger."

"Sheriff Leonard." A man wearing dark green slacks and a lighter green shirt came out of the building and we walked forward to meet him. "I heard voices, figured it was you."

"Jasper," Cal Leonard nodded. "Wanted to introduce you to Henry Biggston. Might be joining my department."

The man was of medium build with short, jet black hair. He extended his hand and we shook. "Jasper White," he said. "What brings you out this way?"

"Work," I said.

"Darn shame what happened to Deputy Shepard," he said, turning to Leonard. "She was good people. But I imagine that's not what you came out here to talk about."

"When you requested backup from Deputy Lynch, I know you

were planning to meet down Squaw Creek road. I didn't see in the report I got from ISD where you were actually heading."

"Wasn't in the report because he never showed up," he answered.

"What was the call?" Leonard pushed.

"I had reports of poachers back on the north branch of Squaw Creek road," he said, doing his best to look earnest under Leonard's withering gaze.

"Where?"

"Down towards Rock Canyon. I didn't have an exact location," he said. "After waiting about an hour for Deputy Lynch, we gave up and started in. Figured he got another call."

"You find anything?"

"No. We'd been hiking for about an hour when we got the call about Lynch."

"Thanks, Jasper," Leonard said, his face softening.

Jasper White looked relieved. "ISD still doesn't have anything?"

"They're saying it was a hunting accident," Leonard said.

"What a way to go," White answered.

"Yup," Leonard seemed finished and started to turn.

"Did you ever get back out there?" I asked, before White could walk away.

"Where?" White asked.

"Rock Canyon via Squaw Creek road," I said.

"No, I guess we didn't," he said. "It's been over a month. I doubt we'd find anything."

I nodded and Leonard looked at me with raised eyebrows.

"Anything else?" Cal asked.

"You were on foot?" I wasn't done with White yet.

"That's right. Terrain's too rough for four-wheelers," White said, shifting uncomfortably. "Why?"

"Trying to get an idea how much terrain you would have covered," I said.

"Not much," he answered. "It's slow going in that area. Lots of hunters this time of year too. Need to be careful."

"Thanks for your time, Jasper," Leonard said.

"No problem. Hope to see you again, Henry," White replied.

Cal led me back to the truck and away from the Crawford Ranger Station. I could feel White's eyes on our backs as we left.

"What's the relationship between rangers and the sheriff's department?" I asked.

"Rangers are responsible for conservation and park management - think poachers and parties," Leonard said. "They carry weapons and make arrests. If it's more than a summons, though, they'll give us a call."

"He seemed nervous," I said when we got into the truck.

"That's Jasper," he said, pulling out of the parking lot, retracing our path back to the main highway. "Your family property is about five miles over that way." He pointed east toward the national forest.

I took out my phone and opened the map. "By Squaw Creek?" I asked.

"Creek goes right through the ranch land. It's low this time of year, but there's always a bit of water in it." Cal slowed and turned onto gravel. The road, simply enough, was named after the creek. "If we cut through here, it'll take us over to 385, which gets us back to Wood Creek."

At sixty miles an hour, I soon became uncomfortable with the gravel sliding beneath the vehicle especially when we hit washboards. Leonard was either a crazy man or in a hurry. On my map application, I traced our path as we drove up and down the steep hills with deep, unforgiving drop-offs only inches beyond my door. Like an old billy goat, however, the hills seemed like Cal's good friend. He navigated the terrain confidently with one hand draped lazily over the wheel, lost in thought.

"Turn south here and you get out of the forest in three miles," he said. "We'll turn up Table Rock Road and be back to town in an hour."

Once I got past the possibility we might die, I found it cathartic to be surrounded by the pine-forested hills. Nature had always called to me and the raw beauty of the snowy slopes and tall trees was breathtaking.

—

"Feel like a steak?" he asked as we finally pulled into Wood Creek.

I looked at my phone. At one thirty, I was starving, having mostly ignored breakfast. "Who doesn't like steak?" I asked.

"I knew I liked you," Cal said, pulling into the parking lot of a nice-looking stand-alone restaurant. The sign read *Coppermill*. With a fancy copper-colored steel roof and broad windows that looked out over a lush golf course, I realized this wouldn't likely be a regular lunch stop for me.

A greeter wearing black pants and a white shirt met us at the door. "Sheriff Leonard, welcome." The girl looked to be all of fifteen years old. "Two today?"

"Thank you, Sadie," he answered. "Regular spot if you don't mind."

"No problem," she said and led us past a large stone fireplace where embers glowed amongst a dwindling fire.

"You know what's next, I assume?" Leonard asked, after we ordered.

"I figured steaks meant you were offering me the job."

"I'm asking you to commit to a year," he said. "Butte County takes some getting used to. I think once you do, you'll come to love it like I do."

"It's beautiful country," I said.

"This job is more than being a deputy," he said. "I plan to retire in a few years. With your service in the Rangers and your family roots here, I think you could make a real run at sheriff. Especially if I backed you."

I sat back in my chair. I'd prepared for a lot of possible conversations, but this wasn't one of them. "Me? What about Ellis and Butler?"

He shook his head. "Despite your introduction, Raff is a good man. Ellis too. But neither of them are leaders. Raff is too easily drawn into the petty stuff and Ellis is on cruise control."

"Do they know how you feel?" I asked.

"Raff does," he answered. "No reason to bring it up with Ellis."

"Did Raff know I was coming in yesterday?"

Leonard smiled. "You think he was looking for you when he pulled you over?"

"It would explain some things."

"He knew."

"Do we have any budget for the Lynch investigation?" I asked.

"All the gas you want to burn," he said. "And monthly lunches here at Coppermill. What were you thinking?"

"I have a friend who's an expert with all things electronic," I said. "I'd like to have him look at the GPS systems."

"We have a guy in town who does that," he said. I raised my eyebrows. "And right, we've had some failures. Your friend make house calls?"

"I think I could convince him," I said. "What about Lynch's truck? Did ISD give it back yet?"

"Vehicle choice is a matter of time on the job," he said. "I doubt Raff will turn down that truck if Ellis does."

I shook my head. "Not what I was after. I wanted to go over the truck myself," I said. "If it's up to me, I'd drive my Bronco on patrol."

"You might have to since the truck's in the shop waiting for a new seat," Cal said. "The state took the old seat out as evidence. You can go over there any time, although I'm not sure how that's going to help."

"That fifty-cal didn't stop when it hit Lynch," I said. "The seat didn't stop it either."

"The bullet wasn't recovered," he said.

"Which means there's a hole in the cab."

"Body shop already took care of that," he said. "But no reason for you not to look at it."

"They'd have pictures for insurance," I said.

We paused as the server slid steaks onto the table.

"Perfect timing." The sheriff pulled an object from his pocket and set it next to the sizzling steak. It was a bronzed badge with five points. *Deputy Sheriff* was etched on the top and across the bottom, *Butte County*. A black band was stretched around the badge. "Time to make a decision, Biggs. I'm offering you the job of Deputy Sheriff of Butte County."

"I accept," I said, picking up the badge. It had seen a lot of use. The number twelve was indistinct beneath the black mourning band.

"That was George Lynch's badge," he said. "Ordinarily, I'd have retired it and given it to his widow, but she wanted you to have it."

"I don't even know her," I said.

"She told me to give it to the man who'd find her husband's killer. I think that man is you."

━━

"Here to collect on that beer?" Faith Hudson asked as I walked across the mostly empty room and sat on a high stool at the bar. With her hair up and her t-shirt covering her stomach, she looked different. I suspected, as pretty as she was, she'd been hit on in every possible way while bartending.

"Nope, but I'd like to pay for one all the same," I said. "I had a big lunch, how about an Ultra?"

"Hey, Reagan, come over here," she called as she pulled out a cold bottle and set it in front of me atop a square napkin.

A woman who would easily be mistaken for Faith came out from the other side of the bar. She was taller than Faith and not quite as pretty, although if they hadn't been standing side by side I might not have thought that.

Reagan smiled. "Geez, he is good looking."

My face must have turned red because they looked at each other and laughed. "Biggs. Nice to meet you, Reagan," I said, holding my hand out to her. "Sisters?"

"What was your first clue?" Faith asked.

"You're both so ..."

"Don't finish that sentence," Faith interrupted, but I finished anyway.

"... pretty. Sorry, I know you guys must get hit on a lot. Wasn't my intent."

"Faith, don't be such a bitch," Reagan said and walked off. "Nice to meet you, Biggs."

"I thought you were going to say tall, but you saved it," she said.

I grinned. I'd been thinking it, but I knew most tall women didn't like being reminded of their height. I appreciated it, mostly because it almost always cut the shorter guys out of the competition.

"I stopped by to thank you for coming by the station this morning," I said. "You kind of saved my bacon."

"Bacon. That's funny," she said. "How'd your interview go?"

"You knew about that?" I asked.

"Not last night, but I heard about it this morning. Small town. Word travels fast," Faith said.

We heard giggling. Reagan Hudson and a blonde woman stood whispering together across the room. The blonde was younger, shorter – five feet six, at the most – and curvy, where Faith and Reagan were narrow. She was just as pretty as the two Hudson sisters I'd already met.

"Another sister?" I asked.

"That's Lexi." Faith raised her voice. "You can come over, Lexi. He won't bite."

"Matt over at Coppermill said you got the job," Lexi yelled back. "Said they gave you Widow Lynch's badge."

I drained the beer and set it back on the bar along with six dollars.

"I told you I owed you that," Faith said, trying to slide back the money.

"I was hoping I could drink *that* beer with you at some point in the future. I'm heading back to Sutherland tonight," I said.

"You didn't take the job?" Lexi yelled.

"Would you *please* take her away?" Faith asked, looking over to Reagan pleadingly.

"Geez, I just want to know what's going on!" Lexi complained, but allowed Reagan to lead her outside.

"Future? When will you be coming back?" she asked.

"My first shift is a week from Sunday," I said. "I have some things to take care of back home, but I'll be back at the end of the week."

"You've still got my number," she said. "Another beer?"

"One's my limit when I'm driving," I said. "I really just wanted an excuse to talk to you before I took off."

As I stood to leave, I was rewarded with a broad smile. "Drive safe."

━━━

I rolled into Sutherland around midnight, bypassing my rental house in town and deciding instead to sleep out at my grandparent's farm.

Late the next morning, I stumbled down to the kitchen, the smell of bacon too overpowering to ignore.

"We didn't expect you back last night," Pappi said, closing his newspaper and setting it down on the kitchen table.

I heard the soft scrape of a shoe a moment before Pearl leaned in, wrapped her arms around me, and kissed the side of my cheek.

"Heya, beautiful," I whispered, bringing my arm back around her.

She placed a plate on the table in front of me. "Missed you."

Pappi smiled. He'd always enjoyed the relationship Pearl and I shared. "You'll never guess who I ran into," I said.

Pearl sat at a chair and looked at me, her expression tight with worry. "Hannah Quinn?" she asked.

I nodded. "And Luca," I said.

"Is that what happened to the side of your face?" Pappi asked.

I recounted the story of my introduction to Pearl's side of the family.

"I knew I should have told you about them before you went out there," she said, wringing her hands.

"You couldn't have known he'd run into Luca," Pappi said.

"Hannah isn't a very happy woman, but I kind of feel sorry for Luca." I said. "Sheriff Leonard said he thought you still owned land on Squaw Creek."

Pearl shook her head. "Hannah and your mother both have their demons," she said. "I thank God every day that Alice let you go when you were young, Henry. I can't imagine you being raised in the same environment Luca grew up in."

"Quinn ranch was originally two sections. Pearl's inheritance was the section of grassland next to the forest. Not good for much beyond grazing," Pappi said. "Her sister, Susie, inherited the farmable land and the homestead. Last we knew, Hannah was living at the farm."

"Is she married?" I asked, switching to cop mode. "Luca's dad. Is he in the picture?"

"We never met Luca's father." Pearl's hands shook as she picked up her coffee mug.

I placed my hand on her wrist. "I'm sorry to bring it up."

"It's not that, Henry. I never got to resolve things with my sister before she died. I hoped Hannah would have gotten her life together as she got older, but it sounds like she hasn't changed," she said.

"Sheriff Leonard sure has fond memories of you," I said, adding quickly, "both of you, really. He said that you were the prettiest girl in the whole county. He said he regretted ever letting you go."

"He's a good man," Pearl said. "It never would have worked between us, though. Butte County was in his blood and I couldn't get out of there fast enough."

"How'd he end up in Sutherland?" I asked. "With Pappi as his TO, even."

"He was a Marine," Pappi said. "When he got back from deployment, Pearl was the one who suggested SPD."

"You weren't jealous?" I asked.

Pearl turned and smiled at Pappi. "Lester knew that I only had eyes for him."

"I don't know if I'm gonna cry or get sick," I said, scooping in a mouthful of breakfast.

"You're going to take the job, aren't you?" Pappi asked, never one to beat around the bush.

I sat back in my chair, pulled the deputy badge from my pocket and placed it on the table. "That belonged to Deputy Lynch. His widow wanted the next guy to have it," I said, unable to bring myself to admit that her request had been even more than that.

Pappi reached across for the badge and held it in his hand. "That's a lot of weight to carry, Henry."

"Emotional blackmail if you ask me," Pearl said, crossing her arms.

"It wasn't like that," I said. "You don't understand how it is up there. DCI is saying it was a hunting accident. Their equipment is failing. And nobody's asking the right questions. I can't walk away from this."

Pappi grinned. "The call of duty is a bitch, Henry."

"Lester, manners," Pearl said.

"Do you have plenty of cold-weather gear?" Pappi asked, slipping a nut through the bracket as I held the new compressed shock in place. We'd spent the last two days finishing needed repairs on my old Bronco and she was in great shape. Even though Sutherland was only five hours from Butte County, I'd miss easy access to Pappi's workshop.

"Pearl had the same question," I said.

"Is that where she went this morning?" Pappi asked.

"I'm meeting her at the western wear store on Highway 2 after lunch," I said. "If you let me know how much she spends, I'll pay you back."

"And have Pearl after me? No way. And what's with western wear?"

"I need a hat," I said. "Leonard said I can wear one of theirs or get my own, but I need a cowboy hat. Pearl said I shouldn't pick out my own."

"What say we take my truck to your rental house and empty it out this morning," Pappi said.

"I'm out. Already gave the keys to the landlord," I said.

"You get things squared away with the D.A.?" he asked.

"You mean for that mix-up at the hotel or my so-called job?" I asked.

"Both."

"As far as I know, they're letting the hotel thing go. If I hadn't had that video, I might have been in trouble. I talked to D.A. Turner's assistant and handed in my badge. I doubt there are hard feelings. It's not like they were using me," I said.

"You want to get back to Butte County, don't you?" he said. "You can't let it go."

I shrugged as I pumped orange goop onto my hands and worked out the grease. "I just don't understand how Sheriff Leonard can be so hands-off. One deputy is dead and another probably won't walk again. Butte should be a dumpster fire. Where are state police? Where's the outrage? It's crazy to me."

"ISD is investigating. Just because you don't see it, doesn't mean it isn't happening. They won't like you sticking your nose in either, especially with that attitude," he said, locking eyes with me.

"They've had two months to solve Lynch's murder," I said. "They came back with *hunting accident*. A two-mile shot, fifty-caliber hunting accident."

"Keep it to yourself and go slow," Pappi said. "You don't know the players. If you go making accusations, you'll end up stepping on toes you might wish you hadn't. ISD has a lot of good officers, but like everywhere else, they're stretched thin, especially in the western part of the state."

"I'd think everyone would want to catch cop killers," I said. "If this happened in Sutherland, there'd be a taskforce and a round-the-clock investigation until the case got closed. Would you let it go if you were sheriff?"

"Careful, Henry," he said. "Cal's not letting anything go. Trust me. He's more frustrated than you are."

"Didn't seem like that to me," I said.

"Don't get fooled by that western slow-play routine of his," Pappi said. "Cal doesn't like showing his hand and those hands are currently tied by ISD involvement. It'll be a lot easier for him to act surprised when a hot-headed new deputy steps on the ISD investigation than to take them head on. Trust me, Cal doesn't believe that hunting accident story any more than you do."

"Can ISD get me fired?" I asked.

"I've been a cop a long time, Henry," Pappi said. "I've never seen a cop fired for chasing the facts. You need to remember exactly one thing. Cal Leonard is your boss. You stay good with him, it won't matter what ISD thinks. Just remember what I said before, though. ISD aren't the bad guys."

                ⬛

"You're really leaving tomorrow?" Snert asked, taking a piece of pizza from the box on his workbench. It felt like old times with me crashing on his couch while looking for a job. "Mel and I were planning to take you out Saturday night."

"There's another storm coming through on Saturday. I'd like to get ahead of it," I said. "You know you could have told me that you and Mel were a thing."

"I didn't know how you'd feel about it," he said. "To be honest, I didn't really know if what we had was real. I mean, talking on the computer was one thing. I figured she was just lonely. I didn't know she was interested in me for real."

I laughed. "I'd say that lipstick all over your face was pretty real. You guys still going hot and heavy?"

Snert's freckled brown face tinted slightly red as he looked away. "I dunno."

"I'm not asking you to kiss and tell. I'm just kind of loving the fact that my little buddy's got a girl in his life, even if he did steal her from me," I said.

"I wasn't trying to steal her," Snert said, suddenly defensive. "It just kind of happened."

"My bullshit meter's going off. You're a dirty dog and you know it," I said. "It's pretty great, right?"

Snert was unable to hold the smile from his face as images I probably didn't want in my head replayed in his mind. "I never understood why people kissed," he admitted. "It's just ... she's so ... I don't even know how to describe it."

I'd be lying if I didn't admit to a momentary bout of jealousy. Mel Garcia not only had an infectious personality but was great-looking to boot. I could have seen us getting along but in the end, my happiness for Snert overrode any personal loss.

"Did you give any thought to a road trip? Are you interested in submitting a bid to look at the GPS units on the Butte County vehicles?" I asked, changing subjects.

"Mel and I talked about bringing the work van up for a visit." He pulled an envelope from his desk and handed it to me. "Eight hundred plus travel. It's all in there. If I had access to personal phones, I might be able to recreate location history. Depends on their settings. Any decent forensic investigator would know that, though."

"I didn't think about that," I said. "State investigators wouldn't miss that, would they?"

Snert shrugged. "Wouldn't they tell the sheriff?"

"Apparently not," I said, shaking my head in disbelief. "There's something going on here that I don't understand."

"I know that look. Last time you had it, you got your truck blown up and Diva shot." Diva perked her ears at the mention of her name.

"Did I mention the sheriff said I can take Diva with me on patrol?" I said.

"Is he paying you more? K-9 units are expensive. Seems like he's getting one for free."

"It didn't come up," I said. "I'm just glad to have her along."

"Don't get her shot again," Snert said, setting a piece of pizza on a plate and sliding it across the floor to Diva. I frowned but didn't stop him. Snert had babied Diva during her recovery and she was starting to put on weight. He pulled a package off the desk and handed it to me.

"What's this?" I asked.

"Open it." Inside was a tan dog coat and harness. Along the spine was a handle and a leash clip.

"Her fur is pretty thick," I said. "I think she'll be okay."

"It's not for warmth," he said. "It has three layers of Kevlar. I assume you'll be wearing armor, so Diva needs some too."

"That's a nice thought, Snert," I said. "Thank you."

"Look at the side," he said.

I turned the coat around and found the Butte County Sheriff's Department logo with the letters K-9 beneath them and Diva's name above. "That's perfect. Now she'll know her name if someone asks."

"Don't be a smart aleck," he said.

"I'm gonna missing hanging out with you," I said, tipping back my bottle of beer and sinking further into his couch.

"You don't have to," he said. "That tablet I gave you will do video chat. I already checked; city of Wood Creek, the seat of Butte County, has excellent internet service. Have you figured out where you're staying?"

"Sheriff is putting me up at the Sage and Rosemary Inn for a couple of weeks until I find a place," I said. "If you guys come out, you'll want to stay there. Owners are a couple crazy old guys that I think you'd find interesting. They run the town newspaper too."

"Mortimer Cook and Denholm Campbell are hardly crazy old guys," Snert said. "They were a crime reporting team in Chicago and received a lot of recognition for a piece they did on mob influence in politics in the late nineties. The article was considered for a Pulitzer."

"Um, you might reserve judgment until you meet 'em," I said. "Especially Morty."

⸻

The miles passed slowly as Diva and I made our way west. While it was a nice drive with bright blue sky overhead and sunlight streaming in the driver's side, I was impatient to get to Wood Creek. To make matters worse, I had to wait until Monday morning for my official swearing-in. It was dark when I finally parked behind the Sage and Rosemary.

"Come on, girl," I urged Diva after she'd taken care of her business. During my previous stay, I learned that the back door to the inn was never locked, so we entered through there. I did have to check in, however, because having been gone for a week, I'd lost the room originally assigned to me.

Diva must have smelled the boozy old crime reporter, because she trotted off, wagging her tail and disappeared around a corner. I didn't feel quite as familiar with the place and dinged the bell on the small counter in the lobby. I looked around while I waited. I loved old buildings and this one had a great smell that put me at ease – ancient wood and tung oil.

"Back already?" Denholm Campbell smiled as he met me on the opposite side of the wooden counter. "I thought I heard you'd be coming back on Sunday. Morty and I were just catching a bite to eat. Care to join us?"

"Oh, I couldn't," I said. "I can come back."

"Nonsense," he said. "It's nothing fancy. Just a sandwich and some soup. You just get into town?"

I was torn. My instinct was not to take advantage of people, but I was hungry and didn't want to offend anyone. "Are you sure?"

"I make a mean pastrami on rye," he said. "Get my meat from a deli back home."

"Chicago?" I asked.

He quirked his head and looked back at me. "Someone's been doing his homework."

"Lucky guess," I said. "A friend of mine found Morty's mob article."

"Keep that to yourself," he said. "He's already hard enough to live with. We don't need to be reliving all that."

"I heard that, Denny," Mortimer called from a room away. "Didn't I, girl?" His voice had changed and I could imagine he was scratching the sides of Diva's face affectionately as he spoke.

"She's all he's talked about since you've been gone," Denholm said. "Impossible to live with."

We found Mortimer in an antique high-back chair positioned in front of a dwindling fire. Diva sat with her face in his lap, her back to the fire and her tail thumping on the floor as she soaked up his attention. "You get to brag about your pastrami sandwich and I can't talk about an article that exposed corruption at the highest levels?" His voice didn't match the implied irritation of his words as he continued to baby-talk Diva, who wasn't taking her eyes off him.

"It's a pretty great sandwich," Denholm answered his partner, heading toward the kitchen. "And there aren't five people within a hundred miles you haven't bragged to about that article. Tomato soup okay with you, Deputy Biggston?"

"Sounds perfect. And just Biggs, remember?" I said.

"Biggs it is," Denholm nodded. "Have you figured out where you're going to stay yet?"

"Haven't even started looking. Might be a little harder with Diva, but we'll see."

"Nice thing Cal's doing; not kicking Mary out," Denholm said, positioning himself behind a modern countertop that separated the galley kitchen from the living space the two obviously shared. He pulled a beer from a refrigerator that looked exactly like fancy wood wall paneling when it was closed and slid it across the counter to me.

"Mary is Deputy Lynch's wife, right?" I asked, thinking back to the conversation I'd had with Sheriff Leonard.

"That's right," Denholm answered. "There are a couple of folks around town who rent out from time to time. I could ask around if you'd like."

"That'd be great." I took my pocket knife out and used the church key to open the beer. "I doubt I'll be there much. Sheriff said to expect nights and weekends for the foreseeable future."

"Person can't work all the time," Denholm said. "We did a little digging on you, too. You're a little over-qualified for a Butte County deputy sheriff position. Can't help but raise a few eyebrows around here."

Morty joined us at the kitchen counter and opened a glass jar filled to the top with dog treats. He wore a silky bathrobe that resembled a Japanese kimono, sheepskin slippers and he reeked of cigar smoke. "A more discerning type of individual might wonder if the sheriff is bringing in a ringer," Morty said, waggling bushy white eyebrows.

"Ringer?" I started to wonder if the dinner invitation had been an invitation to an interrogation. I knew what they were digging for but wanted to buy time.

"Yeah. Ex-Army Ranger who has a flair for investigating unsolved crimes suddenly shows up when the State Patrol Investigative Services Division runs out of gas?" Morty scoffed. *"Runs out of gas –* nope – that phrase just doesn't work for me. Den, how would you phrase what's happening?"

"Mired in bureaucratic red tape and manpower shortages," Denholm answered, looking over to me. "Pepper jack or provolone?"

"What kind of red tape?" I asked.

"Provolone it is," Denholm answered. "Same red tape ISD always runs into – money. According to sources, they've blown their budget and don't have anything to show for it."

"As in, it's easier to call the shooting of an officer a hunting accident? Luckiest bullet ever fired." I let my annoyance show, immediately regretting it.

"Just like that," Morty said with just a hint of triumph in his voice. "Glad to know we'll have a competent investigator working that case."

"I'm not sworn in yet," I said. "And I haven't been assigned any cases."

"I'll be sure to point that out," Morty said.

"Be nice, Mortimer," Denholm said. "Biggs is a guest and we're just having dinner."

I took a pull on my beer. I was out of my league with these guys.

"You know, you could stay at Sage and Rosemary," Morty said. "We have a small suite on the third floor. It's only eight hundred square feet, but that's more than you'd get in Chicago. I'd even throw in free dog sitting."

"Mortimer, we've talked about this. It's a dusty old attic, not a suite," Denholm said. "And it's filled with your crap from Chicago. Where are you going to put that?"

"When's the last time you were up there?" Morty asked, defiantly. "I'll have you know I've taken out all but a few boxes. We'd just need to move a bed and a dresser up from the basement. I've a couple of overstuffed chairs he could take as well."

"What are you thinking for rent?" I asked.

"See! He's interested," Mortimer gloated.

"Biggs, don't do this sight unseen. You're getting into more than you might think," Denholm continued to pull items from the fridge as he cooked. "Why don't the two of you run upstairs and look at the space."

"So exciting," Morty said, racing back to his chair to grab a large glass of deep red wine. "He's not even arguing about the dog."

"Ten minutes to dinner," Denholm said. "Don't be late. I don't like serving cold food."

Morty rolled his eyes. "He's always been like that."

I followed Morty to the back stairs and we wound our way up to the second level. From the front, the inn looked to be two stories, but from the back there was a small third level that didn't extend all the way across.

"Why doesn't the third level go out toward the street?" I asked.

"Characteristic of the time it was built. These small towns wouldn't allow anything over two stories tall within a block of the courthouse. In 1885, Sage and Rosemary was called Wood Creek Hotel and the space was mostly reserved as worker's quarters. They got around the building code by keeping the top level away from the street," he explained.

"You've obviously thought about what's been happening in the county. What's your take on Deputies Lynch and Shephard?" I asked.

"With no evidence collected – at least that ISD will admit to – and Deputy Shephard not saying anything, one can only speculate." He opened a door I had pegged for a closet. Behind the door, however, was another wood-paneled staircase. Morty flipped a light switch and gestured for me to go up first.

"What's your speculation, then?" I asked.

"Denny would say that I'm overly dramatic and that I see conspiracy where none exists," he said. "But I believe someone is hiding something."

"You don't buy the hunting accident?" I asked.

"As you said. Luckiest bullet ever. If either shooting was accidental, whoever pulled the trigger would have confessed a long time ago. Ranchers are a rough lot and as a group, they drink and talk too much. There's also a twenty-five-hundred-dollar reward for information pertaining to either shooting. That's a lot of money for men who live paycheck to paycheck. Someone would talk."

"What makes you think it had to be a rancher?" I asked.

"You're not listening. I don't think it *is* a rancher," he said. "But I see your confusion. The location of the deputy's vehicle suggests the shot came from the northern plains. At least, that's what ISD would have us believe. Northern plains are all ranch lands. My point was, if it was a rancher, we'd know already."

"Got it," I said, stepping up into the suite. "Any other nuggets of wisdom?"

"The majority of drug traffic coming through the state runs along I-80," he said. "Over the last several years, the State Patrol upped their seizure rate. There's a lot of speculation about how they do it, but the fact is, they're very effective. In the last two years, Butte County Sheriff's department has turned over eight seizures to ISD."

"Are you saying you think someone running drugs is targeting deputies?" I asked.

"I'm not saying anything of the sort. It's all speculation," he said.

My mind turned. The attic offered more possibilities than I had expected. The same rich wood paneling adorned the sloped walls and the floor was made from worn, narrow hardwood planks. A bank of windows ran floor to ceiling on the wall facing the street, giving a great view of the night sky. In the middle of the windows was a door that opened out onto the roof and a low drift of snow from the last storm still blocked access to the small deck.

"What do you think?" Morty asked, gesturing grandly. "I think it's the most charming room in the entire inn."

Dozens of boxes, trunks and random moving debris had been shoved to one end of the room. What I didn't find was anything that looked like normal amenities. "It's cool but what about a bathroom and a kitchen. I don't see how it's heated either."

"Bathroom's on the second floor. There's a radiator in here some-where for heat and you look like a hotplate kind of guy – something I'd know about since that's me until I met Denny."

"Do you have a place for all the stuff?" I pointed at the pile that was bigger than he'd originally implied.

"There's room in the basement for most of it, especially once you bring up the bed and dresser," he said.

I looked at him skeptically. "There's a lot up here."

"You could stay in the Victor Victoria Room where you spent last Thursday until you've got this space ready," he said. "What do you say?"

"I say we should talk to Denny."

"I just knew you'd like it," he said and started back downstairs.

"Sheriff is giving you a five-hundred-dollar housing allowance," Denholm said as we joined him in what Morty had informed me was the parlor. "Seems like we could work with that. Might even cover a couple of meals. Is it pretty well cleaned up?"

"No, Denny, it needs some work," Morty said, irritated at being called out. "Mr. Biggston said he wouldn't have trouble moving the remaining boxes to the basement when he pulls out the bed and dresser."

I chuckled as I hadn't said anything of the sort. But he assumed and I went along with it.

"Tell you what," Denholm said. "You clear it out and move a bed up there and I'll get the cleaning staff to vacuum and get you some linens. Once you get a radiator wrench, you'll have more heat than you'll want."

He handed me a steaming bowl of soup and followed with a thick grilled sandwich, heaps of pastrami and cheese dripping from the edges. "This looks amazing," I said. "You didn't need to do all this."

"You'll earn it. Trust me," he said, replacing my beer.

And earn it, I did. I spent the rest of the evening ferrying poorly packed boxes down three flights of stairs to the basement and then dragging heavy furniture back up those same stairs. I finally finished at eleven thirty and popped into the shower, the idea of a beer at Hootskill's burning a hole in my brain.

"Faith's not here tonight."

I was leaning across the bar, but Lexi Hudson still had to yell over the rowdy Hootskill crowd. "What are you drinking?"

"Draft light," I said, placing money onto the bar top. The stool next to me freed up and I grabbed it.

Lexi tipped a tap handle back and drew beer into a disposable plastic cup.

"Where's she at?" I asked.

"Over at Press Box," she said.

"The college bar?" I asked, confused.

"Yeah, Mom owns both Press Box and Hootskill," she said. "We're indentured servants."

"That woman at Press Box is your mom?" I asked, surprised. I'd put the woman at thirty-five but that wasn't possible. "She can't be old enough."

"Save your sucking up," she said. "I'll be right back."

I took a drink of the cold beer and watched as the youngest Hudson girl went down the length of the bar to talk to a waitress. The young server's t-shirt was tied in a knot just under her breasts, showing off a lot of flat abdomen. Given that at least two-thirds of the bar's patrons were male, I would bet the entire staff made out like bandits on tips.

"So, do you like my sister, Faith?" Lexi shouted over the din, filling a tray with Tequila shots and a pitcher of beer.

"I don't really know her," I shouted back.

"She and Reagan got full-ride volleyball scholarships," Lexi said. "Wood Creek won state championships five years running."

"What are they doing back here?" I asked.

Lexi disappeared to fill more drinks.

"Where else would they be?" she asked. "You know what collegiate volleyball players do after college?"

The easy answer was to say *bartend*, but it felt dismissive, so I just shrugged.

"Yeah, there's no NFL for volleyball players," she said. "You know it's okay, right? You can leave. Nobody's going to judge you for going over to Press Box."

I smiled. "That transparent?"

"You keep looking at the door." She dumped my beer into the sink, took money out of her apron and placed it on the bar. "Just go, already."

"Have a good night, Lexi," I said and left without picking up the money.

The music outside the smaller Press Box bar was just as loud as at Hootskill. As I'd noticed the last time I'd been here, we'd changed the radio station from country to alternative. Instead of pickups, sedans filled this parking lot.

I caught Faith's eye about halfway to the bar and she smiled. It was a pretty great smile. Her whole face lit up, starting with a widening grin that showed off her big white teeth. Her cheeks flushed and her light blue eyes twinkled mischievously.

"I didn't think you were back until Sunday," she said, setting a bottle of light beer in front of me. I pulled out some cash and set it on the bar, but she made no move to pick it up.

"Got into town earlier this evening. Had dinner with Mortimer Cook and Denholm Campbell," I said. "They're my new landlords."

"I didn't really think you were coming back," she said. "We're pretty podunk around here."

I feigned looking around the bar. "Lot of pretty girls who might be impressed with a city boy and a badge," I said.

A crash preceded a momentary lull in the loud conversations. I had a flash of déjà vu as I turned to find two young men squaring off behind me. The first had already taken a swing at the second, connecting as well as any ornery college kid who'd been drinking all night can. I set my beer down and started in their direction.

"I got this," Faith said, tapping me on the arm with the end of her pink baseball bat and waiting for me to grab it. In one smooth move, she jumped up, set her bottom on the bar, spun her knees around and jumped off the other side. It was a move I'd seen before – although, I'll admit to paying much more attention this time around. She moved with the confidence and grace of a well-trained athlete.

"Bat," she prompted, grinning at what I suspected was the witless look on my face. I'd probably stood there watching her a little longer than was polite.

I handed Faith the bat and followed her to the ruckus. Without warning, she thwacked the table next to where the drunk college boys were locked in an awkward dance – moves they obviously considered fighting. The noise was thunderous, startling the boys enough to separate them.

"Get out," she demanded, holding her bat up behind her shoulder like a softball player eager to swing.

"But he started it!" The kid who spoke was doughy-faced and had red splotches up and down his neck where he'd been hit. Indeed, he'd been the one I'd seen get tagged first.

"You stupid motherfucker," the kid's belligerent opponent shouted, half lunging and half stumbling back into the fight. Unfortunately, his aim was way off and his fist was headed straight at Faith. I'd carefully watched both boys and was ready. I kicked out with my foot, catching the boy's leg just behind the knee. Without much effort, I grabbed the arm flying toward Faith, twisted it and flipped the boy to the ground.

"You'll stay down if you know what's good for you," I said calmly, my face not far from his. His expression changed immediately to one of remorse and I grew afraid he might actually cry. I straightened and looked over to Faith. This could go one of two ways. She'd either be pissed that I'd stepped in or grateful that I'd saved her from a fist to the face. I was rewarded with a quirky grin and a lifted eyebrow. The small group around us even applauded.

"Bobby Quinn, I said beat it," Faith demanded, grasping the bat with one hand and slapping it menacingly into the other.

"Geez. You don't have to be a bitch about it," he said, apparently having recovered his nuts.

Another Quinn. Did my family have to create all the trouble in town? I stepped toward Quinn, but Faith put her hand on my arm as she pointed the bat at the kid. "Don't think I won't kick your ass."

"I know who this guy is," Quinn said. "He's my cuz. We're just getting to know each other."

"Just leave, Bobby," Faith said.

"Sure. Whatever. See ya 'round, cuz," he said.

I helped the kid I'd put on the floor back to his feet. He looked at me like I'd grown a second head and couldn't get away fast enough.

"You lead an exciting life," I said as we returned to the bar.

"You would have met Bobby Quinn sooner or later," she said. "He's been in more trouble than Luca, except most of the time Bobby's troubles disappear. Thanks for your help back there. You move pretty fast. Is it true you were a Navy Seal?"

"No," I have to admit, I was a little hurt when a flash of disappointment crossed her face. "Army." Bragging about my service wasn't something I did.

"My beer debt is getting out of control," she said. "Are you sure I can't buy you one?"

"How many beers until I can trade up for dinner?" I asked.

"Settle for breakfast?" Faith's face turned red and she took a quick breath, suddenly realizing how that request might have sounded.

"I'd settle for anywhere without quite so many drunk people," I filled in smoothly.

"We close at two," she said. "Takes me about half an hour to clean up. I've got a place we could go after that if you're interested."

"Count me in," I settled back into my seat at the bar, taking a long draw from my beer.

By closing time, the bar had mostly emptied out. Only a few patrons lagged, locked deep in philosophical conversations only made possible after several beers. Faith allowed them to stay as she cleaned up but finally urged them out the door.

"Where are we headed?" I asked.

"You're not much of a drinker for someone I've only seen in bars," she said, looping an arm through mine as we walked out.

I shrugged. "I like to relax as much as the next guy," I said. "I don't like what drunk does to me the next day, though."

"My drinking days are behind me. Two DUIs will do that."

She stopped next to a large white one-ton GMC pickup and searched my face for judgment. I raised my eyebrows. "That seems like second date material to me," I said, making a joke that didn't seem to go anywhere.

"I have a kid, April," she said. "She's ten." I chuckled, which was absolutely the wrong thing to do. She slapped my chest with an open palm and turned away. The truck beeped as she thumbed the remote to unlock the door. "I knew you were too good to be true."

"Wait," I said as she stepped up into the truck.

"Bullshit," Faith yanked the door and it closed with a bang. I watched as she started the truck and roared off.

"Well, damn," I said to myself, as I was the only one left in the parking lot. "That could have gone better."

The next morning, Diva woke me at six. She hadn't wanted out when I got back to the Sage and Rosemary at three and I'd been too tired to push the matter. I slept fitfully in the cold attic room and finally gave up trying around nine. I'd have to get the heat fixed pronto if I was going to get any sleep. At a minimum, I'd need blankets and a pillow.

The night before, I'd brought all my gear up from the Bronco. My organizational skills could have been better, but I'd been focused on finding Faith at the time. I went about setting up an area of the room where I could keep track of the information I'd gather on the two unsolved shootings. I started by hanging a map of Butte County on the back wall, which was the only vertical space that wasn't glass. The territory was unfamiliar. The sum total of my exposure to the county had been the road between Butte and Sutherland and the time I'd spent driving around with Cal Leonard.

The sheer number of square miles the county encompassed was daunting from a law enforcement perspective. Patrols would have to be completely different from the type I'd learned in Sutherland. One deputy could barely circumnavigate the major highways in a single shift, much less do any meaningful police work.

"Want to go for a drive?" I asked, looking down at Diva. There was only one way I could imagine becoming more familiar with the area and that was to get out and see it. Diva was game and wagged her tail excitedly.

"Where are you headed?" Morty caught me on the back stairs just before I went out the door.

"Going for a drive," I said. "I need to learn the area. Thought I'd check out north fork of Squaw Creek today. Maybe get a hike in."

"Wear some orange. It's hunting season," he said.

"Maybe archery," I said. "Deer season is four weeks out."

"It's antelope season." His words sent a chill down my back.

After loading Diva, I took a quick pass through town to check out the major streets and businesses. I'd studied the online map before coming out for the job interview and had a decent memory, but there was no substitute for experience. After zig-zagging through town a few times, I headed out. Table Road turned out to be gravel and I missed the turn and had to head back to pick it up.

An hour later I turned onto the north fork of Squaw Creek Road and started a steep climb deep into Squaw National Forest. There's not a lot I enjoy more than being immersed in a forest and when we arrived at the end of the road, I was excited to find several trailhead markers.

"This is living, don't you think?" I asked Diva, jumping out. The trailhead sign showed the northern branch going out fourteen miles before it intersected with another trail. Previous research told me there were numerous trails that spiderwebbed across the forest and connected to this main entry point. We couldn't possibly hike the entire distance with a storm bearing down on the region, but we could easily put in a few miles. Without hesitation, Diva and I set off, happily crunching down the trail.

A gentle snow fell during the last hour of our return leg. Without any wind, the pines did a great job of trapping the snow. I didn't even realize how much had fallen until we reached the parking lot where the Bronco sat and found it covered in three inches of powder.

Diva was tired and curled into a ball in the back seat, falling asleep almost immediately. We hadn't run into a single hiker, but I hadn't really expected to. We were in a remote area at the start of winter. What I found surprising, however, were tracks in the road. At least four vehicles had come and gone since the snow started. From the depth of the impressions, two had been through within the last fifteen minutes. I drove slowly, following the tracks to where they branched off and went into the forest. I didn't recall seeing a trail big enough for a car when I pulled in, so I slowed, then jumped out and took pictures of the tracks.

I knocked on the glass front door of the sheriff's station at eight-thirty Sunday morning. I probably groaned a little when I recognized Raff

Butler rounding the corner from the stairwell and crossing the lobby. But it was a chilly twenty-eight degrees and as long as someone was opening the door to let me inside, I'd be pleasant.

"You're late," he grumbled, holding the door open.

"Good morning to you too, Deputy Butler," I said. I felt conspicuous wearing my new Stetson Drifter buffalo-hair cowboy hat, but no more so than I had when I wore the black SPD uniform or my army fatigues. Butler wore a greenish-brown baseball cap with the Butte County Sheriff's logo on it and I wondered why Leonard had insisted on the cowboy hat.

Butler locked the door behind us and headed for the second floor. I jogged up the stairs two at a time. The glass door leading into the main part of the station was open and I recognized Gene Ellis, the other deputy who'd helped cool things off with Raff, and the dispatcher Hollie Wilder.

"If I'd known it was you, I'd have called Raff off last week," Gene Ellis said, grinning and offering his hand. "Welcome to Butte County, Henry."

"Good to see you again, Gene," I said. "Call me Biggs."

"Not our finest start last week, Biggs," Hollie Wilder said, approaching and offering her hand. "Glad we didn't scare you off."

"Your team has had a rough couple of months," I said. "No apology necessary."

"She wasn't apologizing," Raff Butler said.

"Stow it, Raff," Gene Ellis said.

"I see we're still learning to get along." Cal Leonard cut short Raff's retort. Instinctively, I straightened and brought my heels together. I fought the urge to come to attention, something relentlessly instilled in me by the Army. "Deputy Butler, do you have something you need to say?"

"I don't like him," Raff said.

"You didn't give him a chance, Raff," Hollie quipped. "You rousted him before he'd made it twenty miles into our county. You're acting like a spoiled brat."

"Whatever," Raff said.

"This isn't how our team's going to work," Leonard said. "Raff, apologize to Biggs. You're out of line."

"Sure. I'm sorry for breaking up a bar fight by myself. And I'm sorry for making a good stop on a man with a violent dog and a truck full of weapons," he said sarcastically. "I'll try not to repeat these mistakes."

"Knock it off, Raff. We're short-staffed. That's on me, but you need to check that temper or you'll be riding a desk," Leonard said.

"Yeah, right," Raff grumbled under his breath.

Leonard clenched his jaw and I could feel him struggling with some sort of decision. "Deputy Grace Fox from Blaine County will be out next week for an interview," he finally said, looking away from Butler. "She has family in the area and I think we've a good chance of picking her up."

"That still leaves us down two," Raff pushed.

Leonard looked around the room. I could feel him seething but he kept his tone level and continued, "Hollie, grab the Bible, would you?"

Hollie Wilder picked up a worn Bible from her desk and stood next to Leonard. She was dressed up this morning and I suspected she'd be off to church after our meeting. She smiled and held the Bible flat out in front of her. "Henry, put your hand on the Bible and take your hat off," she said.

I placed my hat on the desk and put my right hand on the Bible's leather cover. I wondered how many deputies' hands had rested on this Bible. In that moment, I felt the weight of the commitment I was making.

"Henry Lester Biggston, do you solemnly swear that you will support, protect and defend the Constitution and Government of the United States and of our good state; that you are duly qualified to hold office under the Constitution of the state; and that you will well and faithfully perform the duties of Deputy Sheriff of Butte County?" Leonard recited the oath from memory, locking eyes with me.

"Without reservation, I so swear," I said.

Leonard smiled and nodded. "Wear your badge with honor, Deputy Biggston," he said and turned, picking a worn 357 magnum revolver from the desk behind him. "This is your service weapon and Gene will get your personal weapons registered before you go out this morning."

"That might need to wait," Hollie Wilder said, cradling her desk phone against one ear. "Gene, you've got a call over on the Benson Ranch on Highway 20. There's been a shooting."

"Copy that," Gene said and looked at me. "We'll grab a belt and a couple of shirts on the way out. If you need to use the restroom, this'd be the time to get it done."

My heart raced. "No, let's get moving," I said, unable to mask the urgency in my voice.

Raff shook his head and grumbled something about rookies, but I didn't care. I plucked the revolver from Leonard's hand and spun the cylinder to see that it was unloaded. Gene was already at the door and I caught up with him as he took the stairs down to the first level. Together we turned toward the back of the building.

"Figure you're a size large?" he asked.

"Tall if you have them," I said, following him through a locked door. There were a dozen official shirts hanging next to varying weights of jackets. He pushed them apart and handed me an XL.

"Looks like we're out of large," he said. "Talk to Hollie on Monday, she'll make an order. There are duty belts on the wall there. Most of us don't use our department-issued service weapons. Leonard lives in the sixties. What do you carry?"

"1911 forty-five," I answered.

"Nice weapon. Glock man, myself," he said, pulling back his service jacket to expose a nylon belt with a Glock G22 holstered inside. "Have it with you?"

"It's in my truck," I said. "I didn't know the rules about weapons in the station."

"You'll share a desk with the next deputy," he said. "Lock up your weapons when working from the station."

I shrugged my coat off and pulled the tan collared service shirt over the rest of my clothing. It fit across my shoulders, was too short on my arms, and way too baggy in the body. I was swimming in the material. I pushed the shirt tails – as much as I could – into the waistband of my jeans. Eyeing the belts on the wall, I found a worn leather one with a holster that would fit my 1911. The utility part of the belt had spaces for additional magazines, hand cuffs and pepper spray. I wasn't sure what my kit would be long term, but this was a good start. I tested the length and buckled it on.

"That used to be Leonard's," Gene said. "Back when he had a waist."

"Oh? Sorry," I said and started to take it off.

"Keep it. It's department owned and looks like it fits you," he said, handing me a brown service jacket with a faux fur lining. "You have gloves? Wind's up. It's gonna be cold out there."

"He wore a 1911?" I asked.

"No, Raff did briefly," he said, tossing me a pair of cuffs. "But he can't wear that belt either. You feel like driving?"

"Best way to get to know the area," I answered.

"Good man. My rig's out back." Gene led me out through the processing area Raff had introduced me to only a week before.

Gene's vehicle was a newer Chevy Tahoe SUV. The inside looked similar to the patrol vehicles I'd driven while training with SPD. Unlike Sheriff Leonard's vehicle, Gene's had a computer. The rest of the equipment was standard and included the radio, light controls and an empty shotgun bracket. Gene handed me the keys and stowed a small stack of magazines so he could occupy the passenger seat.

"What do you do when you don't have dispatch?" I asked. "Is there someone other than Hollie?"

"It rolls over to one of the two court deputies, Jay or Jerry," he said. "I'm not sure who has this weekend, but Hollie must have picked it up since she was in the office for your swearing-in."

"We need to call this in?" I asked, backing out of the parking space. My training in the city had us updating dispatch with each change to our status.

"Nope," he said. "They already know we're taking the call."

I pulled up next to my Bronco and jumped out to unlock the gun safe I had bolted to the floor beneath my seat. I exchanged the .357 for my 1911, slipping two spare magazines into my belt. I threw my coat into the back seat, locked the truck, and jumped back into Gene's Tahoe.

"You don't seem all that worked up for a shots-fired," I said.

"Head north and take your first right onto Highway 20. Benson ranch is twenty minutes out," Gene said, flipping our strobe lights on but neglecting the siren. The Tahoe responded immediately when I hit the gas. It was Sunday morning and I assumed the light traffic was people heading to church. Surprisingly, they all pulled to the side as I caught and passed them. Wood Creek was a small enough town that we were on the highway in a few minutes and I pushed our speed to a respectable eighty miles per hour.

"For every person in Butte County there are ten cows," Gene said, once we were clear of town. "Benson Ranch butts right up to national grassland and it's opening weekend for antelope rifle season. I'll bet you a Hay Spring donut there's a dead cow on this call."

"You're on, but wouldn't that be a Fish and Game call?" I asked.

"It is if we find a hunter," he said. "Otherwise, we just file a report."

"What's a Hay Spring donut?"

"Turn's about half a mile up here," he said. "You'll want to take it slow. Benson doesn't keep his road up."

A teen dressed in dirty coveralls waved us down at a cattleguard crossing before we made it all the way up to the main house. I slowed and rolled down my window.

"What's going on, Donnie?" Gene asked, leaning across the seat when the young man approached.

"Trespassers on the east pasture," he said. "Dad's got 'em corralled."

Gene unlocked the back door. "Hop in." He pointed. "Follow the road up that way. East pasture is just over that hill. Right, Donnie?"

"They were coming up from the river bottom. We got no trespassing signs all through there," he said.

Yesterday's snow was still on the ground and tracks headed in the direction Gene pointed, so I followed them. It was rough going, but we soon crested a hill and the scene unfolded below us. Two men, mounted on horses and wearing cowboy hats, sat on opposite sides of two downed animals. A few steps away stood three more men dressed in white camouflage.

"Looks like you owe me a donut, Biggs," Gene said as I pulled to a stop on the side of the snowy hill. The scene might as well have been a century old. Under the bright blue sky, the grassy hills stretched on for miles in every direction. Not far away, a herd of cows crowded around a bale of hay. Idly, I wondered how many years ranchers like these had ridden this land, defending the hills and the animals from interlopers. What had this area been like when the invading Europeans had taken the land from the native Americans?

"Took you long enough to get out here, Gene," a gruff voice called from atop a proud brown mare with white socks and a white blaze on her neck.

"Need you to put that gun away, Don," Gene called back. "Stay close," he said in a quieter voice to me.

"I'm out here doing your job, Gene," Don answered. "Don't see why I can't just shoot 'em."

"Put the gun away, Don," Gene pushed again. This time Don grunted and slid his rifle into a leather scabbard and swung a leg over the back of the horse.

"Everyone okay here?" I asked, looking at the visibly relieved hunters who'd been rounded up and held at gun point.

"He's been holding us here for almost three hours," one man said. "Nearly ran us down with those horses."

"We'll get everyone's statements in due time," Gene said. "Deputy Biggston, see what they have to say. I'll talk to Benson."

As I'd discovered when riding with SPD, people have difficulty telling the truth when describing events to law enforcement. It just comes with the job. The fact that a dead antelope lay only ten yards from a dead cow refuted the hunter's story of following a wounded animal onto the ranch for retrieval. I listened to the story and recorded the hunter's names, driver license and social security numbers. Back in the vehicle, I punched in their information and came up with no warrants.

The sound of an approaching vehicle caught my attention. The truck was dark green, like those used by the state game wardens. Sure enough, I recognized Jasper White as he got out of the truck.

"Deputy Biggston," he said, smiling like we were old friends, his nervousness from our first meeting no longer in evidence. "What's your assessment?"

"Gentleman in the middle admitted to taking the shot," I said. "He insists he wounded the animal down by the creek, still on state property. Says they followed the animal up here where it died and that's when they discovered the downed cow. He doesn't believe the events to be related."

White smiled. "No. Of course not."

"I ran them for warrants. They're clean," I said.

"Appreciate your help. I'll take it from here," he said.

I looked over to Gene who nodded and started back to the Tahoe. "What's that about?" I asked.

"We get a few of these calls every year," Gene said. "Technically, Benson could be charged for holding those men. The problem is, if he didn't, the hunters would be long gone and Game and Fish would have a hell of a time running them down. As long as no one gets hurt, we let Game and Fish handle the summons. Judge prefers to hear from the wardens on these matters."

"What about the dead cow? That's worth something, isn't it?" I asked.

"Destruction of property, but on the other side, Benson would probably face kidnapping. Not sure what the judge would do there. No, Jasper will seize the guns since it was poaching. He'll then offer to give them back once Benson is made whole on the beef. Judge might decide to take their hunting privileges if they push it. Most folks just pay the fines and head home with their tails tucked between their legs."

I could see the logic, but allowing someone to take the law into their own hands went against the police training I'd received. With SPD, laws were strictly obeyed. If I'd taken the call on my own, Benson would be sitting in the back of my squad car.

"I can see this doesn't sit well with you," he said. "We're not all that far removed from the frontier days out here. This is a good outcome. Think of it from Benson's side. He lets those guys go and he's out a couple thousand for his heifer. That happens two or three times this year and it could be the difference between break-even and a loss just because a few hunters decided they didn't need to pay attention to posted signs."

"That's gonna take some getting used to," I said. "What now?"

"We'll wait. Jasper will need help transporting those hunters back to their vehicles."

9 / DANGEROUS PEOPLE

THE TRIP to the tiny town of Hay Springs took fifteen minutes from the parking lot of the national grasslands where the hunters had parked. As Gene had predicted, the youngest of the three hunters still retained his rifle. The other two tried complaining to Gene, but when he offered to call Warden White back for a renegotiation, the party declined, taking the rest of the trip in silence.

"How many people in Hay Springs?" I asked.

"Six hundred, give or take," Gene answered. "Fantastic football program. D6 champs last year and they're headed back again this year."

"How do you field a team in such a small town?" I asked.

"That hat says cowboy but you're all city," Gene said, unconsciously adding a bit of drawl as he spoke. He pulled to a stop in front of a house sporting a white sign that read *Hay Springs Bakery*. "Farm boys and ranchers. Lots of big families call Hay Springs home, but they actually live outside of town."

I followed him up a broken sidewalk to the side of the house and through an old screen door. I felt uncomfortable, like we were just walking into someone's home.

"Hey, Gene. Be right out." A plump middle-aged woman stuck

her head through a doorway and then disappeared again. The room we'd entered was the home's original kitchen that had been converted to a small retail space. Two small round tables were pushed against the outside wall. On the counter sat two ten-cup coffee makers, only one of which still had coffee in the glass carafe. The cabinets over the counter were glass-fronted and contained a variety of pastries on the lower level and bags of sugar and flour on top. "I'm about out of coffee. Be a dear and throw on a new pot, would you?"

Gene opened one of the cabinets and pulled out an oversized chocolate cake donut with sprinkles. "Donut?" he asked.

The sign over the cabinet read, "Donuts: $1. Specialty Donuts: $1.50."

"No thanks," I said, pulling a couple bills out and placing them on the counter.

Gene picked up one of the dollars and handed it back to me. "Only a buck for the donuts," he said.

"Who's this?" The woman smiled as she made her way into the shop area.

I pulled my hat off and offered my hand. "Henry Biggston, ma'am."

"Beth Bowrey. Just call me BB," she said. "I've heard about you. Big SPD policeman, served in Desert Storm."

"Afghanistan, ma'am. Desert Storm was a bit before my time."

"Polite *and* cute as a button," she said, turning away to pick up the tray she'd set down before greeting me. With her back to us, she filled empty shelves with new product. When she turned around, she'd loaded a large glazed donut onto a napkin and pushed it to me. "First one's free. I like to think of it as my version of healthy crack." She giggled and I found there was no polite way to refuse her. I accepted the gift graciously even though doing so was something I had specifically been warned against in my SPD training. Things were very different out here. I had a lot to learn about small town ways.

"Anything shakin', BB?" Gene asked, dumping coffee grounds into a trash bin.

"Class of 2020 made their mark on that metal building down on 513," she said. "Principal seems to have a line on the trouble makers. How's Char doing?"

"Still in the hospital," he said. "We were headed over there this afternoon. Wanted to introduce her to Biggs."

BB handed him a wrapped tin of caramel-covered cinnamon rolls. "You give this to her for me. Tell her we're all pulling for her. Darn shame what happened. Hope you catch whoever did that and put them in a deep dark hole. Hard enough raising a child on her own. What's she going to do for work now?"

"One day at a time," Gene answered, pouring water into the coffee maker and replacing the carafe. "I'm showing Biggs the sights today, so we'll get out of your hair."

"Nice to meet you, Deputy Biggs," BB said, smiling.

"You too, BB," I answered and followed Gene back to his Tahoe.

Back in the vehicle we toured the small town of Hay Springs, driving past a small but well-kept high school that boasted a brand-new football field with tall stands that I felt could hold most of the town's population.

"You going to eat that?" Gene asked, eyeing BB's donut that I'd placed on the seat next to me. Between driving and absorbing the town, I'd forgotten about it.

"Go ahead," On the edge of town, I spotted the sign for Road 513 and turned south. I kept my eyes peeled for the steel building BB and Gene had talked about being vandalized.

"High School principal is Bob Tanner. He's also the mayor and defensive line coach for the football team. Started for the university for a couple years back in the day," he said. "He runs a tight ship. People around here really like him."

"That's a lot of jobs."

"Small town," Gene said. "Most people do more than one thing. Only way to stay afloat."

"Does that include deputies?" I asked.

"Sometimes," he answered. "Not me. Been a bachelor all my life.

County pays for my house. Hunting in the fall, fishing in the summer – it's a good life."

"Didn't Lynch live here in Hay Springs?" I asked as we came upon a half-pipe steel building sitting at the edge of a farmer's field. Indeed, at least one side was emblazoned with bright spray paint. In addition to a fair number of cuss words, I clearly saw the graduation year 2020. As far as vandalizing went, this was pretty tame.

"His widow, Mary, and the kids still do," he said. "We should stop in. She'd want to meet you. Turn back on 560th street and north on Highway 87 – that'll take us by the airport."

I didn't love all the introductions, but I knew they were inevitable. In small towns, everyone wanted to be involved or to at least be in the know about changes in the community. I'd remember the faces, but had no chance of remembering all the names. With Deputy Lynch's widow, I anticipated emotions I wasn't excited about dealing with. I pushed my feelings down as we walked up the steps to her front porch, hats in hand.

"Gene." Mary Lynch greeted Gene with a warm hug. A woman in her mid-thirties, she wore loose jeans and a muted brown sweater. She looked more put together than I anticipated, but I saw the sadness in her eyes as she looked up at me after releasing Gene.

"Henry Biggston, ma'am," I said.

She took me in for a moment and then reached out, her fingers coming to rest on the badge I'd placed on my belt. "Cal said you were a good man," she said, her breath catching. "Thank you for accepting George's badge. He'd want to know a good man had it."

"I'll do my best," I said, not exactly sure what to say.

She nodded. "I'm sure you will. Where are my manners? Please, come in."

"Sorry, Mary. We can't this morning," Gene said. "I just wanted to bring Biggs over so it wouldn't be weird when you bump into each other."

"Very thoughtful, Gene," Mary said. "Could you tell Cal that I found some of George's old papers when I was cleaning up? I don't know if he wants them or what I should do with them."

"I'll pass along the message," Gene said.

On the way back to the truck, I pulled out my notebook and wrote down BBs name and that I owed her a dollar. I also recorded that we needed to tell Leonard about the papers.

"They teach you to take notes at the academy?" Gene asked as we got back in the Tahoe. Before I could answer, he continued, tapping his finger on his head. "Me, I keep it all locked up here. Take Table Road west and we'll grab Bordeaux back through the forest up to Wood Creek. We can stop by the hospital and drop these rolls off for Char."

As we drove, Gene continued to point out names of the farms we passed. I didn't recognize any of them and wished I wasn't driving so I could record what he was saying.

"Table Road continues south," Gene instructed as we came to a T intersection. "Turn north and take Bordeaux. That's the Hudson ranch there. Nice property and backs onto the forest. Old man Hudson used to run a guide service outta there when he wasn't ranchin'. Wife took the insurance money when he died and bought both bars in Wood Creek. Girls all live at home still. Little weird if you ask me. Nice looking bunch if you like 'em tall."

Driving slowly, I glanced over and saw Faith's white pickup truck parked in front of the barn. In a nearby paddock, a small figure bounced atop a young brown and white Paint horse. I guessed by the size, that the girl was April, Faith's daughter. Movement caught my eye and I saw Faith walking across the yard between the house and barn. Sensing our presence, she turned and looked, reaching up to hold her cowboy hat in place as the wind caught it. Her hair followed the wind as did the ends of the long coat she wore. Tall and angular, she looked fantastic backdropped by the forest and the aged barn. If she'd been smoking, the scene would have made a perfect Marlboro cigarette ad.

"None of them married?" I asked, speeding up. Faith turned away and continued over to the arena, not bothering to wave.

"That's Faith there," Gene said. "Hard woman. That's her kid, April. You'll never guess who she had her with."

I shook my head. I knew maybe twenty people, not one of them would I have paired with Faith.

"Raff Butler," he said, nodding as he allowed the discontinuity of his statement to sink in.

"No way," I said.

He grinned broadly. "He was a senior. She was a sophomore. Back in the day, Raff was a halfway decent football player – for C1 at least. Played tight end. That was before he got fat and lost his hair."

"Geez," I said. "I thought she played volleyball. State titles and all that."

"Three months pregnant her sophomore year. Kept it a secret until after the tournaments. Man, was it a big scandal when everyone found out. People wanted to kick her out of school and off the team. You know how that goes. Didn't matter though 'cause that was Reagan's senior year. With Reagan graduating, we wouldn't have had a shot at state the next year without Faith, so the town got over it," Gene said.

"They get married? Her and Raff?" I asked.

"Lasted about a year," he said. "Raff's always been an asshole, but he's a decent cop."

"What's his problem with me?" I asked.

"Raff has in mind he's the heir apparent when Cal steps down," Gene explained. "Cal talked you up before you came out and I think he's worried you're his competition. He'll settle down."

I shrugged and continued driving. Bordeaux Road was gravel and the trees on both sides had thickened as we climbed into the hills. I didn't recognize the part of town the road dumped us into, but Wood Creek wasn't that big. "The hospital is between Eighth and Tenth, just take Tenth there," Gene said, pointing.

The hospital was a single-story brick building with a large

parking lot off to the east. Like all hospitals it smelled of antiseptic. We made our way into the building and past an unoccupied nurse's station. Halfway down the hall, Gene knocked on a door and let himself in. I followed behind, hat in hand.

Gene said something I didn't catch and the woman I presumed was Deputy Char Shephard laughed, adjusting her bed so she sat up. I'd spent more than my share of time in Army hospitals visiting friends and felt a familiar rock in the pit of my stomach. Char Shephard would likely never walk again. The bastards who'd taken her legs had taken more than that. They'd taken her shot at having more kids or holding down a normal job. Hell, just going to the bathroom would be a major event for the foreseeable future. I wasn't sure my anger about this kind of injustice would ever be resolved and it must have shown on my face.

"Biggs, you okay?" Gene asked, suddenly appearing in front of me.

I looked around the room, my eyes darting to Char and then back to Gene. "Yeah, sorry, what'd you ask?" I wasn't sure how long I'd been standing there getting angry. An Army psychologist told me I had PTSD and that I needed to get counseling as soon as I got stateside. I hadn't, of course. It just wasn't my thing.

"I was just introducing you to Char, here," he said.

"Sorry," I extended my hand and smiled. "It's great to meet you, Deputy Shephard. Brave thing you did all by yourself. Glad you made it out."

"Go figure," she said. "I'd have thought it would have been an IED that took me down. Not a bunch of damn poachers."

"You served?" I asked.

"Six years in Army Reserves," she said. "Had a tour in the sandbox."

"Hooah," I said.

"Hooah," she answered instinctively. "Word is you spent some time in Afghanistan with the Rangers. You tabbed or the real deal?"

"Third battalion out of Benning, ma'am," Uncomfortable, I looked to change the subject. "I hadn't heard ISD decided it was poachers."

Char's face clouded and she looked away. "I don't honestly know," she said. "One minute I was out on patrol and then I woke up in the hospital."

"Still no memory of what happened?" Gene asked softly.

"Nothing. Doctor says it might come back in pieces or maybe it never will," she said. "You boys need to be wearing armor. I took three to the chest that day and somehow drove myself out. I'd have been dead without that armor."

"Nato 5.56 is an odd choice for hunting," I said, recalling what I'd read in what little information the ISD team had given out. "It's a little light for deer."

Char nodded. "There are some dangerous folks around," she said, her face clouding again. "They don't like the law. You be careful, Biggs. Back home, we don't always get to know our enemies by what they're wearing."

"When you getting out of here?" Gene asked.

"Drains come out at the end of the week," she said. "I start PT on Monday up in Rapid City. Mom's been helping with Chad. I might send him home with her for a while."

"Back in Wyoming?" I asked, recalling what I'd read in Char's file.

"Casper," she said with a smile. "Someone's been doing some reading."

"Just wanted to know what I was getting into up here. You guys have had a rough ride lately," I said.

"Remember the armor," was her only response.

"We'll get out of your hair, Char," Gene said. "You need anything, just let me know. I'll be by in a couple of days to check on you."

"Thanks, Gene, and thanks for looking in on Chad. He really looks up to you," she said. "Nice to meet you, Biggs. If you want to come by sometime, I could give you an outsider's rundown of all things Butte County. Might be a better perspective than you'd get from Mr. Home Grown, here."

"Careful," Gene said. "I don't need you city folk ganging up on me."

I pushed my hat back on and smiled. "You know, I might just do that."

On the way out of the hospital, I stopped. "How is it that three deputies cover an entire county?" I asked. "There's not enough hours."

"We're always on call," Gene said, nodding toward his truck. The wind was up and the afternoon was cooling off. "At least that's how it'll feel. Weeknights we don't have an active deputy from midnight until eight the next morning. Friday and Saturday nights we double up for the bar calls and ditch parties.

"Once you're done riding with me, you'll probably catch four ten-hour shifts starting on Thursday. Hollie keeps track of it all. It wasn't too bad with four of us. But Raff and I have been hitting it hard lately. I hope this interview Cal has next week pans out."

"What's on-call look like?" I asked.

"Most of us prefer to pull a double: work the first shift then on-call for the second. You get quarter time for being on call. Works out to decent money. If you get called in, you'll get time and a half. We've got budget for six deputies so Cal's a soft touch on the overtime. Expect to get pulled out of bed at least once a week."

"Sounds about right," I said.

"Are you hungry yet? I figured we could grab some grub, head back to the station and get you keyed up and those weapons registered."

———

Diva spun in the snow, thrilled to see me back from my shift. We'd finished up about five, having spent the afternoon at Gene's favorite speed trap location. There was no doubt Leonard ran Butte County differently than a metro police department, but life certainly seemed to run more slowly out here.

"She give you any trouble?" I asked as Morty joined me in the back.

"Best behaved girl ever," Morty said, pandering to Diva with a high-pitched voice. "She has a knot on her back though. Wonder if you've had it looked at?"

"Off the record?" I asked, remembering I was talking to a journalist.

Morty's eyes took on a predatory glint. "So young to be so cynical," he said. "Off the record is fine."

"Scar tissue," I said. "She was shot last year."

"On that Richard Manning sex trafficking case?" he asked.

"We got lucky, Diva should have been killed or at least severely disabled. There are a couple of vertebrae fused together under the scar. She saved my life that night."

"Bossians were shooting at you and you're still walking around?" he asked, astounded.

"Like I said, I got lucky."

"Why do I think there's more to this story?"

"Messing with the mob was a bad idea," I said.

Morty threw his head back and let out a high-pitched laugh. "My boy, you seem to have mastered the Midwestern art of the understatement. How was your first day on patrol?"

"A lot of introductions," I said. "I met Mary Lynch."

"Ooh, how'd that go?" he asked.

"Sad," I said. "My grandfather was a police officer. I can't imagine my grandmother going through that."

"Let's head inside, I'm getting cold," he said. "Maybe a drink? Denny was mixing margaritas when I left. I think he's hoping you'll stop in."

"Diva, come," I said, slapping my thigh. Diva turned from snuffling around in a snowbank and happily joined us.

"Who else did you visit?"

"Don Benson lost a cow to a group of antelope hunters," I said. "I lost a donut bet on that one. Which, of course, meant we dropped by BB's bakery in Hay Springs."

"The conquering hero returns," Denholm announced as we walked into the parlor. He must have anticipated my arrival, because waiting for us on the counter were two tall margarita glasses. "How'd your first day go?"

"Char Shephard said something odd today," I said.

"Oh?" Denholm asked, his interest piqued.

"Relax, Denny, he's already requested asylum," Morty said.

Denholm quirked a smile. "Go ahead kid, we're out of the exposé business."

"She warned me to be careful – that there were dangerous people around," I said. "Any idea what she was talking about?"

"That's a tough one," Denholm said. "Between her car being shot up and Deputy Lynch's death, she's not wrong."

"Any idea who she's talking about?" I asked, taking a sip of a very strong margarita. "According to her, ISD believes she ran into a group of poachers."

"Sounds like you're not buying the party line," Morty said.

"Disproportionate response," I said. "Who kills a cop over a poaching charge? One *maybe* gets you a fine and your weapon confiscated. The other gets you life behind bars."

"It does seem thin," Denholm said. "But we do see a lot of violations around hunting season."

"Hunting accident doesn't attract quite the attention as an attempted murder," Morty said. "Someone's trying to keep a lid on something. I can feel it."

"Don't start that," Denholm warned.

"CAN'T STAY AWAY?" Hollie Wilder asked, looking up from her desk adjacent to the station entrance. I opened the box of donuts I'd brought from the grocery store and held it out to her.

"Purely self-defense. It's nicer here; there's not much heat in my apartment," I said as she plucked a frosted chocolate cake donut from the box.

"Is that the Diva I've been hearing so much about?" Her voice shifted up a register. She set her donut in the middle of her desk and rolled around. Diva wagged her tail but made no move to leave my side.

"It's okay, girl," I said, relaxing the tension on her leash. Diva was generally wary about new people and the smells within the station had her on edge. With my permission given, she passed Hollie's desk and then with a whine, lay on the floor.

"Such a good girl," Hollie encouraged. "I think she likes me."

Diva was probably alerting to a weapon in her desk, but that wasn't information Hollie needed. "Where is everyone?" As far as I could tell, the station was empty other than Hollie.

"Cal's getting breakfast at Boone's and Raff's out at an accident by

Highway 20," she said. "You need something? I don't have you working today."

"I wanted to get a look at Deputy Lynch's truck," I said, setting the donuts on the edge of her desk.

"Don't put those there. I shouldn't be eating this one," she said. "I'm afraid you're too late on the truck. I think the body shop is just about done with it."

I picked up the box and looked at the desks against the windowed wall on the north side. The largest desk belonged to Gene – at least it had a picture of him and a few other men standing in front of an elk. On the next desk was a picture of a man I didn't recognize. Standing next to him, however, was the widow, Mary Lynch.

"I'm sorry, Biggs," Hollie said, following my gaze and standing up abruptly. "I'll get that cleared off today. Raff will move over to George's desk and you'll share Raff's with the next deputy."

I set the donuts next to the coffee maker. The coffee smelled burned, but the pot was full. "Which body shop?" I asked. I'd already used the rugged tablet Snert had given me to identify the only two body shops in town.

"Rick's on Main and Niobrara," she said.

"Does he do maintenance work too?" I asked.

"Nope, that'd be Norm over at Bard's Auto on Twentieth and Bordeaux," she said. "Need me to write this down for you?"

"Not so far," I said. I pulled out an envelope containing Snert's contract and set it on Cal's desk.

"What's that?" Hollie asked.

"I talked to Sheriff Leonard about having a friend of mine do an independent inspection of the vehicle GPS sending units," I said.

"Hand it to me and I'll get it signed. That desk is a black hole," she said. "You know you might want to take it easy for a couple of weeks. Might rub some the wrong way if you appear too eager."

I handed her the envelope. "Appreciate the advice," I said.

She smiled. "Didn't think so, but at least I warned you," she said.

"And if you're going to wear the hat, make sure you tip it when dismissing a lady."

I nodded my head and pinched the brim like I'd seen Leonard do. "I don't always play well with others."

"That's what Cal said."

"Heel." Diva popped up from where she'd been lying next to Hollie's desk. She had brown crumbs in her whiskers, but I pretended not to notice.

Bard's Auto was closer than the body shop, so I decided to go there first. The shop's design was classic, with three mechanic bays, a small glass store front with a register, glass-fronted pop cooler and four old gas pumps outside. I hadn't filled the tank since my arrival, so I pulled up to the first island. I was barely out of the truck when a scruffy-looking man in coveralls walked out from an open mechanic's bay.

"Full service," he said, pointing to a weathered sign.

I shrugged and twisted off my gas cap. "I've got it. You Norm?"

"Yup. Raff said they'd replaced Lynch," he said. He had a large fading bruise on the side of his face. "That you?"

I held my hand out to him. "Biggs," I said. "That's quite a shiner you got there."

Norm looked at his greasy hands and then tried wiping his palms on the rough fabric of his coveralls. Given their condition, I wasn't sure that action would be enough. "Sorry, just pulled a water pump. Nice truck you've got here. Seventy-seven?"

"Seventy-eight," I said. "Still a work in progress."

"Sounded all right when you pulled in. Personally, I'd load her up with headers and glass packs. Get you another ten, fifteen horsepower," he said and then pointed to his cheek with a lopsided grin. "Luca Quinn. Did my face just before he ran you through the side of Hootskill. Word is, he tuned you up pretty good in that cell."

"You grow 'em big up here," I said.

"That why you're here? Are you filing charges on Quinn?" he

asked. "If so, I've got nothing to say. He and I just had a disagreement."

"Sheriff Leonard said you were the guy to talk to about the fleet vehicles."

"Not many of those left," he said. "I had to get Leonard's old patrol truck back and running so Raff would have something to drive. Someone shot up Shepard's rig real good."

"You saw it?" I asked.

He looked away and spit a stream of tobacco onto the pavement. "Nah. That's what I heard from the boys up at Rick's Body."

The gas clicked off and I peeled off four twenties, handing him the cash. "Leonard said something about corrosion on the GPS sending units."

"Hell, that ain't the half of it," he said, walking around the back of the truck toward the station's front door. "Equipment in those rigs are shit."

"But you didn't get a look at Shephard's or Lynch's?" I asked.

"Not after the fact," he said, counting back my change. "But I'm not surprised."

"That F150 Interceptor Lynch was driving was brand new," I said. "How'd the unit get corroded so fast?"

"We moved the equipment over from an old vehicle," he said, locking eyes with me. "Why? You got an issue?"

"Just trying to figure out why two deputies got shot and nobody knows where it happened," I said. "It's a lot of coincidence."

"Not around here." He turned his back on me and walked through the doorway that joined the retail space to the mechanic's bays. He was done talking.

Diva whined as I slid back into the truck. She was hitting on some scent I'd dragged back into the truck with me, but she soon lost interest and laid her muzzle back between her front legs. We'd gone for a longer-than-usual run that morning and she was tired. "Norm wasn't feeling chatty either," I said, patting her head before starting the truck.

The drive over to Rick's Body Shop took only a few minutes. The white-painted single-story cinderblock building sat at the edge of town. With a small parking lot in front, the shop backed to a large chain-link fenced lot that looked like it also served as a local junk yard. When I jumped out of the truck, the smell of paint fumes was immediately evident.

"Deputy Biggston?" a woman asked as I entered a small reception area.

"That's right," I said.

"Hollie Wilder called over and said you were coming. She said you wanted to get a look at Deputy Lynch's truck."

"Word is it's ready for paint," I said. "Any chance you took pictures for insurance before you started?"

"Of course. Rick will be right up," she said. "I'm Dawn, by the way."

"Call me Biggs."

Six two and not a pound under two-fifty, Rick was a big man with unruly, curly black hair and scars on his face that were either from acne or chicken pox. "And you can call me Rick." The man's voice was higher than his frame would suggest. "That F150 is done," he said. "Just needs a new seat since the staties took the old one."

"Was there a windshield when you got it?" I asked.

"Some," he said, waving me on to follow him. "It broke out on the tow, though."

I followed him down a narrow hallway and into a wide-open bay where six different cars were parked, each in varying stages of repair. "You stay pretty busy out here?" I asked.

"Always better in the winter. Those last two snow storms were good for business," he said, pushing through a door at the back. I followed him out into the yard where another dozen vehicles were parked. The F150 Interceptor sat proudly in line, a new coat of white paint gleaming brightly in the sun. "Decals will be in later this week. Should be on the road by the end of next."

"Nice looking truck," I said. "Show me where the bullet hole was?"

"Holes," he corrected.

"Two?" I asked.

"Yup," he said opening the back door. The seats had all been removed and the metal frame had been patched and buffed smooth. "Didn't find the second one until we pulled the back seat."

"State police know about that?" I asked.

"I sent pictures."

"Mind if I get copies of all those pictures?" I asked.

"Nope. Hollie said I was to help you 'much as I can," he said. "Give Dawn your email address. She'll send 'em right over."

"Where were the holes?" I asked.

"First one was right here," he said, placing his finger on the metal wall just below the back window. "Second one was down here." Rick slid his finger down until it was only an inch or so off the floor.

"Top one would have gone through the bed," I said. "You know if ISD recovered it?"

"Aluminum bed," he said, as if that explained everything. "Punched all the way through the tailgate."

"What about the bottom one?" I asked.

"Just nicked the metal under the bed," he said. "About here."

"That's quite an angle," I said, holding my arm out to mimic the bullet's trajectory. "You have a stick or something?"

"Sure," he said, picking up a piece of rebar from a nearby pile of junk.

We worked for a few minutes attempting to align the bar with his memory of the hole placements. From my estimation, the bullet would have come through the top six inches of the windshield. The shooter had to have fired from an elevated position.

"I'm going to need those pictures," I said.

"You want to look at Shephard's vehicle?" he asked, nodding to a car that was covered by a tarp.

"I sure do," I said.

There's nothing that quite prepares you for seeing the remnants of a firefight. Char Shephard's vehicle was riddled with bullet holes.

Just how she survived was beyond me. "Shit," I said, under my breath. "ISD didn't take this with them?"

"Not yet," he said. "They had their guys over here for a few days doing a workup on it. Far as I'm concerned it's totaled."

I put my hand on the door and started to open it.

"Not supposed to let anyone mess with it," he said, stepping forward and placing his hand on the door. I looked at his hand and then to his face, giving him my best steely-eyed glare. He got the message because he pulled back. "Yeah, I suppose you're somebody."

The smell of blood and feces assaulted my nose when I opened the door. Unlike Lynch's truck, the state had left the seats behind. There was something else I hadn't smelled for a long time – sweat mixed with fear. I could almost imagine the horrific moment when Char Shephard had come under attack.

"How many bullets did ISD recover?" I asked. I heard the rattle of something in the door as I opened it.

"A bunch. I don't know," Rick said putting some distance between himself and the vehicle.

I snapped on some black gloves and poked my finger into several of the myriad holes in the vehicle's seat. On my fourth entry, I hit pay dirt. Opening my pocket knife, I extracted a slug.

"Shouldn't you be careful how you extract that?"

"You a hunter, Rick?" I asked.

"A little," he said. "Deer mostly."

"What do you use?" I asked.

"Two-forty-three," he said. "I'd like to get a six-five Creedmore though. Don't like the drop off on my two-forty-three."

"What's that look like to you?" I asked, handing him the slug.

"It's small," he said, rolling it around on his hand. "I'd guess two-twenty-three or five-fifty-six. All these holes, I'd guess AR-15. Not really hunting rounds."

I walked around and looked at the vehicle. On the passenger side, the bullets had entered the front quarter panel and the door, just below the glass. It was hard to trace the angles, but I found no holes lower than waist height and the glass was broken out. The holes in the hood suggested a higher shooting position. On the driver's side, however, the bullets had entered low – none above knee level – and from somewhere in front.

In my mind's eye, I could see the ambush as if it was happening now – two shooters, one in a ditch, the other on the side of the hill. Shepard's vehicle entered a kill box, past the point of no return, only something spooked her and suddenly she stopped. The shooter in the ditch on the driver's side, keyed up from anticipation, fires early. Whatever suspicions Char had were confirmed and she jammed the car into reverse. The other shooter, knowing he has no option, joins in, only it's too late and she's already moving out of the box.

"It rained the day she got shot, right?" I asked.

"A little," Rick answered. "I remember being glad she was found on pavement. Seems kind of petty, doesn't it?"

I crouched next to the rear tire and shined my penlight up behind the tire. Caked mud and gravel mixed with green pine needles was splattered against the front of the wheel well. It fit with spinning tires on a remote portion of a forest road. I flaked off a sample into a plastic baggy.

"What'cha got there?" he asked.

"Not sure."

———

"You hear the news?" Gene asked. He'd picked me up behind the Sage and Rosemary Inn early on Tuesday afternoon. My next shift wasn't until Thursday, but he'd called the night before and explained there'd been a change of plans.

"Not sure," I said, loading Diva into the back seat of his Tahoe as he moved around to the passenger seat.

"Grace Fox accepted the deputy position," he said.

"That's great," I said. "Where's she from?"

"Two years at Faux Hills, South Dakota. That's north of Rapid City a piece," he said. "I imagine she's looking to climb the ladder."

I tried to keep the smile from my face as I wondered how small a town would need to be for Butte County to be climbing the ladder.

"That should help," I said, keeping my voice neutral. Privately, I was concerned that Butte County wasn't currently the sort of place a fresh officer should be making her mark. "Any military experience?"

"Not from what I heard. Associates in criminology, though," he said. "She's starting next week. That's why we're picking up shifts today and tomorrow."

"Oh?" I asked as he pulled out.

"My job is to make sure you're ready by game time," he said. "You're graduating early."

I'd been surprised that I was only required to have two training weeks with Gene and now one of those was being trimmed off. I wasn't sure I was ready.

"Sounds great," I said. "I'll be honest though, I wouldn't have known what to do with those poachers. My TO drilled me pretty good on state law, but conservation law isn't something I've had much experience with."

"It's not really your problem," he said. "This is peak season for hunting. Jasper and the rest of the wardens get calls all the time. Heck, I still call 'em and I've hunted this area my whole life. Even though Raff and I aren't riding in your rig, we'll still be available for backup and questions. Worse thing you can do is not ask. Now, let's head over to Crawford and down Highway 71. I'd like to run you through some traffic stops."

"Copy that," I said and pulled out.

As it turned out, traffic stops on a remote highway weren't really a lot different from ones done in town. It did seem like a certainty, however, that drivers way out in the boonies had easy access to at least one weapon – oftentimes right on the seat next to them.

"I don't know what you're worried about," Gene said after our fourth speeding stop. We'd only handed out a single ticket to a

Colorado license where the driver had been doing eighty-two in a sixty-five. The driver hadn't been the fastest we'd pulled over, but apparently local plates and a humble attitude got you a warning in Gene's book. "Those are textbook stops."

"Feels like we're a little loose on the speed limits," I said.

"Sheriff is an elected position," he said. "Folks around here don't like getting pulled over for speeding on an empty highway."

"Is that why Raff pulled me over? Because my license plate was from the eastern part of the state?" I asked.

"No. He's just a jack wagon when he's grumpy," Gene said. "Really not that bad of a guy. Give him some time to come around. I understand you were up at Rick's Body shop. I haven't wanted to go look. Hard enough for me to see Char in the hospital. I don't think I could see her rig after what happened."

"She was ambushed," I said. "Those weren't poachers."

Gene nodded his head. "Leonard said you were a fire pisser. And you're right, nobody believes that shit," he said. "You need to be careful, though."

"How so?" I asked.

"You've probably already noticed we do things a little differently out here," he said.

"You mean different rules for sixty-nine prefix plates?" I asked. Each county had a numeric prefix for its license plates and Butte County's prefix was sixty-nine.

"That's nothing," he said. "I don't care if you bust locals for speeding. I hand out warnings and if I get repeats, I'll hand out tickets. No, I'm just saying, take it slow when making accusations."

In that I hadn't made any accusations, I was confused and felt like Gene was holding back on me. "I'm not aware that I've accused anyone of anything."

"Norm Bobbins said you came on pretty strong," he said. "He feels like you accused him of bad maintenance on the rigs. I'm not sure you want to be pissing on his leg since he's the one who works on your brakes."

"You think he'll sabotage my vehicle because I'm asking questions?"

"No. Why would you say that?" he asked, frustrated. "But the way you turned that conversation on me is exactly what I'm saying. You need to be more sensitive."

I nodded. "What'd you mean when you said you needed to get me ready by game time?"

"I keep forgetting you didn't grow up in a small town," he said. "Around here, Friday nights are all about football. Until they're all about basketball ... and volleyball ... then softball and baseball."

"Lot of problems at the games?" I asked.

"Almost never," he said. "But an elected sheriff can't buy better publicity."

"Let me guess, our goal is to be seen but not draw attention."

"And here I thought you hadn't been listening to me," Gene said.

"You KNOW where Hemmingford High School is?" Hollie asked, holding a wallet-sized card out to me.

"Can't I just follow any car in town?" I asked, taking the card. "What's this?"

"Fleet gas swipe card. While you're driving that blue dinosaur of yours for Butte County, you can refuel at any Corn Pride station."

"What happens when I need to drive somewhere personal?" I asked.

"Do your best," she said. "Hopefully it's a temporary situation. Did Norm get your grill lights and radio installed?"

"Nice and clean," I said.

"I'll be sure to tell him you said that. Seems he's not your biggest fan," Hollie said. I smiled and tipped my hat to her as I walked out. The move earned me a return smile. "You're learning, Biggs."

During the drive, I had time to think. How long could I be happy with the slower life of a rural deputy? I thought of my job in Butte County as just a one-off. I was here to find who'd killed Deputy Lynch and put Deputy Shephard in a wheelchair, but was there something long-term for me in Butte County? I just couldn't tell. The ruggedly beautiful country appealed to me, but I didn't think that'd be enough to keep me here.

Hemmingford was buzzing with activity when Diva and I arrived. Locating the high school field turned out to be easy. Giant field lights stood out as great beacons that drew the townspeople like flies to a bug zapper.

"Aww, Deputy Bagstown," A heavy woman wearing a bright red and white jacket met me at the chain link gate where ticket sales looked to be brisk. I snapped Diva's leash and pulled her in to my knee as the woman lunged at me, her hand outstretched. "I'm Mayor Ruth Holling. Welcome to Hemmingford."

"Nice to meet you, Mayor Holling," I said, shaking her hand.

"Well, I need to be off," she said. "The band is about to perform their pre-game show. I never miss it. I hope you enjoy the game."

I watched her leave. She reminded me of a large red and white butterfly as she touched down on various groups of people on her way through the stands. For a small town, the citizens seemed to be out in force.

"Ooh, can we pet your dog?" The gaggle of girls who approached as a unit were wearing short red skirts and white sweaters that didn't cover their stomachs.

I stepped between Diva and the girls. "Sure, just take it slow, she's a working dog. We don't want to make her nervous," I said, extracting a handful of small treats I'd brought along for just this possibility. "Diva, sit."

"She's so pretty. Has she killed anyone?" one of the girls asked, which caused them all to giggle.

"Her job is to sniff out drugs and bombs," I said, ignoring the question. "What are your names?"

"I'm Harper, that's Ella, Zoey and Brook." The girl who seemed to be the spokesperson performed the introductions. "We're the cheer squad for Hemmingford."

"She's gentle but keep your hand flat," I said.

In general, people avoid German Shepherd service dogs due to their intensity. Diva was no exception, but we'd worked on receiving treats from strangers. She brought her ears back and slowly wagged her tail as the girls each in turn handed her a treat.

"Thank you, Mr. Policeman," Harper called as she skipped away, two of the other girls falling in line behind her. The last cheerleader had yet to provide her gift to Diva and she seemed nervous and unwilling to approach. Of all the girls, hers was probably the sanest response. Diva wasn't a pet and it seemed she sensed it.

"Zoey, isn't it?" After she nodded her head and met my eyes, I held my hand out. "I can give it to her. Why don't you catch up with your friends?"

Zoey glanced at my hand, then back at my face, and, still nervous, dropped the treat into my hand and ran off. I wouldn't have thought anything more about her reaction if, when I turned back, Diva hadn't been lying down with her paws stretched forward. She'd gotten a whiff of something on the girls. I groaned. Arresting cheerleaders on my first solo outing would certainly not be popular.

Hemmingford was a town of several hundred people and the smallest town in the county with its own high school. As I walked through the crowd, I estimated a minimum of four hundred in attendance with the visitor's stands nearly as full as the home town's side. I couldn't help but smile as I shared the anticipation with the bustling crowd around me.

I tracked Hemmingford's cheer squad as they ran out onto the running track that separated spectators from the football field. I caught Zoey staring at me as she unpacked pom-poms from her bag. When my eyes met hers, she looked away and hustled to fall in line with her friends as they started working on their cheers.

"Deputy?" A man approached from my side and I turned to meet him. He was in his fifties, wearing a red and white baseball cap that sported the school's bobcat mascot.

"How can I help?" I asked, directing Diva to sit next to me. I pulled out my notepad and wrote down the names of the four girls, adding that Diva had alerted on one of them, likely Zoey.

"I think there's been a fender bender in the parking lot," he said, trying to read my notes upside down. "By the back entrance to the school."

"Want to show me?" I flipped my pad closed and gave him my full attention.

"Uh, sure. It's just right in the lot, though," he said, eyeing one of the few remaining open seats in the stands.

"Why don't you drop your blanket first?" I said.

"Yeah, I could do that," he said, visibly relieved. I followed him out to the large L-shaped parking lot. Our trip was made more difficult by the excited fans milling around, many of whom he knew. We stopped frequently as he returned greetings and chitchat. "You're new, aren't you? I'm Adam. Adam Duncan"

"Just started this week," I said. "Came up from Sutherland. Henry Biggston."

"Shame about Char Shephard and George Lynch," Adam said. "People around here support you all. Hope you catch the bastards who did that."

"Appreciate that," I said.

"See, right over there." He pointed as we cleared the edge of the school. Sure enough, an old pickup had backed into a gravel-dusted white sedan.

"Appreciate it, Mr. Duncan," I said. "I'll get it from here."

"Happy to help."

From the field, a band started to play, the music wafting over the top of the school. I'd seen a stream of uniformed band members gathering in the endzone and imagined they were taking the field for the pre-game show.

"Anyone hurt?" I asked, approaching a young man who sat on the tailgate of the truck. The truck had been pulled away from the sedan but was still blocking the driving lane.

"Not yet," he said as I got a whiff of alcohol. "But Olivia's gonna be pissed I hit her car."

A shout from across the parking lot had us both looking around. A high school girl ran directly at us, her arms raised in alarm.

"Is that Olivia?" I asked.

"That's her," he said.

"Could I get your license and registration?" I asked. He didn't skip a beat, pulling both from a front pocket and handing them to me. Todd Hood looked like every farm kid I'd ever known. "Have you been drinking tonight, Todd?"

"Had one on the way over. I'm not drunk though," he said. "Her car's too small. I didn't see it when I was pulling out."

"Damnit, Todd, you hit my car!" Olivia's voice easily cut through the band's muted song.

"Sure enough," he said.

"Could I get your license and registration, miss?" I said.

"Aren't you going to arrest him?" Oliva turned abruptly on me. "He just admitted to hitting my car."

"Probably no need for an arrest tonight," I said. "License and registration?"

"I'm missing the game and my dad's gonna be pissed," she bemoaned as she opened the passenger-side door to dig through the glove compartment. While she searched, I wrote Todd's information into my notebook and handed the papers back to him. He smiled patiently as we both observed Olivia's search. "I don't know why I have to find this stuff when *he's* the one who hit *me*," she complained, finally emerging from her car. "What am I supposed to do now?"

"The good news is your vehicle is operational," I said, taking her information, transcribing it and handing her a card with my name and the station's phone number on it. "Give your insurance company a call and tell them I'll have a report filed within the next forty-eight hours."

"Is that all? Can I go?" she asked, taking my card.

"That's all I have," I said. "You're free to go."

Todd mistook my releasing Olivia as his sign to get moving. "Hold on,

Todd." I pulled out my phone and took pictures of the scene as I'd found it. I'd chronicled a number of accidents under the supervision of my SPD training officer and even one with Gene. This was my first solo report, so I wanted to be thorough, and ended up taking more pictures than I needed.

"About that beer," I said.

"I'm sober," he said, pulling worn cowboy boots off. "Give me a line, I'll walk it."

I smiled. The young man was full of confidence. "Why aren't you playing ball tonight?" I asked. "Sounds like you know the drill: nine steps forward, then turn around and come back."

"Problems with authority," he said, not wavering as he walked forward and then back.

"You know underaged drinking is illegal?" I asked.

"I do. Figured that you smelled it, so lying wasn't really an option," he said.

"Right foot: six inches off the ground and hold it," I said and he complied. Todd was neither oppositional nor was he impaired.

"I pass?" he asked.

"You did," I said. "You're going to get a ticket for running into Olivia's car. My book's over in the truck. Why don't you park your vehicle and follow me over."

"No lecture?" he asked, closing his tailgate.

"About drinking?" I asked.

"Yeah."

"Would it help?"

"Nah."

It took another thirty minutes to process Todd and get him on his way. Before leaving the truck, I opened the tablet Snert had given me. When I checked my email, I found a couple from Snert. I guess I was feeling a little homesick, so I poked the video chat on the messaging program we used.

"Henry, thanks for calling," Snert answered, his face appearing on the screen, his apartment in the background. "How's life on the western plains?"

"More forest than plains out here," I said. "But it's dark and cold right now."

"Oh, that's right. I had forgotten Wood Creek is on the southern tip of the Black Hills," he said. "Are you working right now? I see your uniform."

"I'm at a high school football game in Hemmingford," I said. "Just processed an accident. I saw your email and thought I'd give you a call."

"Did you read it?" he asked.

"Nope," I answered, grinning. He found it annoying when I ignored his emails and called him for the details instead.

He sighed. For some perverse reason, the sound lifted my spirits. "I received acceptance of my proposal to provide technical assistance to Butte County. Melinda and I are thinking of coming up next weekend. Would that work?"

"Sheriff has me working graveyards on the weekends," I said. "But I can make it work. I'll just have to adjust when I sleep."

"What if we came out Sunday? We could drive back on Monday and I'd only have to close the shop for a day," he said.

"That'd work," I said. "I don't have next week's schedule, but I bet I'll be off Sunday, Monday, Tuesday."

Diva whined and sat up in the passenger seat.

"I'll ask Mel if that works for her," he said.

I tracked where Diva was looking. Two teens had walked across the lot, stopping next to an old conversion van. Instead of just getting in, they knocked on the side cargo door and waited. My curiosity was piqued when I recognized one of the pair as cheerleader Zoey.

"Hey, I hate to do this to you, but I need to get going," I said.

"Call me back sometime. I have some thoughts about GPS data," he said.

"Okay," I said and hung up.

One side of the cargo door opened and smoke billowed out. The wind was up and it quickly cleared the smoke, allowing me to make out two people inside. Flashes of light from a ceiling-mounted screen suggested the occupants were watching a movie. I couldn't make out more because the door quickly closed behind Zoey and her partner. I strained to make out the vehicle's license plate, but it was too dark and my night vision monocular was in my go-bag in the way back. It was a mistake I wouldn't repeat.

"Looks suspicious, doesn't it, girl?" I asked, placing a hand on Diva's mane. She was tense, her attention fully on the van into which Zoey had disappeared. A few minutes later, Zoey and her friend emerged and scanned the parking lot. We were far enough away that both teens looked right past us. Satisfied, the two jogged through the parking lot, back to the game. Seeing the pair, Diva whined, her whole body trembling in anticipation.

I gave it a couple of minutes and then started the Bronco, backing out of the spot where I'd parked. The van was parked on the outer edge of the lot. I didn't want to give away my intent, so I circled wide, finally ending up in the last row where the vehicle sat. I pulled to a stop with my passenger door only a few feet from the end of the van.

Seeing no immediate reaction to my presence, I snapped Diva's leash to her harness, went around behind my truck and unsnapped the buckle that held my weapon in place. With Diva on my left, I walked her over to the van and carefully peered into the side window. Two men, one large, the other smaller, held game controllers, their shouting drowned out by the sounds of game-generated gunfire.

I backed away a bit and we moved forward to the cab. At the front passenger door, Diva alerted, jumping up, placing her paws on the window.

"What was that?" one of the occupants asked. Since they'd been staring at a video screen, I was pretty sure their night vision was shot and that they couldn't see me very well. I hustled, bringing Diva around the hood to the left side, just in time for the door through which Zoey had exited swing open. Diva barked and pulled against her harness.

"What the fuck?" the man yelled in surprise, slamming the door closed.

"Butte County sheriff's department," I announced, placing one hand on my pistol, the other holding Diva back. "Step out slowly from the vehicle."

"Brad, it's the cops!" a muffled voice from within exclaimed.

The van rocked in response to chaotic movement inside and a figure slid into the front seat. "I've got you blocked in. Turn off your vehicle," I shouted, pulling my pistol free.

"He's right there!" the driver yelled, looking out the window at me.

"Go, go, go!" the passenger urged from somewhere in the back.

I backhanded the window with the butt of my pistol, shattering it, just as the vehicle lurched forward, jumping onto the low cement block that indicated the front of the parking space. I thought the van would be stopped by the block, but its squealing tires found purchase and the vehicle jumped and bumped onto the icy grass. Gaining speed, it careened down a steep hill that separated the parking lot from the road and freedom.

"Come," I ordered, racing back to the Bronco. Diva didn't need any urging. She jumped in, clearing the driver's seat in a single bound. I cursed as I realized that by parking so close to the van, I didn't have an easy shot at pursuit without first reversing. I pushed back at the adrenaline that fought for control of my focus. In battle, soldiers lose peripheral vision, often looking past otherwise obvious problems or solutions. Such was my case. Twenty feet down were a pair of open parking spots and I raced forward, pulling my seat belt on and snapping Diva's harness in, all while I navigated out into the hardened ground beyond the lot.

"Butte Base, this is Butte-4, come in," I called over the radio, working to slow my speech. Hollie wouldn't have dispatch, but one of the guard service personnel would be monitoring from their home.

By the time I'd made it to the hill, the van was already a half block away on the street and accelerating.

"Butte-4, this is Base, over," a man answered, just as my new shocks bottomed out in the ditch. My Bronco had beefy tires and plenty of torque to spin them and I climbed out and bounced onto the road. Unfortunately, what I had in power, I lacked in maneuverability. I fought to maintain control as I switched surfaces. Diva barked loudly as I popped on both lights and siren.

"Butte-4, this is Base, can you read me?" Base asked again.

"Butte Base, this is Butte-4. I'm in pursuit of an older, white conversion van headed south on Donald Avenue," I said. "Suspect is turning west on Highway 2. Over."

"Copy that, Butte-4. I'll call it in to Butte-1. Over," Base answered.

I set the radio microphone into the cradle and mashed on the accelerator. Without a police interceptor engine the Bronco was working hard to obey my request for speed, but I wouldn't call her overpowered for the task. Fortunately, old conversion vans weren't well known for their sporty behavior either. The chase was on.

The school was on the western edge of Hemmingford and we were soon free of town. Ninety-two miles an hour looked to be the van's max speed and while the Bronco wasn't topped out, it had to be close. For several minutes, I simply followed along.

"Butte-4, report in please, over," Base called.

"Base, we're continuing on Highway 2 and are three miles from intersection with 71," I said. "Speeds are in excess of ninety miles an hour. I'm moving in for a license plate, over."

"Copy that, Butte-4. Be advised, Butte-1 and Butte-3 are en route. Butte-3 advises intercept in twelve minutes if chase turns north on Highway 71. We've informed Niobrara County in case chase continues on Highway 2. Please advise on course adjustments, over," Base said.

"Copy that, Base," I answered. "License plate is six-niner-alpha-one-four-two. I repeat six-niner-alpha-one-four-two, over."

I saw lights at the intersection ahead. If the chase continued down Highway 2, any seizure would likely occur in Wyoming and mean we'd lose the suspects. I didn't trust interstate politics and decided right then to keep things in Butte County. As we approached the intersection, I pulled into the left lane and started drawing even with the van. The driver, believing I'd overcommitted, seized his advantage and locked his brakes, sliding toward the intersection with the intent to turn north onto Highway 71.

To the extent of his limited thinking, he was right. I was overcommitted and slid past the intersection. What he failed to consider, however, was that I now had two police vehicles coming right for him.

It turned out the van's driver had more immediate problems as a front tire exploded under the heat generated by his skid. With little control, I watched in amazement as he successfully kept the van from flipping over. The vehicle slid through the intersection and ended up in the ditch.

"Base, this is Butte-4." I spun my tires as I reversed back into the intersection. I'd overshot but stayed safely on the highway. "Suspect has left the road at Highway 71 and Highway 2. I have two suspects on foot, over."

Unlike the van, which had buried its nose into the opposite side of the shallow ditch, my Bronco had no trouble navigating the terrain. I drove down and popped up on the other side, plowing through a three-strand barbed-wire fence and landing in a field. The two men saw the lights of my truck getting closer and split, running pell-mell for the safety of the forest a quarter mile away.

"Butte-4, I copy, over," Base answered.

Catching someone running through a field isn't hard, especially when you're driving a truck. Catching two, however, gets interesting. I oriented on the driver, who had chosen to run through the field. My rationale was simple, the danger to my vehicle would be a lot less. Plowed land had minimal holes or gullies, but the same couldn't be said of the pasture land near the tree line. The field had been picked in the fall and while corn stalks slapped the bottom of my truck, they did little to stop me.

I flipped off the sirens and jumped from the vehicle, keeping Diva's leash in hand. We ran him down, catching him easily within the first twenty feet. "On your face, Brad!" I yelled, remembering the name the passenger had used. The minute I touched the man's back, he dove forward, landing roughly on the ground, breathing heavily and obviously exhausted.

"You're under arrest!" I landed on the guy with my knee across his back. Diva wanted a piece of him and barked angrily. I had to call her off not once, but twice as I cuffed the man behind his back. I frisked him and found an oversized knife but nothing else.

With Brad under control, I tried to locate the second perp, but he was nowhere to be found.

"Get up!" I ordered, pulling at Brad's cuffed hands.

"Why?" He resisted.

"Now!" I ordered, yanking him up and looping an arm under his.

"What are you doing?"

"Shut up," I ordered, turning to call out, "This is Butte County Sheriff's Department. I have a dog and I'm going to release it if you don't give yourself up right now."

With no response, I pushed Brad forward into the dark. "Butte County Sheriff," I called again. "I have a dog. I'll release her if you don't give yourself up immediately."

Controlling Diva and an exhausted Brad took some doing, but I pushed him across the field in the direction I'd last seen his companion fleeing. "Damnit." I finally said. The guy had me. Weighed down with a suspect while my truck door was wide open and the engine still running, I was putting myself in too much risk. The passenger could lure me out too far, circle back and grab my truck. Even worse, the perp could somehow get around me and get the van out of the ditch, although I didn't think that likely.

"All right, come on." I walked Brad back to the truck.

"Aren't you gonna go get him?" Brad asked.

"Who?" It was worth a try.

"Um. Nobody."

Back at the truck, I leaned in and called back to base, letting them know I had one in custody and one suspect still on the run. I locked the truck and brought the keys with me as the three of us walked back to the van.

"What are you selling?" I asked.

"Selling? Nothing."

"Why'd you take off, then?" I asked.

"You scared me," Brad said. "I didn't know you were police."

"So when your buddy yelled, 'Brad, it's the cops,' that wasn't enough of a clue for you?" Brad shook his head and looked at the ground, defeated.

I pulled one of Brad's arms through the steering wheel and relocked his wrists together with the cuffs. The van reeked of marijuana, but I didn't initially see any obvious signs of it as I scanned the interior. I let Diva loose inside.

"Hey, you can't do that," Brad complained. "You got no probable cause."

"You gave up that argument when you vandalized school property, fled the scene, and resisted arrest," I said. "Want me to continue?"

Diva pawed at the grimy shag carpet. When she didn't leave the area alone, I suspected there was something more than just some dropped weed flakes on the floor.

"She's causing damage to my ride, man," Brad said. "I'm gonna sue."

"Worried about that, are you?" I asked. In the distance, I heard a siren. I looked north out the van's window but couldn't see anything yet.

I flicked open my pocket knife and pulled at the edge of the carpet, exposing a neatly cutout flap.

"I don't know anything about that," Brad said.

Beneath the carpet was a loose piece of sheet metal that looked like it hadn't been seated back in place properly. I pulled the metal up, exposing several plastic gallon-size zipper bags of pot and a quart-size bag half full of tiny packets of white powder.

"What'd you sell to Zoey?" I asked, taking a quick picture of the stash with my phone.

"Zoey who?" He asked.

"Look pal, you're looking at serious time here. Right now, I've only got you as the driver. If I don't find your friend, all this weight is yours. You got weed and what looks like meth. What kind of idiot drives this dirty?" I asked.

"I'm serious, it's not mine. I was just hanging out, getting loaded," he said.

"Hear that siren?" I asked. "That's Deputy Butler. And you know who's not ten minutes behind him? That's right, Sheriff Leonard. You might want to get your story straight. Now, tell me what your friend sold Zoey. If you were just along for the ride, I might be able to make this easier on you."

"I don't know," he said. "I was playing video games. It was just a quarter."

"Quarter of what? Meth?" I asked.

"Yeah. She wanted something for a party. Look, it's just a bunch of teenies. They'll share the bag and get a little bump. No harm, no foul," he said.

"What is your partner's name?" I asked.

"I'm not a snitch," he said. "He'd kill me."

I jumped out, jogged over to the Bronco and brought it back over next to the van. "Sit, girl," I ordered as Diva came up next to me. I slipped her harness off and pulled on the vest Snert had made. I slid two water bottles into the specially made pouches. She looked up at me like I'd grown a second head.

A minute later, Raff pulled up in his old Crown Vic cruiser, dramatically sliding to a stop.

"What's going on, Biggston?" he asked, jumping out, hand on his weapon.

"Hand me your cuffs, would you?" I said, pulling on my heavy coat and grabbing my go-bag. To Raff's credit, he didn't question my request and handed me the cuffs from his belt.

"What are you doing?" he asked.

"I've got Brad – not sure of his last name – cuffed to the steering wheel. There's a load of drugs in the middle seat." I pulled my Henry .30-30 rifle from its leather sheath and slammed the tailgate shut, locking it. "His partner took off cross country."

"Luca Quinn is most likely the other," Raff said. "If he made the trees, he's long gone."

"I'm going after him."

"Like hell you are," Raff said. "You don't want to be chasing Quinn by yourself. He knows these hills. You don't."

I looked north. A second set of lights was racing down the highway, Sheriff Leonard no doubt.

"I have my phone. I'll check in every two hours if I can get cell coverage." Diva and I loped off toward the thickly forested hills that I had absolutely no familiarity with.

"Hunt 'em up, girl." Diva sniffed the air, keeping her head a foot off the ground as I played out her lead to its max of twenty feet. I knew the direction the second perp had taken and given the odor of pot coming off Brad, I wasn't concerned about Diva's ability to track this guy.

I resisted Diva's pull urging me to sprint across the frozen field. With my quarry having a fifteen-minute head start, it would likely turn into a long night and I was already feeling the heat build beneath my coat. As I reached the edge of the field, I saw Leonard's truck pull in next to Raff's. I wondered if I was in for a good old-fashion ass chewing when this was over. If I was honest though, I didn't care. If he wanted to run, I'd oblige with a chase. It's just part of who I am.

Just past the field was a small gully where excess water collected from both the hill and the field. Along with the sunlight today, the temperature had reached forty-five degrees, melting any exposed snow. The eastern edge of the field, however, was blocked from the afternoon sun by the slope of thick trees. I was facing a nice hard bank of crystalized snow. It was a good break.

I slung the .30-30 over my shoulders, resting it sideways atop my backpack and securing it with a Velcro strap. It wasn't an overly stable configuration but would free one hand for a penlight. Diva pulled me south along the snow line, dipping her head low. She was on scent and never hesitated as she jumped into a snow bank.

"Slow, girl," I said. I sank to my thighs in soft snow as my boots broke the tenuous crust that had formed in the thaw/freeze cycle common with fall snows. Scanning with my light, I found deep boot prints and slogged toward them. Only a single set of prints went through the drift. These were recent.

Coming out of the gulley, the snow depth lessened as we started up the hill. My perp's strides were long, like he'd been running. I pulled Diva to a stop and crouched next to his tracks, inspecting one of the perfect imprints. The boot tread showed thick lugs, not unlike my own. I stepped in next to the print. While a person tends to slide forward when running on this type of slick surface, making comparisons more difficult, his shoe size was larger than my twelve and a halfs.

I shrugged my backpack off and unfastened my gun belt. Running with a belt full of equipment is something a person can do for short distances, however, I wasn't going to tolerate the restrictive feeling for the entire night. I removed my pistol, two magazines, and Raff's cuffs and then hung the belt on a nearby tree branch as a trail marker for those who came behind me. While I had my pack available, I pulled out my night vision monocular.

Diva whined as I burned precious time fooling with my load-out. "I'm ready, girl," I finally said, after scanning the hillside with my monocular, not a bit surprised that my target was long gone. "Let's go."

We soon fell into an uncomfortable rhythm as we picked our way up the side of the forested hill. Diva's strap was my only guarantee of keeping her near and was also a constant snare for every limb and shrub passed. I estimated we'd climbed over six hundred feet by the time we crested the first rise and my heart hammered from the exertion. Whoever I was chasing, he wasn't in bad shape.

I scanned the western valley in the direction the perp was headed. Between the trees and the limited magnification of the scope, the move was a longshot. Sure enough, I came up empty. With the sun down, the temperature had dropped fast and although I was sweating in my jacket, I estimated we were in the mid-twenties. I felt fortunate the sky was clear and the waxing moon was half full, providing enough light to avoid major obstacles.

I wasn't about to allow my body to fully recover. I was in good shape and my best bet was to apply pressure to my quarry. "Let's go." Diva didn't need the urging. Her four legs had carried her up the hill almost as easily as running on flat ground. In the pale moonlight, I caught the telltale sign of a fall: a long scrape where a boot had ripped a light covering of earth away from a hidden rocky surface. My quarry had descended the hill at speed and I wasn't surprised when he turned north, cutting across the backside of the hill instead of going directly down. I wondered what went through his head when he realized he was being chased.

The backside of the first hill soon gave way to a new upward slope and while down was less anerobic, I much preferred the heart-pounding, but sure-footed change. As Diva pulled me along, I tried to recall what I'd seen of the area from the road. West of Highway 71, there wasn't much in the way of farms or productive ranches. I recalled it was hilly and forested, but that was all – and not of much help.

At some point this guy had located a deer trail and decided it was his best mode of travel. I haven't always been a big churchgoer, but that doesn't mean I don't think the Big Man's Son doesn't look out for us. My quarry had just made his first big mistake of the evening and it was a godsend. Diva hustled us along on a perp's trail with no reservations, but the strap that held her was a constant source of slowing. A well-worn deer trail, however, had few obstructions and we nearly doubled our pace. Next time Pearl asked me to go to church, I vowed I was all in.

It was just past two-thirty in the morning when I pulled Diva to a stop. We'd given up our jogging gait long ago, having tired after more than four hours on the scent. I sat back on a log and leaned over to grab one of Diva's dwindling water bottles. The move likely saved my life as an angry bee sailed past on my left side a microsecond before I heard the report of gunfire. My left thigh burned with the unmistakable pain of having been shot.

I dove forward onto the trail just as a second shot from up the hill zipped by. With Diva's leash in hand, I lunged off the edge of the trail, trying to recall just how steep this portion was. Two more shots rang out, but Diva and I had already dropped from sight, sliding nearly twenty feet at a sharp angle before running into enough brush to stop us. The shock from the impact was jarring.

"Who are you," an exasperated voice called down the hill. The voice belonged to Luca Quinn.

"Deputy Henry Biggston, Luca. Put your weapon down," I said. I scrabbled in the snow, looking for my .30-30 rifle, but couldn't find it. I'd also dropped my night vision monocular and left my gloves on the trail above. In all, I was alive, but my odds of survival had just dipped precipitously.

as The sound of brush cracking underfoot signaled Luca's movement in my direction. "You dropped your rifle," he said. "And this cool little scope. That why you've been on me so good? I've hunted these hills all my life. I'm surprised you were able to keep up."

I heard the lever of my rifle cycle as he chambered a round.

"Give it up," I called, ducking around a tree, trying to gain my feet, but between the slippery slope and my leg's refusal to operate correctly, I struggled. "If you shoot a cop, there's no coming back for you."

"Mama always said kin was special, but she never much cared for your side. I think we mighta been friends if you'd growed up around here. I'm gonna be sad to kill you," he said. "Now stand still."

Fortunately, in my condition, falling wasn't that hard, so I dove to the side just as a slug buried itself into the bark next to me. "Shoots a little high, don't you think?" he asked when the smoke cleared.

I slid down the hill, putting more distance and trees between us, grateful that Diva was sticking with me. Another shot rang out, striking a nearby tree. "You think you could mount this little scope on the gun. It'd make this a whole lot easier."

His reliance on the monocular gave me an idea. I pulled my pack off and dug out the long-handled LED flashlight. Unlike my penlight, this heavy light had a wide, bright beam and doubled nicely as a club if needed. The sound of rocks rolling down the hill warned me of Luca's approach. I quickly tossed my pack as far as I could back up the hillside.

Luca bit and fired at the pack. In that moment, I released Diva. "Git 'em!" isn't the right command but for some reason it was top of mind. I spun around the tree, flashing my LED up the hill as Luca worked the lever, loading a fresh round into the chamber. I timed my roll to the side to coincide with the sounds of the gun. Luca finished chambering the bullet and as I predicted, fired immediately at the light source, which I'd flung at him.

Unlike people, dogs don't need much light to see. Even though she was tired from the chase, Diva launched herself almost six feet into the air to latch onto Luca's free arm and spin him around. Luca fell face first onto the hillside, dropping my rifle. He managed to pull his arm away, dislodge Diva from his coat sleeve and send her flying.

We were on the dark side of the hill, blocked from most of the moonlight. I struggled to locate Luca and Diva as I pulled out my 1911. For a massive man, Luca was remarkably agile. I felt sorrow that our confrontation would most likely end with one of us dead, but I didn't see either of us giving up. Luca was clearly not bright enough to be running whatever high-stakes game I'd stumbled upon.

In the dim light, I watched as he caught the trunk of a tree with his arm and swung around. Somehow, he'd located his pistol and fired even before he'd stopped moving. I was surprised that I didn't feel the burn of another gunshot – until I heard a yelp of surprise from Diva.

Luca had given up his position by firing the weapon. That was all the information I needed. I settled down on my good knee and fired three shots, hitting him high and right at twenty yards. He screamed in agony as he spun and fell to the ground. A moment later, Diva landed on him, latching onto his arm, growling and tugging like she intended to pull it off. Her actions didn't do much to stop the screaming.

"Diva, setzen!" I ordered. I rarely resorted to the German commands she'd originally been trained with, but they carried more weight with her in tense situations like this. I struggled to gain my feet and slowly limped up to where the two were entangled in Diva's leash. I spun Luca onto his face and pulled his arm from Diva's mouth. "Good girl. Now, sit." I unclipped her lead and tied Luca's arms behind his back with it.

Luca gurgled in pain and having been shot before, I felt for the guy. The fact was, my first priority was to make sure he couldn't hurt either Diva or me any further. "You shot me. We're kin," he managed before he fell unconscious. I felt for his pulse. His heart was beating, although I had no idea what shape he was really in.

I clambered up the hill to retrieve my flashlight and pack. On the way back down, I found my .30-30, but not the monocular Luca had taken. Placing the items out of Luca's reach, I grabbed Raff's cuffs and replaced Diva's lead. I turned him over and shined a light on the green army fatigue coat he wore. The material was soaked with blood where my .45 caliber bullets had ruined his shoulder. He didn't have a great chance of surviving the night.

I pulled out my first-aid kit, sprinkled a clotting agent into the wound and wadded up a spare t-shirt for a compress. I had no idea if I'd stopped the blood loss, but it was the best I could do under our current conditions.

"How are you doing, girl?" I asked as Diva limped back over to me.

I imagined the worst when she gave a pitiful whine and dropped her head into my hands. I searched her over with the flashlight, finding a furrow in the armored vest Snert had provided. "Is that where it hurts?" She whined again when I felt under the vest, pushing gently on her hide. My heart started beating again when I found no wound or anything I felt was permanent damage. It was quite an improvement over the last time she'd been shot.

As adrenaline left my body, my leg gave out and I plopped into a drift of snow the sun had yet to reach. With some difficulty, I located my pack and dressed my thigh. The bullet had cut an angry trench through the skin and exposed damaged muscle. I used the last of my water to clean the wound which was too deep to be left alone. I grimaced as I pulled out the one first-aid item I hoped I'd never have to use: my skin stapler. I'd originally bought it for Diva and had never contemplated using it on myself.

Unfortunately, stapling my body turned out to be exactly as painful as you'd expect. I probably needed more than the four I managed to apply, but there comes a point where the analytical side of your brain is overridden by self-preservation.

"Holy shit, girl," I finally said, flopping back onto the side of the hill. Diva pushed into me and licked my face, wiggling her worried little butt in concern. I pulled out my cellphone and checked for service. Nothing.

There was no way I was getting Luca out of here tonight in my current condition. I rummaged in my backpack and pulled out my emergency food. It was horrible stuff: six hundred k-cals per chunk of yellow, gooey, bland ick. I tossed one to Diva and after filling my mouth, realized I had no remaining water.

Go-bags are all about survival and I'd spent a good amount of time organizing mine. It took nearly an hour to set up a temporary camp, build a windbreak and get a fire burning. I'd wrapped Luca p like an over-stuffed baked potato in two of my space blankets. With snow melting into water in my pot, I prepared to boil tea so I could rest with my back against a tree and wait for dawn.

"Hey." The kick on my boot woke me, shooting pain up my leg. "I gotta pee."

It probably wasn't right, but the first thing that popped through my head was surprise that Luca hadn't died in the night. The fire had long since burned down to embers and I leaned over to push a few small branches into the coals to stoke it back up.

"Did you hear me?" Luca asked.

"Not sure what you want me to do about it," I said, dumping out the pot and refilling it with fresh snow. Getting water from snow was time consuming, but once boiled, it was safe to drink. Having lost a lot of blood, Luca would need to drink plenty of water. I had refilled the two quart bottles I'd brought along before drifting off to sleep a few hours before, but we'd run out shortly.

"I'm dying of thirst," he said.

I scooted over on my butt, dragging my injured leg along as carefully as I could. I pulled back one of the space blankets I'd secured around Luca. There was a lot of blood on his jacket and my compresses were saturated. I couldn't imagine how the man was even talking. I crouched next to him and dribbled water into his mouth until he was satisfied.

"You gonna make me pee my pants?" he asked.

Diva growled a warning as Luca tried to move.

"It's okay, girl" I stood, testing my leg carefully. Skin pulled at the staples but held. Every muscle in my injured leg hurt, but I was able to help him to a standing position. I removed Diva's lead and clipped the dog-side to his cuffs and held the other end. "So pee."

Luca stumbled as he walked a few steps to the base of a tree. I turned sideways to give him a bit of privacy, but when I looked back, he'd collapsed in the snow. Any hopes I had of Luca Quinn making it off the mountain by himself vanished in that moment. Instead, I set about making a litter from pine poles, paracord and my lean-to tarp.

Around eleven o'clock, I was finally ready to roll my distant cousin into the sling and start up the hill. Slow going doesn't begin to describe the speed in which a three-hundred-pound man can be dragged up a steep embankment by an injured man. On the plus side, I managed to locate my night vision monocular.

It was sometime after noon when I stopped to rest, no more than a mile from where I'd made camp the night before. Dragging Luca along the deer trail had taken every bit of strength I had and I was going to be pissed if the asshole died on me before we made it back to the truck. Somewhere during the trek, one of my staples had pulled free and my boot had become squishy with my own blood. I rewrapped the thigh tightly, unwilling to try the stapler again.

Thankful for the afternoon's bright sunshine, I rejoiced when we ran across a stream. I vaguely remembered it from the previous night, but this would allow me to refill the water bottles. I had a Life Straw but chose instead to use purifying tablets since they required the least effort. Somewhere along the line, Luca had slipped into total unconsciousness. If I didn't pick up the pace, I'd be spending a second night on the mountain, something I didn't believe Luca would survive.

At that time of year, darkness hit Butte County around five in the evening. I watched with some dread as dusk caught me on the trail. I wasn't sure how much longer I could keep going. I'd tied paracord onto the handles of the sled and looped a length over my shoulders to bear some of the weight, but the technique provided only a small amount of relief to my hands. A few times, I thought I heard the sounds of ATV motors, but mountains play tricks with your ears, sometimes masking close sounds behind a rise while amplifying distant sounds through a draw. Without a sighting, I refused to stop. I was pretty sure I wouldn't be able to get myself moving again.

An hour after the last flicker of sun blinked out from the western sky, I caught a glimmer of light across the valley between me and what I believed to be the final rise. It was a cruel joke of mountain travel that to get anywhere, there was always a descent before you just had to climb again. I wondered what shape I'd be in by the time I made it to where the will-o-wisp of light had flashed. My mind wandered at the thought of will-o-wisps. Extreme fatigue does funny things to a person and I dwelt on the notion for a while. I couldn't recall what they were exactly, but seemed to remember they were bad news.

A second flash of light from across the hill got my attention and I realized that maybe I wasn't hallucinating, that the light was possibly someone coming to help. I slowed and pulled Luca to the side of the trail, shaking my bleeding and beleaguered hands. If the light wasn't help coming, then it could be trouble. Either way, I'd meet them on the trail and make it easy for them to find me.

I pulled up my .30-30 and fired into the air three times – a universal signal of distress. The light I'd seen flashed again and I realized it was a signal. I rummaged for my big LED and waved it in a wide arc oriented on the signaler.

Fifteen minutes later, Diva barked excitedly just before I heard the sound of horses' hooves. I'll admit, I got a lump in my throat when I recognized the angular figure of Faith Hudson as she raced up on her brown and white Paint. In a single fluid move, even before the horse had stopped, she swung a leg off over the horse's back, the long tails of her coat following dramatically. Releasing the reins, she simply stepped from the horse and raced over to me.

"Shit, Biggs, is that you?" she asked.

I worked to release the .30-30 and found I couldn't uncurl my hands. More riders were headed toward us on the trail and soon Sheriff Leonard came into view, riding a much larger dark-brown Quarter horse. While not at all the athletic figure Faith was, he looked comfortable on his high perch. Diva whined and ducked her head as she pulled in next to me, wagging her tail at Faith's approach.

"Tell me I'm not hallucinating," I said.

"Your hands are bleeding," Faith said, running a flashlight beam over my body. "Are you shot?"

"Luca's hurt," I said. "Got him in the chest. We need to get him off the mountain."

"Luca Quinn?" Leonard asked, pulling my heavy coat back from Luca's face.

"He hasn't moved in a while," I said. "Can we get a Flight for Life?"

Leonard leaned down and then walked over to me, gently working the rifle from my hands. "Son, Luca Quinn is dead."

"What about the other guy?" I asked.

"Brad O'Neil's in custody. State Patrol is processing the van," Leonard said, shaking his head. "We have twenty LEOs from five counties out searching these hills for you."

I looked at Faith who'd taken it upon herself to wrap my left hand which had been bleeding from the stress of holding the litter. "Are you a deputy?" I asked.

She shook her head.

"Terrain on this part is too steep for four-wheelers," Leonard said. "Hudson Ranch has the best mountain horses around. Ms. Hudson insisted on coming along. Good thing too. She's the one who spotted my old gun belt on that tree."

"I guess this means we're even on that beer," I said, trying to catch her eye.

"Not even close," she answered.

"BIGGS, CAN YOU RIDE?" Leonard asked. "We're only a mile and a half from the highway."

I nodded. I'd been raised around horses. "What are you thinking?"

"You've got a gunshot wound and I've got a radio," he said. "Take my horse. Hudson can get you down to the command post. Jasper from Fish and Game is already on his way. We'll take care of getting Quinn out of here."

"What about her?" Faith asked, looking at Diva, who lay on the ground, exhausted.

"I'll carry her in front of me," I said.

"That trail is steep, Biggs. You're going to have a hard enough time with your leg banged up," she said. "Put her up with me. She and I will get some bonding time."

Leonard approached Diva and leaned in, as if he were about to pick her up. "Hold on there, sir," I said, just as Diva's eyes flew open. She startled and growled. German Shepherds have a low, throaty growl that is menacing enough to put ice in your veins.

Leonard stilled, neither withdrawing rapidly nor continuing forward, which showed a lot about his understanding of animals.

"It's okay, girl. We're all friends," I soothed.

Diva turned to look at me, her eyebrows flipflopping as she worked through the situation.

When her ears stayed back, Leonard withdrew. "And here I thought we were friends," he said.

"You really are a pain some days," I said, leaning down to pick her up. Ordinarily, her sixty-five pounds wasn't that much for me, but lifting her onto Faith's Paint was about all I could handle. Of course, mounting the tall Quarter horse Leonard had ridden up the mountain with a bum left leg turned out to be equally difficult.

"Before you go." Leonard stopped me. "You should know the state patrol are down at the command center. I want you to push 'em off until you get to the hospital and I can be there with you."

"Problems?" I asked.

"Not really," he said. "We're all on the same team, but I'm pretty sure we both know there's something going on here and it's not about poachers."

"Do you think this is related to Lynch and Shephard?"

He glared at me. "Three times, now, my deputies get shot. Three times, ISD takes the case."

"At least this time nobody's going to pin this on poachers."

"I'll catch you back at the hospital," he said. "Leave your truck keys and we'll get your rig back to town."

"You ready?" Faith asked, circling her spirited Paint back around. Diva gave me a piteous look as she hung on for dear life, half draped over Faith's knees.

"I'll follow," I said, which earned me a half grin.

"We call him El Chubby," she said, once we were a hundred yards down the path. From experience, I knew the deer trail would shortly run out and we'd have to bushwhack back over the final hill.

"Leonard?" I asked skeptically. This earned me a laugh.

"No, dumbass," she said. "That's what Lexi named the horse you're riding. It's the only one we have that's big enough for Leonard, so you're sort of right. Why didn't you take a radio? Finding you would have been a lot easier."

"I don't have one. Since it was Friday night, I had to take my own truck," I said. "Football nights are an all-hands-on-deck type of thing."

"Aren't you military types supposed to always be prepared?"

"That's Eagle Scouts," I said.

"But you were military, right?"

"Yup. Army."

"Way I hear it, you were more than that."

"Not really," I answered. "You mind telling me why you drove off the other night?"

"Seems obvious enough."

"Not from where I'm sitting," I said.

"You laughed at me when I told you I had a kid. Did you already know Raff was the father?" she said, jumping in before I could answer. "Just drop it."

"Is that a big thing out here?" I asked.

"Having a kid? I'm pretty sure that's a big deal even in Sutherland."

"I didn't mean it that way," I said, frustrated that I wasn't able to communicate how I felt.

The horses labored to climb the steep incline and I leaned in close, enjoying El Chubby's display of raw strength. We topped the hill and when I looked down, it appeared the entire valley was filled with strobing lights.

"Doesn't matter," she said. "It's over."

I decided to take a final shot at it. "I laughed because all I was trying to do was ask you out for a drink."

"Why was it funny, then?" She stopped her Paint and turned to look at me. Diva took that moment to jump off. Apparently, she'd had enough of horseback riding.

"It was like you were trying to talk me out of drinks by telling me all the bad gossip about yourself," I said. "I shouldn't have laughed."

"No, you shouldn't," she agreed.

I urged El Chubby forward and down into the waiting chaos.

⊏⊐

"I don't know if I'm horrified or impressed by these staples." Dr. Naples, M.D. was on the name tag of the white-coat-wearing attending physician on duty at the hospital. With a firm grip on pliers, he removed the staple that was sticking out and still attached to only one side. He'd applied a local anesthesia, which made its removal almost pleasant, at least considering what I'd gone through when I'd put the staples in – or when that one had started ripping out. "Why would you have a medical stapler in your pack?"

"They're for my dog," I said, not interested in explaining that I had needed them once before and didn't have them.

"I'm going to leave the other ones in. We'll put you on a strong antibiotic and you need to watch for redness or swelling," he said, bringing out his own fancier-looking stapler. "Hold still. This might pinch."

"You need anything else?" I asked, peeling off the gown I'd been given. For a moment, the doctor stared at the scars across my abdomen.

"Thank you for your service, Mr. Biggston," he said, unexpected tears filling his eyes. "My son served. He didn't make it back."

"Army?" I asked.

"Infantry," he said. "Roadside bomb."

"I'm sorry," I said, pulling on my shirt. I'd never known what to do when someone thanked me, but this felt different.

He placed a hand on my shoulder. "I'm glad you made it back. Maybe you could tell me about being over there some time. I never got a chance to talk to Zach about it."

I nodded. "I'd be honored."

As I pulled my torn jeans back on, Naples gave me an assessing look. "I'd recommend you remain in the hospital overnight and stay on limited duty for at least three weeks," he said. "Infection is a concern."

"I'll be careful," I said, pulling my blood-stained, over-sized uniform shirt on. "I have things I need to do."

"You should know there's a detective lady from the state in the hallway waiting to interview you," he said.

"Is there another way out of here?" I asked. It wasn't that I didn't want to talk to ISD – well, yes, it was that, but not because I was afraid of the questions. I just had something I needed to do.

He pointed to a door at the back of the room. "That exits to the hall next to the stairwell. I wouldn't recommend stairs on that leg, though. You open that wound again and you'll bleed through your dressing."

I nodded and hobbled to the second door, Diva trotting along beside me. "Thanks, Doc. Maybe we could grab breakfast sometime."

Once in the hallway, I found the stairwell just as Doc Naples had said. I pushed open the door and pulled back, startled. There was already someone on the other side of the door.

"Some tricks never get old," Sheriff Leonard said, holding his hat in hand. "Want to tell me why you're ducking ISD?"

"Any chance you'd like to take a drive?" I asked.

He pushed his worn cowboy hat onto his head and grinned. "You're like an old hound dog on a scent. Where're we headed?"

"Hemmingford," I said. "Brad O'Neil confessed to selling drugs to a Hemmingford girl. I'd like to see if we can recover those drugs."

"Something more than ditch weed?" he asked.

"O'Neil said he sold her methamphetamine," I said.

"Damn!" Leonard accelerated. "Are you sure?"

"Hate to think of a bunch of kids getting into that," I said.

"Yup."

We drove in silence for a while, both lost in our own thoughts. I finally broke the silence. "Did you put Doc Naples up to using that exam room because it was near a back door?"

"That's what I like about you, Biggs. You don't miss much," he said. "You think we should get you some clean clothing first? Is that really the best shirt we had for you? You look like a kid playing dress up."

"Hollie has a shirt order in," I said. "I need to locate a cheerleader in Hemmingford. All I've got is a first name. Zoey."

"Start at the beginning," he said.

"Diva alerted on her at the game," I said. "I was going to follow up after, but I happened to see her get into a van in the parking lot."

"Brad O'Neil's?" he asked.

"That's right. I tried to make a stop, but they bolted," I said.

"I want you wearing body armor," he said. "Didn't Gene get you outfitted?"

"I think you're out," I said.

"Talk to Hollie. We shouldn't have anyone out there without a vest," he said, pulling the radio transmitter from beneath his dash. "Base, this is One. Can you patch me through to Mayor Holling on my cell?"

"Butte-1, copy that," a man answered just as we pulled into the parking lot behind the Sage and Rosemary. I wanted to drop Diva off with Morty, but thought I might need her before the night was over.

"You look like hell," Morty said, meeting me at the back door of the hotel. I was hoping to miss my landlords, but I should have known better.

"Sounds right," I said, brushing past him and doing my best to run up the stairs. It was humbling that Morty was able to keep up with me.

"You got shot," he said.

"I don't have time to talk."

"That's not a denial. Let me guess. Poachers," he said.

"Leonard will skin me alive if I give you anything on this without his permission," I said. "It's mostly a good ending though and no poachers involved. Let me clear it first and I'll give you what I can."

Morty followed me into the freezing cold of my attic apartment. I'd volunteered to work on the heating system but had yet to find time.

"Tell him we'll run with what we've gleaned from the radio transmissions if he doesn't want to let you talk," Morty pressed. I dropped my ripped pants and tenderly slipped on a new, not quite as worn pair. I pulled on a clean uniform shirt and tucked the extra material around the back.

"Give me that shirt. Denny is a wizard with blood stains and he'll even drop in a couple of darts to show off that girlish figure," Morty said. "I think your poor pants are a lost cause, though."

"I'll talk to the sheriff about that interview." I turned to head back out the door.

"There's a rumor a body was brought down from Angus Hill west of 71," he said. "Can you confirm that was Brad O'Neil?"

The old man's eyes glittered with excitement as I returned his gaze. He was as much on the hunt as I was. "I can tell you Brad O'Neil's body was not brought down from any hill."

"Ooh, such a careful answer," he said. "Were you after poachers?"

"Game and Fish weren't primary," I answered as I made it to the steps. Spending any more time with Morty right now would be dangerous for my career.

When I approached Leonard's rig, he was on the phone, talking animatedly. Seeing me, he waved me into the truck and hung up as I slid in next to him.

"You're looking better," he said. "Grab a wet wipe under the seat and move some of the grime off your face. We're headed to a party."

"What kind of party?" I asked as he pulled away from the parking lot.

"Butte-1, this is Base. I have a Detective Cropsie asking to be patched through."

"Go ahead, Base," he answered.

"Cal, Roseland Cropsie here," a woman's voice came through the static. "I'm looking for one of your officers. I was told I'd be able to question him at Wood Creek General, but he appears to have given me the slip."

"That so?" Leonard said.

"Luca Quinn was pronounced at eight-thirty this evening. You know the drill," she said. "Your officer needs to stand down while we do our investigation."

"Roseland, you know I'm short-handed here," Cal argued. "I'll bring him in to you in a couple of hours. We have something we need to take care of first."

"Are you with Deputy Biggston?" Cropsie asked. "You need to bring him here, right away."

"When will you finish processing the van?" Leonard asked.

"Midnight, latest," she said. "We're looking to get outta here in the morning, but we can't do that without closing Biggston's shooting investigation."

"I'll personally deliver Deputy Biggston to your hotel by midnight," Leonard said.

"Take possession of his firearm, Cal."

"Copy that. Butte-1 out," Leonard said, hanging up the radio's microphone.

"Morty and Denholm are listening in," I said, pulling my 1911 from a coat pocket and dropping it into the plastic bag he held out for me. I'd switched to a brown service coat but hadn't been allowed to recover my duty belt. "Morty was pumping me for an interview when I got clothes."

"What'd you tell him?" Leonard asked.

"SPD drilled into me that patrol officers don't talk to press," I said. "He wanted me to verify that it was Brad O'Neil who got taken off Angus Hill. I told him I didn't believe that to be the case. For the record, I didn't know it was called Angus Hill until Morty said so."

Leonard's smile took on a slightly predatory look. "Morty can be trouble but careful management can be useful. Did you say anything else?"

I thought for a moment as we sped down the highway toward Hemmingford. "Sort of. Hope I didn't speak out of turn. He asked if all the activity on Angus Hill was related to poaching. I told him that Game and Fish weren't primary."

Leonard tipped his head as he thought about it. "Maybe not the most savvy thing to say," he finally summarized. "But I think Morty's already on that trail."

"Feels coincidental that I got shot at," I said. "Without Diva's alert, I would never have suspected something was up with Zoey and I never would have been interested in Brad's van. What's the link?"

"Butte County is a relatively peaceful part of the country," he said. "Gunshot wounds are almost always one and done. Husband gets drunk, roughs up wife, she finally gets tired of it and gives him a taste of buckshot. Or a hunter gets greedy and a farmer decides to take the law into his own hands. There's nothing subtle about a gun. You can almost always figure out who did it by who got shot and where."

"You're saying that because I got shot in a remote area by a drug dealer, Lynch and Shephard did too?"

"It would explain ISD pointing at poachers," he said.

"And they don't read you in because they think you're in on it?" I asked.

"Me or one of my deputies," he said. "You're fresh enough that Cropsie thinks you're not involved. I seem to recall you ran into a dirty cop in Sutherland."

"Nala Swede made a couple of bad calls, but she wasn't dirty. Do you really think ISD suspects you?"

"County sheriffs have a lot of latitude," he said. "Cropsie's just doing her job."

"Did you know Lynch took two bullets?" I asked.

"What do you mean?" he asked. "How do you know that?"

"I stopped by Rick's Body Shop and had a look. Rick told me they found a second exit on the vehicle. A bullet came through under the back seat, so it wasn't initially found. The angle was way too high for the crime scene to be where the truck was found. As you know, a fifty-cal leaves a mess, so I'm not surprised they missed it."

"Anything else I should know?"

"Not really," I said.

"Out with it."

"I recovered a slug from Shephard's rig. It was in one of the doors," I said. "We've already dismissed poachers so it's not exactly news that it wasn't a hunting round."

"Twenty-two?" he asked.

"Full metal jacket two-twenty-three," I said. "Go right through a deer."

"That's a legal round for deer," he said.

"Most states won't allow such a small round," I said. "Did you see the trajectories?"

"I know the car got shot up pretty good."

"There were two shooters," I said. "Gunman on the driver's side took a low position, either in a ditch or on the base of the hill. The other was high, probably positioned up the hill. It was a classic ambush layout except the guy in the ditch blew it and fired early, probably saving Shephard's life."

"Do I even want to know how you saw the ISD's report?" he asked.

"No report," I said. "I made Rick show me the car."

"And you figured all that out by looking at the car? What exactly did you do in the Rangers?"

"I had a lot of days like today," I said, looking to change the subject.

The small town of Hemmingford was quiet and Leonard navigated to a modest, nice-looking foursquare home with a broad porch that stretched around at least three sides. The porch light was on and light spilled from interior windows.

"Ruth Holling is Hemmingford's mayor," Leonard explained, not knowing I'd already met the woman at the game.

"Zoey's last name is Holling?"

"No, but Ruth makes it her business to know everyone else's business and she has a daughter in high school," he said, hopping out.

I jumped out and followed Leonard up cement stairs to the front door. He hadn't even knocked when Holling appeared behind the glass security door and smiled brightly. "Sheriff Leonard and Deputy

Biggston, it's good to see you even though it's late. Ralph and I had just gone to bed for the night. How can I help you?"

I glanced at my phone to check the time. Already eleven-thirty. Time seemed to be racing away from me. Leonard removed his hat as he stepped inside, and I followed suit. "Ruth, we're looking for one of the school cheerleaders. First name is Zoey."

As he talked, a girl I recognized from the football game came to sit halfway down the broad stairs leading to the second floor. If I was right, she was one of the four cheerleaders I'd introduced to Diva.

"I don't know," Holling said, taken off guard. "Brook?" she yelled up the stairs, not realizing the girl was sitting only ten feet from her.

"I'm right here, Mom," she said.

"Zoey Watts," Holling said. "Do you know where Sheriff Leonard can find her?"

"No," Brook said flatly.

"Come down here, dear. Don't be rude," Holling pushed.

"I don't know anything. I'm grounded. Remember?" Brook said sarcastically.

"Is Zoey in some type of trouble?" Holling asked. "I know her father. He works as a ranch hand. Good man. I could probably find his phone number."

"That'd be helpful, ma'am," Leonard said.

Brook hadn't taken her eyes off me the entire time I'd been standing there. I decided to push my luck. "Could we talk a minute?" I asked, gesturing out the door with my head and glancing at Leonard for approval.

Brook sighed as only high school girls can. "Fine. Whatever. But I still don't know where Zoey is."

I walked off the porch and down the stairs. Brook wouldn't last long in the cold. "Is Zoey a friend?"

Brook shrugged. "Maybe. Is she in trouble?" She'd already started shivering.

I put my hat on and pulled off my coat, glad I'd left the pistol in the truck. I swung it over her shoulders. "Yes and no. If she's your friend, you probably know she's been experimenting with marijuana and maybe some pills."

Brook's eyes widened and I knew I had her. "I ... I don't think so."

"Did you know, in my job, most people I talk to lie when they've done something wrong? It's just human nature," I said. "Zoey's only in trouble because the things she's buying from Brad O'Neil are going to hurt her. Do you know what she bought from him last night at the game?"

"No. Zoey doesn't do drugs."

"Brook, aren't you cold? Come in, dear. You can talk inside," Mayor Holling called.

"Just a minute, Mom," Brook called back.

"Do you remember Diva, my dog? She's sitting right there in the truck," Brook nodded her head. "If I can't figure out where Zoey is, I'm going to ask your mom if I can bring Diva into your house. I'll make up a story about checking for gas leaks or something. You should know that Diva will find even the smallest trace of pot in a backpack or anywhere else it's been stashed."

"You can't do that." Brook's nostrils flared as her eyes cut back to the house. I'd hit a nerve.

I shrugged. "Look, we're not here to make trouble for you. What I want is to find Zoey and help her before she gets hurt. If you would prefer, we can have this conversation with your mother. I just thought maybe you'd like a chance to help your friend without making this a whole big thing."

She stared at me, searching my face, trying to determine if I was bluffing. She finally decided I wasn't. "She's at a ditch party over by Fisher Res."

"What does she drive?"

"Her boyfriend, Bobby Quinn, drives a new blue Camaro." Her face had lost all color and I wondered if she was about to get sick.

"Thank you, Brook. If you think of anything else, give me a call." I pulled out a generic business card for the sheriff's department, wrote my cell number on it and handed it to her.

"WHAT'D YOU GET FROM BROOK?" Sheriff Leonard asked as we climbed back into the truck.

"Zoey's at a ditch party by Fisher Reservoir," I said.

"Been parties out at Fisher Reservoir for as long as there's been beer and teenagers," he chuckled. "I seem to remember tipping a couple barley pops out there with Pearl back when."

"Pearl was a partier?" I asked. My mental vision of Nanna was that she was nothing short of a saint. I wasn't sure I wanted to discover anything different.

Leonard shook his head. "There's not a lot to do around here for entertainment," he said. "Even less back then. Most of the time we were just hanging out, talking around a bonfire. I seem to recall the sheriff back then wouldn't give us too much trouble if we cleaned up after ourselves."

"Do you do the same?" I asked.

"Situational," he said, flipping his lights on but leaving the siren off. "Like old Sheriff Adams, I'm not going to hassle kids for tossing back a couple of beers on Saturday night as long as they don't make a mess and aren't out driving drunk. Thing that's bothering me is that ISD didn't say anything about meth in O'Neil's van."

I shook my head. "I found a hideaway compartment in front of a rear passenger seat. There were bags of weed and another bag with what could have been methamphetamine."

"I guess I just saw weed. Did you tell ISD about the meth?" he asked.

I smiled. "No. Why?"

"Well, I didn't see it and I don't think Raff did. You don't want State Patrol climbing in your ass for something you think you saw." I nodded. If I hadn't taken a picture, Leonard might have been able to convince me not to push the issue. "You do know we're going to talk about you running off into the woods with no backup. What if that bullet had found more than your leg?"

"It was a lucky shot," I said. "If I'd waited, Quinn would have been long gone. But I'd be *all for* a portable radio."

Leonard turned onto a gravel road and flipped off the strobes atop his rig. "We have radios. Gene should have made sure you had one in your truck. I told Mayor Holling about you finding meth. She wanted you to bring Diva to the school and do a locker check. I talked her out of it."

"Why?" I asked.

"If we take your dog into the school, we'll find half a gram of weed here and there. As you know, that's no big deal. But what happens when someone has enough for distribution? We'll ruin lives. And for what? A little weed?"

"What happens when we find ecstasy and crack?" I asked. I had difficulty with just how grey Leonard saw the law.

"We don't have a drug problem in Butte County," he said.

"I hope you're right," I said. "O'Neil was dealing on school property. He had to know we'd have someone at the game."

Ahead on the gravel road, a pair of headlights turned on and a vehicle started toward us. "Looks like we've been spotted," Leonard said. "There's a lot more to being sheriff than busting every small infraction you see."

"I don't know if I can see that line as easily as you and Gene," I said. The vehicle that passed us was an older white pickup with a curly red-haired teen behind the wheel. I wrote down the license plate and time in my notebook.

Leonard laughed out loud. "Son, don't change a thing. I knew who I was getting when I hired you. Remember, your granddad trained me. You know the difference between being an SPD cop and being a sheriff?"

"You're elected," I said.

"Good to see the lights are all on in that noggin of yours," he said. "That's right. Locking up kids for things their parents did as teens is a surefire way of losing an election. Catching a deputy-murdering drug dealer, however, is a surefire way of cementing the next election."

"The gun Luca used didn't match either of the guns used on Lynch or Shephard. How can you be sure the two crimes are related?"

"Call it instinct," he said "State Patrol is already searching Luca Quinn's trailer. I'll bet you a steak they find an AR-15 that matches bullets in Shephard's car."

We crested a hill and saw a flood of vehicles pouring onto the road from a tree-lined drive. "That pickup was the lookout, wasn't it? And you're on for steak."

"Deal," he said. "What are we looking for?"

"Blue, late-model Chevy Camaro. It belongs to Bobby Quinn," I said.

"Nothing's ever easy with you, is it?" he said. "You just gotta poke that bear."

"Brook Holling said Bobby and Zoey went to the party together tonight," I said. "Apparently, they're a thing. Is that a problem?"

"Hannah Quinn is a pain in my ass," he said, leaning over and flipping the light bar back on. "Bobby's her *good* kid. He's goin' to college and is trying to make something of himself. Every time Bobby gets in trouble, Hannah crawls so far up my ass I fart her perfume for a week."

While he'd been talking, I'd been scanning the fleeing vehicles for

Bobby's Camaro. "He's up ahead," I said, pointing unnecessarily over the dash. Half a dozen vehicles separated us.

"Hang on," Leonard said, cranking his SUV off into the snow-packed ditch. It was a move I probably wouldn't have considered unless lives were on the line. He cackled as the vehicle's heavy-lugged tires bit in and the powerful interceptor engine roared. "Give me some siren, how about?"

Bobby Quinn seemed to sense that we were after him. The blue Camaro jumped out to the left of the slower traffic, accelerating fast on the gravel road. Even with Leonard's powerful vehicle, the soft ditch slowed us enough that Bobby pulled away quickly.

"Culvert," I warned just in time for Leonard to swerve up the opposite side of the ditch. For a moment, we were airborne as we jumped the service road that entered the reservoir's property.

"Damn, but I miss this," he said, turning into the ditch and rolling through the bottom and back up the other side. Responding to our lights and sirens, most of the vehicles had slowed and Leonard nudged his way back onto the gravel road. I could just barely make out Bobby's disappearing taillights.

"You're crazy," I muttered, half in awe. My other half recognized that this could very well be my last ride.

"Know these roads like the back of my hand," he said.

"You still see him?" I asked. There were several cars ahead, their drivers also deciding to make a run for it, but I was pretty sure I was tracking the right one.

"Negative. I assume he's still ahead?"

"Roger that," I said, glancing at the speedometer. We were doing seventy on a gravel road, definitely a new record for me. "Front of the pack on the right."

"Expect to drift when you're on gravel." Leonard couldn't help but take the moment to coach me on country living. "Don't overcorrect, just go with the flow. I happen to know the ditches next to the reservoir are well maintained. That fact and the melt and freeze cycles we've had, I wasn't too worried about holes or stumps. If you do take a ditch, though, you'll roll at these speeds, especially if you stick a wheel."

It takes a lot of nerve to keep your speed up on gravel and the drivers who had been keeping up with Bobby soon gave up. One by one, each vehicle slowed and pulled to the side. I tried to catch their license plates, but between the gravel dust and our current speed, all I got was a basic description of the vehicles.

"He's braking," I said. "He's turning."

"That's a mistake," Leonard said, jamming on his brakes and steering toward the ditch. Anti-lock brakes thudded in a staccato rhythm as he dropped the right front wheel over a high lip of gravel on my side of the road. The gravel was soft and the move pulled the truck into the turn. Before I could even process what he'd done, Leonard released the brakes and accelerated forward. It was a move of ridiculous precision, and dangerous beyond comprehension.

"Oh, shit!" I gasped, losing my normally cool façade. My reaction must have been what Leonard was looking for because he hooted with joy.

"Son, you should see your face!" He was nodding his head up and down like a bobble head doll. "I don't suppose your granddad told you I used to race dirt track?"

"That's even more terrifying."

"Don't get your panties in a bunch. We're about to end this," he said, and he was right. Leonard had destroyed Bobby's head start and we were about to overtake the Camaro. "I can't let him get on the pavement and he knows it. That Camaro SS has four hundred and fifty-five horsepower. Doesn't do him a lot of good on the gravel though."

Leonard's Yukon surged forward. He brought the nose of the truck up next to the Camaro and gave it a slight tap on the left back fender. We were both accelerating but probably only doing fifty when he executed the maneuver. The tap sent the Camaro into a spin and Leonard jammed on his brakes as we watched the sportscar slide into the ditch.

"What's Bobby Quinn going to say about that?" I asked.

"He'll probably make Butte County pay for repairs," he said. "Now, let's go talk to Zoey."

"Want me to process the stop?" I asked. "I figure you have him on felony evading."

"Yeah, write him up," Leonard said, "but hand me the ticket once you're done with him."

I nodded and jumped out of the truck. Diva whined at the door, wanting to join me, but I closed her in. The Camaro's engine revved as the driver attempted to climb out of the ditch. The car didn't move, despite the wide wheels spinning and throwing all matter of material behind it. Low slung and on a slope, the car would require a wrecker to extract it from the ditch.

"Driver, shut off your engine and place your hands on the steering wheel," I shouted, holding my CCP and tactical light out in front of me. To the driver's credit, I only had to shout the order twice before the engine slowed to idle and the window was rolled down.

"I need your license and registration," I said, lowering neither my gun nor flashlight as I positioned myself behind the driver's seat.

"You could have killed me!" Bobby Quinn was just as I remembered him from Press Box Bar where I'd separated him and another kid who were fighting.

"Turn off the engine and step out of the vehicle." I waved my flashlight into the back seat and then over to the passenger seat. Zoey Watts was nowhere to be found.

"Which is it? You want my license and registration or for me to get out?" he asked petulantly.

I pushed the flashlight beam into his face. He had a large bruise across one eye and down his cheek. "Did you know it's illegal not to stop when you're being chased by a police vehicle? In fact, it's a felony. You want to lose that attitude and start complying?"

He rolled his eyes and I got a strong whiff of alcohol as he opened his door to push his driver's license into my hand. An open can of beer sat in the console between the two seats. So much for harmless drinking and no driving.

"Not like my mom won't get me out," he said.

"Where's Zoey Watts?" I asked. He shrugged and stumbled as he stood.

"Haven't seen her," he said. "I don't think she was at the party."

I cuffed Bobby's hands behind his back and pushed him against the Camaro. "Don't move," I said and walked back up to where Leonard still sat in the truck.

"He's drunk and has an open container in the vehicle, but no Zoey Watts," I said. "I'd like to run Diva past his car once."

"Do that," Leonard said. "Do a field sobriety and see if we can get him to blow."

Working with drunks has always been one of my least favorite parts of police work. Those under the influence are both mouthy and sloppy. As I walked back to the Camaro with Diva, she showed interest in the car but didn't specifically alert, meaning there'd been drugs in the vehicle at one time or another but at the moment, Bobby was clean. He did, however, fail the field sobriety with a blood alcohol that registered almost twice the legal limit.

"Mr. Quinn. You're being placed under arrest for operating a motor vehicle while impaired. I've also written a ticket for resisting arrest and another for felony reckless evading," I said and mirandized him.

A second set of flashing lights showed up on the scene. I'd expected Raff or Gene and was surprised to discover it was a State Patrol vehicle that pulled up.

"I've got this, Biggs," Leonard said, handing me my bagged 1911 pistol. "I'll run Diva back to Morty. They seem to get along okay."

"You'll send someone over to Zoey's house?" I asked.

"We've got it." He pulled my truck keys from his pocket and tossed them to me. "Your rig's parked behind Sage and Rosemary."

"Morty's going to want an interview," I said. "He's on this."

"I know." Leonard walked away with a grimace.

A very large trooper stepped from the patrol car and adjusted his gun belt. I put him at two-fifty if he was a pound. From the passenger side, an older woman wearing a grey wool suit and black trench coat stepped out. She had grey-streaked hair that was neatly cropped and her black-rimmed glasses gave her a severe look.

The woman walked around the front of the trooper's vehicle and Gigantus fell into step behind her as she approached the scene. "Deputy Henry Biggston?" she asked.

I straightened and approached, removing my hat as I extended my hand. "I'm Deputy Biggston, ma'am," I said. My military experience had taught me that showing respect was rarely seen as weakness.

She pursed her lips, looking from my extended hand up to my face. I felt like she was attempting to peer into my soul as we locked eyes. "Sergeant Detective Roseland Cropsie." She accepted my hand, shaking it firmly. Her grip was practiced but had little strength behind it, something I found unusual given her high rank within the state's highest law enforcement service. "Is that the weapon used in the fatal shooting of Luca Quinn?" She nodded to the pocket where I'd stuffed my bagged 1911.

I pushed my hat back onto my head and extracted the bag from my pocket. Gigantus's right hand jumped to the pistol on his hip, but he stopped short of drawing it. "Easy there, big boy," I said. "The slide is back and the magazine has been removed." I rotated the bag so he could see it.

"Deputy Biggston, given your propensity for flight, I'm detaining you while I conduct an investigation on the fatal shooting of Luca Quinn. Do you have any other weapons on your person?"

"Walther CCP," I said and pointed to my other pocket. "It's loaded hot. I'll go slow."

"Index finger and thumb," Gigantus directed.

"I did not flee the hospital," I said, ignoring his directions. I extracted the CCP, dropped the magazine into my hand and pulled back the slide to eject the bullet in the chamber.

"What would you call it?" the detective asked. "I sat in that hospital for an hour before I realized you and the doctor were gone."

"Brad O'Neil confessed to selling methamphetamine to Zoey Watts. I wanted to find her and prevent harm," I said. "Unfortunately, we haven't yet been able to locate her."

"Do you have any other weapons, Deputy Biggston?" she asked.

"Just these," I said, pulling my pocket knife out and removing a smaller, hidden knife from my belt. She rolled her eyes. I didn't mind.

"You'll play nice?" she asked. "I'd prefer not to handcuff you."

"You have my full attention."

The ride back to Wood Creek was quiet. Detective Cropsie was apparently uninterested in questioning me in front of Gigantus.

There's always a bit of a funk in the back of a police vehicle and the state patrol car was no different. Nonetheless, I drifted off to sleep only a few minutes into the drive and was awakened when my door was yanked opened. I blinked twice and forced myself to calm. I'd dreamed again of being in Afghanistan on a raid and was ready for action when Gigantus's large figure loomed into view.

"Oh, it's you," I said, feebly covering for my overly tense posture. By the look on his face, my reaction hadn't been lost on the big man. We were in an underground garage I didn't recognize. "Where are we?"

"Beneath Butte County courthouse," Gigantus had a high voice that made me question if he was a steroid user. "We have use of a conference room."

I nodded and allowed him to direct me over to an elevator. "Where's the detective?" I asked.

"She's already up there," he said. "I'll warn you once. You behave or I'll put a hurtin' on you."

"Good to know," I said. Idly, I wondered what a grudge match between him and my even larger cousin Luca Quinn would have looked like. I was pretty sure Luca would have kicked his ass, but then we were family, so I was biased.

"Would you like something to drink before we get started?"

Detective Cropsie asked as I was led into a small conference room. There were a few manila folders on the table. "There's coffee on the credenza."

I grabbed a cup and started to fill it. The burned smell told me it wouldn't be fresh, but caffeine was going to be important. "One for you, ma'am?" I asked.

"No, thank you," she answered.

The chairs around the table looked comfortable, but they weren't even close. I chose the one directly across from Cropsie. I'd been through any number of after-action reports and wondered if this interview would resemble any of them. Turns out, the process wasn't that different. I started out by giving a narrative of how I became interested in O'Neil's vehicle and gave as much detail as I could think of for each step past that. Cropsie had a sharp mind and stopped me periodically, asking questions for details I'd left out.

"Thank you, Mr. Biggston," she said, when I was finished.

"And?"

"And I need you to commit that story to writing with as much detail as you have just provided," she said.

"And then what?" I asked.

"I will take your case before a board of senior officers who will make a determination as to the legality of your use of force," she said. "This board will recommend one of several courses of action. These actions range from no further action required to murder charges."

"That's quite a continuum," I said.

She nodded tersely. "Do you have other questions?"

"Do you make a recommendation to this board?"

"I do."

"Will you share that with me?"

"I will. I do not find the events that led to the fatal shooting of Luca Quinn to be outside of the scope of normal policework. That said, I also believe you acted recklessly in single-handedly chasing a fugitive onto the mountain. I can only hope Sheriff Leonard will reprimand you so you modify your procedures during future contacts. What you did was brave to the point of foolhardiness. He could easily have taken you down on that mountain. I've looked at your military record and understand you are highly trained and were chosen for service because of your willingness to make bold actions under adverse conditions. Please understand, Mr. Biggston, you need to curb this desire or I fear I will be investigating your death next time. That would be a shame. We've buried enough heroes."

I nodded, caught off guard by her words. "Could I ask one more question?"

She nodded, tipping her head back, looking every bit a librarian or schoolmarm. "You don't really believe the shootings here were poaching, right?"

With a deep sigh, she said, "Leave it alone, Deputy Biggston. This was hopefully the big break we've been looking for. Now give us time to work."

THE MORNING SKY was just starting to lighten when I walked out from the small parking lot beneath the courthouse. The air was a crisp twenty-five degrees and even though my thigh throbbed, I was grateful to be walking on a flat surface. Trooper Gigantus had offered to drop me somewhere, but Sage and Rosemary was only a couple blocks away and I preferred to be on my own. I glanced at my phone, it was seven thirty in the morning.

The sound of a vehicle approaching caught my attention and I was surprised to see Sheriff Leonard's Yukon slow to a stop beside me.

"Funny running into you out here," he said, having rolled down his window. "I was headed over to drop your dog off with Morty. Doesn't appear she's my biggest fan."

I opened his back door and let Diva out. "Did you find Zoey Watts?"

"Gene ran over to the house. No one was home," he said. "How'd things go with ISD? Cropsie can be a bitch. Did she say how she was leaning?"

"She'll present to the board next week. I'm on suspension until they make a ruling," I said, handing him my badge. "She felt it was a justified shoot."

Leonard coughed derisively. "Well, hell. You think? You chased an armed subject halfway across the mountain and got shot. Damn right it was justified. I talked to the Doc. He said you need to stay off that leg. I told Hollie not to schedule you until a week from Monday. I got something for you."

He pulled a familiar leather duty belt from his passenger seat. It already had my department issued .357 magnum revolver sitting in the holster. "Can I carry if I'm suspended?" I asked.

"You can in my county," he said. "I'm not having one of mine walking around unarmed after taking down a cop killer. And it's looking like you owe me a steak."

"You found weapons at Quinn's house?" I asked.

"He lived in a trailer on the edge of the family farm," Leonard said. "ISD will run ballistics, but Raff says State Patrol pulled out a couple of AR-15s and a fifty-cal. They also found ten more weapons and enough ammunition to start a war. Not many people will miss Luca and you'll be the toast of the town before the end of the week."

"Two shooters fired at Shephard," I said, frowning. "Do you really think Brad O'Neil was the second? What about who supplied them the drugs?"

"Your granddad couldn't take a win either," he said, laughing. "We'll get to all that, but my experience has been that these things are like knitted socks. Pull one string and the whole thing unravels. I'd be surprised if anything more comes of it. You did good, kid. You single-handedly solved the Squaw Creek murder."

I pulled the service belt on and buckled it. "The case doesn't feel complete."

"That's a feeling you'll get used to," he said. "Now, I need to go talk to an old newspaper man. I wonder if I can convince Morty and Denholm to run a special issue."

I adjusted my hat as he drove off to park only a block further down in front of the Sage and Rosemary. Idly, I wondered if that's what it took to be sheriff. No doubt he'd spin the tale to bring maximum attention to the department.

"Let's go, girl," I said, leading Diva down an alley and around the back of the hotel. She wasn't the type to complain about her injuries, but I could tell her feet were sore from our trek through the mountains. We both needed to take it easy for a while. As we walked, I could see the lights were on in Morty and Denholm's parlor. No doubt, Leonard was already inside, drinking coffee and crafting a story about his department's victory over the bad guys. Whatever was going on, I wanted no part in it.

I was exhausted and if not for Diva, I'd have missed the fact that there was an additional vehicle sitting behind the inn. As it was, when I tried to turn for the back door, Diva ignored me and trotted over to a big old white F350 that sat idling. Mentally, I kicked myself. I should have seen the large truck or at least heard it, but I'd been up for hours.

I walked over to the driver's side and grinned as I recognized the lanky figure who'd fallen asleep with her seat reclined half way, a black felt cowboy hat resting over her face. She looked so peaceful that I hated to wake her, but I couldn't imagine what she was doing idling here of all places. I knocked gently on the window.

I had to knock a second time before Faith stirred and then lurched forward, wildly looking around. She calmed as she recognized where she was. After adjusting her seat, she rolled down the window.

"Hey, there," I said, leaning against the side of the truck. The cab smelled of old spilled beer, perfume and horse crap. I'd probably avoid sharing that particular description with her, however.

"Hey," she answered. "What time is it?"

"Sun's almost up. Seven-thirty or so," I said. "How long you been sitting here?"

She rolled up the window, pushed the door open and slid out so we stood face to face, almost uncomfortably close. "I came over after work. I need to apologize."

I shook my head and placed a hand on her elbow, half expecting her to pull away, but she didn't. "You rescued me last night. I don't think there's anything to apologize for."

"It's just, I don't talk to people that well. Lexi says I'm prickly," she said. "I don't mean to be, but working in a bar, I tend to see the worst in people. You've been nothing but a stand-up guy."

I allowed a smile to show on my face. "I can see how a pretty woman like you might get the worst end of bar talk from drunk guys. I don't think you're the problem, though. My buddies tell me I don't have girlfriends because I don't let anyone in. How about we call it even and start over?"

"I'd like that."

"So," I said. "Do you have any kids?"

This brought a crooked smile to her face. "I have a daughter, April. She's ten years old and amazing. She's my life."

"She sounds pretty terrific," I said.

Faith placed a hand on my chest and leaned in, bringing her lips to within a couple inches of my own. She kept her eyes open and searched my face. I tipped my head and closed the distance. Her lips were soft and I breathed in the scent of her as we kissed. I reached around and cradled her back with my hand, savoring the moment, allowing the concerns of the world to disappear around me.

"Thank you," she said, when we finally broke apart.

I searched her face. *Thank you* was far from anything that made sense. "For what?"

"Not deciding I'm just a crazy person. I don't do this very well," she said.

"Oh, you definitely do this well," I said.

She smiled, taken off guard. It was the sort of smile that lit up her entire face. I wished I could take a picture of that smile. "*Relationships*, stupid. I don't do relationships very well."

"We should form a club," I said, willing to say just about anything for the moment not to end. A ray of sunshine chose that moment to peek over the low buildings to the east.

"Damn. I gotta get going," she said. "April will be worried."

"When can I see you again?" I asked.

"Actually, that's why I'm here," she said. "We always have a big Sunday dinner. Lexi said I should invite you over."

"Wow, already introducing me to the parents. You move fast," I said.

She took a mock swipe at me. "You've already met everyone except April."

"Aren't you afraid to introduce me to her? What if things don't work out between us?" I'd seen numerous television shows where this was a concern and it made sense.

"I live in a house with five women. If you think there are any secrets, you're nuts," she said, holding onto the lapel of my coat. "We eat at five."

"Do you want to come up for a while?" I asked, nodding at the hotel. "There's no heat, but it's warmer than out here."

"I gotta get going," she said, her eyes lingering on my face. I leaned in and kissed her again. This time she wrapped her arms around my back and held me tightly for a time span I found difficult to gauge. Faith finally released me and slipped back into her truck, saying nothing more and refusing to make eye contact. Just before the truck pulled from the alley, she turned and waved.

Diva, who'd been very quiet up to that point, whined, rubbing her head against my leg. I think she felt sorry for me, or maybe she was just getting cold. I sighed. The last thirty-six hours had been quite the roller coaster and I was spent in every way imaginable.

I tried to be as quiet as possible when I entered through the back of the inn, then pulled up in surprise.

Denholm stood patiently waiting for me in the hallway, smiling. "I understand you're the hero of the day once again," he said.

"You've already talked to Sheriff Leonard?" I asked.

"Morty's in with him now." He dismissed the sheriff with a wave of his hand. "We already listened to the whole thing on the radio.

That Faith Hudson is a pretty girl. I think she's had a tough time with love. I'd take things slow."

I nodded. "I'm out of my league with her."

"That's how you know you're doing it right," he said with a wink. "I found my tools. You think you'd have time to work on that radiator today? I imagine we just need to open a valve. It'll be stuck, but I've got a cheater bar."

My eyes went to a long steel pipe leaning against the wall and then to the heavy wrench Denholm was waving around. I desperately wanted to sleep, but I was tired of sleeping with my coat on. "How hard can it be?" I asked.

"We'll know in a few minutes," he said, following me up the stairs.

"It's not really that bad up here," I said, throwing my coat onto the bed next to a neatly folded uniform shirt that hadn't been there when I'd last left. "Thank you for getting the blood out of my shirt. You didn't have to do that."

"I know," he said. "When you get to my age, being useful is its own reward."

"How did you know Morty was the person for you?" I asked, accepting the wrench from him as I crouched next to the radiator.

"I suppose it's different for everyone," he said. "Mostly, we're best friends, have been for as long as I can remember. You get to a point in your life where you can't imagine living without your best friend."

I placed the wrench on the bolt atop the outlet valve of the radiator. I'd seen radiators with more sophisticated valves – not so much with this one. I strained to move the rust-fused bolt and was about to give up when the material cracked away and the bolt turned slightly.

"How much should I open it, do you think?"

"Start with half a turn," Denholm answered. "Kind of early to start talking seriously about Faith Hudson, isn't it?"

I sat back on my heels and looked over to him. "You're right," I said. "I just don't have a good compass where women are involved. I missed a really great girl a while back because I didn't communicate very well."

I moved to the inlet side and similarly opened the valve. Fortunately, there wasn't as much rust on that side.

"Seemed like you were communicating with Faith pretty well in the parking lot," he said.

Steam entered the radiator and the whole unit banged loudly, making me jump back. While I'd grasped the basics of radiators, fine tuning was beyond me.

Denholm chuckled. "We haven't bled that one in quite a while. The noise is just trapped air. He tossed me a small brass tool. You have enough left in the tank to grab that bucket in the broom closet on the second floor?"

I nodded. "If I'm not back in ten minutes, send a search party." On the way to the stairs, I noticed that Diva had curled up on the bed and made no move to join me. I might have felt bad, but she'd earned the downtime.

"Your leg is bleeding through a little," Denholm noticed, when I got back a few minutes later. "I shouldn't have sent you after the bucket."

"It's been doing that," I said. "The staples are holding fine. I just need to get off it for a few hours."

"Let's get this heat going and I can take your pants with me," he said.

I grinned, placing the bucket under the bleed valve. "Won't people talk?"

Denholm shook his head, grinning. "Just turn that bleed valve until all you get is water. Be careful, the water is hot," he said "Do you believe in fate, Biggs?"

"I think we make our own fate." I shook my hand as scalding water squirted out onto my fingers.

"What happened with this woman you let go?" he asked.

"She's dating my best friend," I said. "When she deployed, he stayed in touch with her and I kind of didn't."

"How'd that make you feel?"

I closed the bleed valve and grabbed a t-shirt from the floor to wipe off my hands. "Mostly thrilled for my friend. Snert's never had that much interest in women, but he came out of his shell with Mel. Doesn't change that I feel like I blew a relationship I thought was a slam dunk."

"Oh, ho, ho, dear boy. Tell me you haven't used those words in front of this woman, Mel," he asked.

"No. I assume we've got doctor/patient confidentiality here," I said.

Denholm nodded. "Of course. Except I'm a newspaper man and you should never trust a secret to a newspaper man. But I do see your problem."

"I wasn't interested enough?" I asked. "Mel is fantastic. We got along great and I think we'd have been good together."

"This Mel was too safe. It doesn't take a genius to see you're not looking for safe," he said. "Now take those pants off."

I was just coming awake when my phone alarm rang out. I stumbled across the floor and turned off the alarm, my leg stiff and complaining. I pushed through the fog of sleep and checked my wound. I'd bled through the bandage, but that was to be expected. Probably not the best idea, but I'd wrapped flexible plastic wrap around it before I went to sleep, not wanting to stain the bed. The bandage was a bit of a mess and the skin underneath was wrinkly and white, but I'd had enough experience cleaning up wounds that I knew the look would improve. The crease in my thigh actually wasn't all that bad, considering.

When I was as cleaned up as I was going to get, I made my way downstairs. I wanted to stop by the grocery on the way out to the Hudson ranch. Pearl had taught me that it was impolite to show up at someone's house for dinner without bringing something. I was at a loss as to what that something should be, but I'd figure it out.

"You should leave her with me," Morty said, catching Diva and me at the back door. I wondered if I needed to look for cameras on the back stairway, since my two landlords always seemed to know when I was coming and going.

"Are you sure?" I asked. "She's moving slow, but I figured she'd be able to sit a lot where we're going anyway."

"I like having her around," Morty said. "It's like being a grandparent. All the joys of parenting and none of the messy stuff."

"How'd your interview with the sheriff go?" I asked.

"He laid it on pretty thick, but there's a story in there somewhere," he said. "It'll be in Wednesday's edition. That Luca Quinn was a piece of work. You came out sounding pretty good. Do you agree with Leonard that we're done with this story?"

"Off the record?"

"If you must," he said. "It'd be a better story the other way."

"It doesn't add up for me," I said.

"You don't think Luca Quinn was involved in Deputy Lynch's murder?"

"I don't know," I said. "State Patrol's ISD has some weapons they're processing. I don't think the bullets that killed Lynch were ever retrieved. They have a better chance of tying him to Shephard."

"Leonard said ISD recovered a fifty-caliber rifle. Isn't that what was used on Lynch?" he asked.

"Sure. Without ballistics, I don't think we'll know if it's the same gun," I said. "And I'm not saying Quinn wasn't involved."

"You think there's another shooter. What about O'Neil?"

"Maybe," I said, not believing it. Brad O'Neil was a lightweight in my opinion. "What about motive, though? Murdering a cop will get you the death penalty. The drugs found in O'Neil's van carry a few years, if convicted."

"I like the way your mind works," Morty said. "I'll keep this between us for now, but you gotta let me use it when you get to the bottom."

"If I'm right, I think you can expect a visit from Leonard once we're done," I said.

"Do you have any leads?"

I grinned. "I could ask you the same thing."

"What me?" he asked, feigning innocence. "Why do you think I know anything?"

"Do you?"

His face grew more serious. "In my experience, crime is about the money. Follow the money, find the criminal."

"Not sure I follow," I said. "There's no money in this."

"Sure there is," he said. "You just haven't found it yet."

HUDSON RANCH WAS LOCATED on the eastern edge of Squaw National Forest. A cluster of buildings that included two large barns and an American Foursquare, all painted the same bright white with blue metal roofs, were neatly arranged on a grassy incline and back-dropped by thousands of acres of federally protected land with old-growth pines.

Next to one of the barns, two angular women leaned against a wooden fence, watching a smaller figure work a horse inside the outdoor arena. From the end of the drive, I couldn't immediately discern Faith from her older sister Reagan. From the back they looked nearly identical, although I seemed to remember Reagan was a hair taller than Faith.

I parked the Bronco in front of the barn and was met by Faith as I approached the arena. "Hey Biggs," she said, giving me a quick hug. "April was just finishing her barrel racing practice, although I think her timing is suspicious."

April drove a small horse around the end of a row of barrels. She raced back toward us, throwing a rooster tail of sand up behind her.

"She looks good," I said. While I'd grown up around horses, I'd never participated in racing, although I'd seen my share of it. "Does she compete?"

Reagan had turned at my approach, smiled and gave me a quick hug. "She's a Hudson," Reagan answered before Faith could. "She doesn't compete, *she wins*."

I gave Faith a sidelong glance as she finished the phrase with her sister.

A sharp whistle from the back of the house filtered across the yard. I looked back to see the girls' mother standing on a covered wooden porch. She gestured for us to come her way and then disappeared back into the house.

April approached at a quick trot, smiling in triumph at her clean run. "What kind of name is Henry?" she asked, without any introduction.

"I don't know. What kind of name is April?" I shot back, without thinking.

"I was born in April," she answered. "You can't be born in Henry."

"April, be nice," Faith interjected.

"How about you call me Biggs," I said. "You sure got after those barrels. I bet you're hard to beat."

This brought a smile to her face. "I could beat you," she said defiantly.

"April!" Faith scolded.

I laughed. "No. It's okay. She's right."

"We're working on humility," Faith said. "Mom already called, so go put Hermione up and make sure you brush her down this time."

"Aww, Mom," April said. "Can I do it after dinner?"

"Don't you have homework?"

"No."

"Okay, but don't think you're getting out of it," Faith answered. "I'll be right in to help with the saddle."

A hand grabbed my own and I looked over to find Reagan standing next to me. "So exactly what are your intentions with my sister?" she prodded, giving me a slightly mischievous look.

"Um," I stammered. "Well ..."

"Go easy, Rae, we haven't even been out for drinks yet," Faith said.

"I've got this, Faith. Go take care of April." Reagan pulled me toward the house.

"Quite a place you have here," I said as Faith shrugged.

"I'm serious, Biggs. What are you doing?" Reagan pushed as soon as her sister was out of earshot.

"I don't really know," I said. "I was hoping to get to know her."

"Are you? Or are you trying to get back at Raff?" She stepped into my space, pinning me with her eyes. There was something about a woman who was tall enough to look straight across at me that I found intriguing.

"Not one to mince words, are you?" I asked.

She raised her eyebrows and nodded her head.

"My interest in Faith has nothing to do with Raff."

"You know he's going to hear about it, right?" she asked.

That gave me pause. "Are they still a thing?"

"Heavens, no," she answered. "He only has custody every other weekend or so and even that he manages to screw up."

"There you are," Mrs. Hudson said, stepping onto the back porch. "I thought I saw you pull up. Everything okay out here?"

"We're fine, Mom," Reagan said. "I was just talking to Biggs here about Raff."

"I thought we agreed we weren't going to talk about him tonight," Mrs. Hudson said.

"You and Faith agreed. I said it needed to be out on the table."

"Don't be rude, dear," Mrs. Hudson said. "Come on in, Henry. Welcome to Hudson Ranch."

"Call me Biggs, Mrs. Hudson. I was just telling Reagan what a great-looking home you have out here," I said, remembering that I'd left the wine I'd brought for her in the Bronco.

"Only if you call me Darlene. Mrs. Hudson sounds like my mother," she said.

"You know you'll never get a drink in this town if you hurt my sister, right?" Reagan wasn't giving up.

"Reagan Hudson, you stop now," Darlene said. "You'll run him off before we even get dinner."

"Um, actually, I left something in the truck," I said. "Mind if I run back out to grab it?"

"Run now and I won't hunt you later," Reagan said.

I had to inspect her face to determine if she was joking. It was a fifty-fifty proposition at best.

"Reagan, I need help with something inside," Darlene said, rolling her eyes. "You're a friend now, Biggs. Just let yourself in."

I walked back to the truck, hearing voices as I grabbed the flowers and bottle of wine I'd bought at the grocery store on the way out of town.

"Running away already?" Faith asked, smiling and looking at my gifts.

"I know it's cheesy, but someone recently told me that I don't do a good job of communicating." I held out the flowers. "These are for you."

"Aww, they're pretty," she said, taking them. April caught up with her and pulled at her mother's hands, burying her nose in the bouquet.

"Good." I hated that I felt so off balance. If I could have been back on the mountain fighting with Quinn, I'd have made the swap. I just didn't do social situations well, especially with a houseful of women.

Faith must have noticed my anxiety because she looped an arm through mine. "Come on. I'll protect you."

"Protect him from what?" April asked, skipping along next to us.

"Aunt Reagan," Faith said.

"Oh."

The smell of fresh-baked bread permeated the kitchen as we entered the mudroom at the back of the house. "Boots off, April," Faith said, kicking off her own and setting them on a shelf full of women's shoes and boots. I took the cue and knelt to untie my own boots.

"You don't have to, Biggs," Faith said, but I was already committed.

"What kind of dumb boots are those?" April asked, having removed her own in short order.

"Just something I got used to in the Army," I said.

"Mom said you got shot chasing down Luca Quinn. Is that true?"

I looked up to Faith for help. I wasn't sure what was okay to say to a ten-year-old and didn't want to overstep my bounds.

"April." Faith's voice held a warning.

"I have a little wound on my leg," I said, standing back up. "It's no big deal."

"Then why is there blood on your pants?" she asked.

I looked down, disappointed to see a few bright red dots on my thigh. "Darn it," I said. "I'm sorry, Faith, I need to go back out to the truck. I thought I had it bound up. Doc said I shouldn't be moving around much."

"Mom," Faith called. "April, go play. Just sit on the bench, Biggs, we've got a kit."

"What's up, dear?" Darlene asked, leaning into the mudroom. "We're just about ready to sit down."

"Biggs' leg is bleeding and my hands are full of horse. Can you help a minute?" she asked.

"Of course. Lexi grab my bag," she called over her shoulder, taking charge. "Pants off, Biggs."

I briefly thought about arguing, but the look on her face told me it would be easier to go along. "It's nothing, Mrs. Hudson. I probably opened it up when I got out of the truck. I just need to add a little gauze to the top and maybe a little plastic wrap if you have some."

"Like Saran Wrap?"

"Keeps the blood from seeping through," I said, unbuckling my jeans and pulling them off. I felt awkward as I took off my ankle holster with my concealed CCP inside and placed it on the bench next to me. If Darlene noticed, she didn't say anything.

"Nonsense. You need to stay off that leg until those stitches set," she said, pulling a pair of sweatpants from a stack of laundry. "What were you thinking, coming out here after getting hurt like this?"

"Faith invited me?" I said weakly. "I didn't want to turn her down."

She shook her head. "I swear I don't know why women don't rule the world. This bandage is soaked through."

"Ooh, pants off already. That has to be a record," Lexi said, setting a bag next to her mother. "Pasty white legs. Looks like a rancher to me."

I felt no small amount of embarrassment as Darlene clipped off my dressing and set to wrapping strips of quick-clotting gauze around my leg. "You really don't have to," I started once, but she ignored me.

"No shortage of injuries on a ranch," she said, taping the top of the bandage in place. "You should probably get your money back from the hospital, though. Those staples look like they were attached by a five-year old. You're going to have a crazy-looking scar."

She grabbed the dark sweatpants and pushed them over my feet. "That was me," I said. "It was dark."

This got her attention and she searched my face to see if I was joking. "It's true then? Luca shot you on the mountain and you brought him in?"

"Faith was there," I said. "She didn't tell you?"

"She just said Luca was hurt and they'd found you hauling him out in a sling," Darlene said. "I can't imagine walking very far with this wound."

I nodded. "I was pretty happy to see Faith show up on that horse."

Darlene packed her first-aid supplies and stood, using her hands to push against her thighs. It wasn't hard to tell where the girls got their good looks. Up close, it was clear Mrs. Hudson had some years under her belt, but I could have been convinced she was an older sister.

"Well, I hope you're hungry. We've got a mess of food." She swept up her bag in one hand and old bandages in the other.

"Starving." I strapped on my ankle holster, pulling the leg of the sweatpants over it. I accepted Faith's hand to haul me up from the bench.

"What kind of wine is that?" Faith asked, as we walked through the kitchen into the dining room. A large table had been set with a spread that would put most thanksgiving meals to shame.

"I got this for your mom," I said, shrugging slightly. "I don't really know anything about wine though. The women at the grocery said it would go with just about anything and it was the most expensive one in its row."

Faith laughed. "Chardonnay. I'm sure it's nice," she said, handing it to her mother. "You want a drink?"

"Not tonight," I said. "I have to drive yet."

"You're not going home," Darlene said. "You need to stop working that leg if you ever want it to heal."

"Can we eat already?" April pushed, sliding into a chair next to Lexi on the opposite side of the table.

For the second time that evening, Reagan, who'd taken the chair to my left, grabbed my hand. Looking across I noticed that Darlene, Lexi and April were already holding hands. I reached for and found Faith's, bowing my head as Darlene prayed over the food and thanked the good Lord for the safety of her family. It was a sincere and unpretentious prayer that reminded me of Pearl.

After grace, attention at the table turned to the mechanics of passing food around. A comfortable quiet settled in as the six of us ate.

"Rumor is, you're a Quinn," Darlene finally said, breaking the silence.

That got Lexi's attention. "Are you serious? You're related to Luca Quinn?"

"I think that's right," I said. "His grandmother would have been my grandmother, Pearl's, sister. I didn't really know that before I came out here. I think there's some bad blood."

"Shame about Luca," Darlene said. "Can't help but think under different circumstances his life would have gone differently. Hannah Quinn is a hard woman."

"I met her after that dust-up at Hootskill. She came down to the station to talk to Luca. She seemed pretty upset," I said.

"You've had a couple of big weeks," Darlene said quietly. "Wood Creek will breathe a big sigh of relief now that George Lynch's murderer has been caught."

"I hope that's right," I said. "I guess we'll see what the state has to say about it."

"You don't sound convinced," Lexi said. "Trust me, Luca Quinn was a big-time bad guy."

"Maybe that's not the best dinner conversation," Reagan said. "So, Biggs, we didn't get to finish our conversation. Why don't you tell us what your intentions are regarding Faith?"

"Mom," Faith complained.

"Reagan, that's enough. Let Biggs finish his dinner in peace."

"I couldn't eat another thing," I said, pushing my plate forward.

"I'd like to know," Lexi joined in and I looked over at her. I thought she was on my side, but clearly that wasn't the case.

I'd had some time to think about Reagan's question since the first time she'd asked. "Right now, I'd just like to get to know her. Maybe catch a movie or go to a barrel race. Go for a hike. Whatever she'd like to do."

"How about a horse ride in the mountains? There's trails that start right at the back of our property," April asked. "I could come along and show you how to ride."

"I'd love that," I said, grateful for her enthusiasm.

"The only thing Biggs is going to be riding for a while is a couch," Darlene said, standing up and carrying a handful of dishes out to the kitchen. "And you better not be full. I made pecan pie. Your only choice is ala carte or ala mode."

"Have you ever watched that show *Ranchers?*" April asked, jumping up. "The new season just started. It's about a family that ranches. It's not real, but it's kind of funny. We should watch it."

"Not tonight, April," Faith said. "Maybe you should ask Biggs what he'd like to watch while we clear the table."

"Oh, I'm a big *Ranchers* fan," I said, allowing her to drag me from my seat. I'd seen the show but rarely had enough time to watch. It was the right thing to say as she smiled widely and sat next to me on the couch, firing up the TV.

I woke up the next morning about five thirty. Faith and I had stayed up late, talking after the others had gone to bed. While we hadn't solved any of the world's problems, it had been nice to just hang out. Something woke me and I suspected it was the scraping sound coming from outside the house. I slowly extricated myself from Faith, lowering her to lie more comfortably on the couch and adjusting the oversized quilt to cover her from the cold morning air.

Padding into the kitchen, I noticed an outside light was on. I pulled on my boots and winter coat and pushed through the back door onto the porch, then froze, startled to realize that the noise was coming from a very large bull elk rubbing his rack against a nearby tree. Sensing my presence, he turned to me, not overly concerned. I'd never been that close to an elk before and felt a great privilege as he returned his attention to the tree. I watched for a few minutes and he finally jogged off, leaping easily over a horse fence that stood in his way.

"We call him Bob," Faith said in a low voice, wrapping her arms around me from behind and laying her head on my shoulder. "Last night was nice. I think April really likes you."

I rested my arms over hers and turned toward her, kissing her on the cheek. "She's quite a kid. Hard to imagine she's only ten."

"Living in a houseful of women makes you grow up fast," Faith said, shivering. I didn't want to lose the moment, so I shrugged off my coat, put it around her shoulders and wrapped my arms around her waist. "Thank you for not getting pushy with me on the couch last night."

"And have Reagan jump out of the shadows with a baseball bat?" I asked, only half joking.

"This isn't the right time, but I need you to hear this from *me*," she said. "Raff was abusive. I hid it from my family. Reagan took it pretty hard. She's been overprotective ever since."

I gritted my teeth. Like Reagan, I had a strong protective instinct and abusive men were something of a trigger for me. "I'm sorry he hurt you," I said, wanting to say something stronger but knowing I needed to check myself.

"There's more. It's important," she said, pushing back from me, tears spilling onto her cheeks. I reached for a tear and wiped it off but didn't say anything. "He beat me one night when I was pregnant with April and I almost lost her."

I shook my head as I absorbed the pain in her words. I couldn't imagine why she would tell me all this. I pulled her to me and hugged her as she sobbed. "She's a great kid, healthy, intelligent. It's okay, Faith."

"It's not," she said, pushing back so she could look me in the face. "I can't have any more children. The doctor was able to save April, but Raff ruined me, Biggs."

I pulled her back to me and allowed her to cry as my mind raced with the information. It took me a while to realize that she was trying to tell me again why she was unqualified to be in a relationship. This time I didn't feel like laughing.

"I'm so sorry, Faith," I said, my own eyes stinging with emotion.

"Why would anyone want to be with me?" she said, pulling away. "I know I'm a mess. I'm sorry. You should go."

I carefully slipped my hand down to grab hers. For a moment, we played a game of tug of war as she tried to escape. Her heart wasn't really in it and there was no way I was letting go, so she soon stilled.

"Walk with me?" I asked.

She nodded and followed me down the stairs toward the main barn where I could hear horses stirring in the early morning. "My mother left me when I was really young. I don't know why and to tell you the truth, I never asked. I guess I just never wanted to know. The idea that she didn't love me enough to stay has always hurt so bad that I locked that part of my life away."

"She loved you," Faith said.

"Who knows?" I asked.

"Every woman who's ever had a child knows," she said. "I don't know why she left, but I guarantee she thought she was doing the best thing for you by leaving you with your grandparents."

"They're amazing," I said. "I won't lie to you, Faith. I'd hoped someday to have children."

"I know," she said, wiping tears from her eyes. "Of course you do. That's why I had to tell you before we got in too deep."

"Let me finish," I said, stopping in the middle of the yard. "I'm drawn to you, Faith. Maybe it's not meant to be. Maybe the way I eat granola pisses you off, or maybe I can't take that you can dunk a basketball over me." I gave her a half smile to see if she was listening.

"Did you really just make a tall joke?" she asked.

I raised my eyebrows. "Maybe. Can you dunk?"

"Maybe with a volleyball," she said. "I used to get pretty close with a basketball, but I'm only five-ten."

I shrugged. "What if you're the one for me, Faith? What if I'm the one for you? We gotta trust that if we're meant to be, everything else is going to work out."

"I'm never going to have any more children, Biggs," she said, crossing her arms defensively.

I stepped forward, gently pushed the coat apart and drew her to me. "Okay, I hear you loud and clear. Now, hear me. We'll work through it. Heck how do we even know if all my equipment works?" I gave her a small smile. "I've been blown up a lot."

For the first time that morning she grinned as she grabbed my hand, placed it on her breast, and leaned in for a kiss. The move caught me entirely off guard and I'll admit, I got a little dizzy as she pulled me tightly to her.

"Seems to me your equipment's in good working order, Private Biggston," she said.

"Sergeant," I corrected, enjoying our closeness and the kiss. Subtle was one thing Faith Hudson was not.

She pulled away and laughed, giving me a mock salute and then running off. "We should grab some eggs. I'll make you breakfast."

"Wait." I hobbled after her, not wanting to break open my wound. "What if that hadn't worked? Would you have dumped me?"

"I guess we'll never know," she said as I caught up to her at the back of an elevated shed that looked to be a chicken coop. "Hold your hands out."

I complied. She opened the back of the coop and plucked eggs, handing them to me one at a time.

"Do you remember that first night at your bar, when Luca Quinn got in a fight?" I asked.

She laughed, flicking her sandy brown hair over her shoulder. "Of course. What about it?"

"Who was he fighting with?" I asked. "I think one of the guys was Brad O'Neil."

"Nope. Tom Williger was one. Jepp and Tom Huber too," she said.

"Three on one? That was hardly a fair fight," I said.

"Yeah, they needed at least two more guys if they wanted to take on Luca," she said. "That's kind of a strange question. Why?"

"What were they fighting about? Luca's mom, Hannah, was super pissed that next morning. Something about having to do all the work while he was locked up. I figure they're farmers, but it's winter. Do they raise livestock?" I asked.

"I don't think so," she said. "Last I heard, they lease out their farm and live off the income. Hannah's sick."

"My grandmother still owns the ranch land next to Quinn's farm," I said. "Maybe we could take a run out there sometime this week."

"What are you up to?"

"Doc said I needed to take it easy. I thought maybe some sight-seeing would be nice."

"Is Brad O'Neil going to keep his mouth shut?" Cal Leonard set his expensive cigar into a glass ashtray and picked up his glass of scotch. The small group sat next to a massive fireplace where the embers of a poorly tended fire crackled. Long rays of the afternoon sun reflected off the snow-covered field outside the picture window, providing the only light within the wood-paneled den.

Hannah Quinn picked a split log from the adjacent wood rack and set it carefully into place. She stared, mesmerized by the small tendrils of flame that quickly licked at the dry wood. "Luca was a good boy," she said. "He didn't deserve to be hunted down like a wild dog."

"I know it's a blow to lose your boy, Hannah," Leonard said. "But he was dealing meth and he ran from a cop. Luca should have just let Biggs catch him. We could have worked it out. Only he couldn't, could he? He was carrying meth."

"Does State Patrol have the meth?" Quinn asked, turning from the fire.

"No," Leonard said. "And that's how it stays if O'Neil keeps quiet."

"My boy goes down for the murder of Lynch and Shephard's

shooting?" Quinn asked. "And you're worried about what happens with O'Neil? I lost my boy, Leonard."

"I'm sorry for that, Hannah. Really, I am. But your boy is doing us a lot more good with his death than he ever did when he was alive."

"You're a real asshole," she said.

"Does O'Neil know anything? ISD is going to put the screws to him pretty hard," Leonard said.

"He doesn't know anything about Lynch or Shephard," Quinn said, the building rage draining from her face. Leonard found it disconcerting how quickly she shifted moods. "Wouldn't take a lot on his part to link Luca's supply back to me, though."

"Will he talk?"

Hannah Quinn's face twisted into a menacing grin made all the more sinister by the unhealthy grey pallor of her sagging skin. Illness and rapid weight loss had taken a major toll on her body. "Not if he knows what's good for him. I have a couple of boys in lockup. I'll have them explain things when he makes general pop."

"We had an agreement to keep your meth out of my county," Leonard said. "Don't shit where you eat, Hannah. This all could have been avoided."

"Don't blame this fucking mess on me," she growled, coughing wetly. "You were supposed to keep Lynch off my fucking ranch."

"We've been through this," Leonard said, picking up his cigar and puffing deeply. "He was there to serve papers on Luca. That's what deputies do. It would have been suspicious if I'd stopped him."

"Then you bring in someone like Biggs? What the hell were you thinking?" Quinn asked. "He's got a damn drug-sniffing dog and now he's killed my boy."

"In case you hadn't noticed," Leonard said. "I'm receiving quite a lot of scrutiny from State Patrol's Investigative Services Division. Biggs bringing down Lynch's killer is just the break we've been looking for."

"That's not a price I agreed to pay," she said.

"We'll let things settle down a bit before I fire Biggston," Leonard said. "We can hunt him down then if it makes you feel better."

Hannah shook her head slowly. "Don't patronize me. Now what's this I hear about a specialist coming in from Sutherland to look at your patrol vehicles?"

"How'd you hear about that?" Leonard asked.

"I've got my sources. Word is they're going to look at the GPS units – try to figure out where Lynch and Shephard got hit," she said. "Don't play dumb. You signed the invoice."

"Who do you got in my department? Surely not Hollie."

Quinn smiled and lifted her eyebrows. "Like I'd tell *you*."

"You need to learn some subtlety, Hannah," Leonard said. "No electronics tech is going to find more than ISD. Worse case is, we'll have a report that says our equipment is old, which we already know. But they're breathing down my neck. They know there's something rotten and I can't look like I'm just rolling over. So, I bring in a virtuous rookie hotshot who got lucky once against organized crime during a private investigation. That rookie kills a known drug dealer and voila! We miraculously find the very guns used to murder Lynch and disable Shephard. Hell, we may even end up with a grant from the state for new equipment. Take the win already."

"We're not out of this yet," Quinn said. "What are we doing about our other problem?"

"I thought we'd get to that," Leonard said, standing and draining the last of his scotch. "Let's go have a little chat."

Quinn nodded and followed Leonard through his modern, sprawling log-style ranch. He led her into a breezeway that separated the house from a four-car garage and turned to open a door to the basement.

"Did you kill him, too?" she asked, no small amount of fury in her voice.

"Way I see it, he's not my problem," Leonard said, flipping on the lights and illuminating the wide carpeted steps that led down.

"Won't it be suspicious if he just disappears?" Hannah angrily pointed out.

"Nope. I've got tape back at the station that shows me releasing him this morning," he said. The basement, like the upstairs, was huge and decorated in a western theme. Trophy heads hung on the walls surrounding the pool table that sat adjacent to a large bar.

"Don't you think State Patrol would find your lifestyle a little ostentatious for a sheriff's salary?" Quinn asked.

"Family property. Far as anyone knows, I used my inheritance to fix the place up," he said.

They passed through the game room and into an unfinished area with no windows and a bare lightbulb hanging from the ceiling. Against one wall, steel hooks were embedded into thick timber cross braces at both waist and shoulder level. Two unconscious people were manacled tightly to the structure, long chains threaded through the hooks to keep them pinned to the wall.

Hannah Quinn held a hand up to her nose. She easily identified the unmoving teens, despite the black hoods covering their faces.

"You've crossed the line," Quinn said, her mouth set in a hard line. The room reeked of urine and worse.

"Don't get your panties in a bunch," Leonard said, kicking the young man's leg, causing him to stir. "I just shot 'em up with a little Ketamine. Might have overdone it on Zoey. Looks like she pissed herself."

"What are you going to do?" Quinn asked.

"You're not listening," Leonard said, pulling the black bag from Bobby Quinn's head. "Bobby pulled Zoey Watts into this and you need to deal with her."

Leonard squatted next to Bobby and slapped his face violently. The first strike had little effect and he followed up with a backhand. "Bobby, are you in there?" he asked. "You just gotta know how to talk to 'em. The Ketamine makes it so they don't feel much."

The sound of a revolver being cocked caught Leonard's attention and he looked over his shoulder to find Hannah pointing a nickel-plated .38 Special at him. "You sick fuck," she said.

"Well now, Hannah, don't be hasty," he said. "Truly, I'm sorry about your boy, Luca. I had no idea Biggs would run him down like that."

Hannah Quinn shook her head. "Shut up, Cal. You brought a drug-sniffing dog and a man hunter into my county. How else did you think that was going to end? Now you've taken my good sweet boy and kidnapped this girl."

"The girl fingered you, Hannah," he said. "I picked her up and gave her a little push. She gave up Bobby in a heartbeat. She knows about the ranch. Put the damn gun away already."

"What's next? You send Biggston out to the farm to finish the job he started?"

"I had to drug your boy here because he has issues with authority," Cal said. "I want him and this girl out of my basement tonight. What you do with them is your business, but I'm telling you, Bobby has to clean up his act. State Patrol wanted a chat with him and I had to dance a jig to keep that from happening."

"Call off your deputy," she said. "I need him out of my shit."

"You're going to shut things down for a few weeks and let the dust settle. ISD will close the Lynch and Shepard investigations soon. Next spring, I'll fire Biggston and we'll be back in business."

"You don't get it," she said. "We've made promises to people you don't want to disappoint. And don't you worry about Biggston. I'll take care of him."

"Biggston is your blood," he said. "I don't want you doing anything crazy. Let things settle."

"Pearl Quinn died when she left Butte County. Fitting that her daughter's boy will die here too," she said. "I'll tell you where to find the body."

"What's on your plate today?" Faith asked, setting a silver mixing bowl on the granite island centered in the large, modern kitchen. If the finish of the house was any indication, the Hudsons were doing well. "Are you working?"

"I'm not supposed to show up until Thursday," I said, sliding painfully onto a stool. I hadn't kept up with the pain meds and my leg hurt like the dickens. "State Patrol should clear me by then. Leonard said I could show up earlier if I wanted. Do you work tonight?"

"We don't open on Mondays," she said, cracking a fresh egg into her bowl. "April has a 4-H thing after school, but otherwise I'm all yours. I could probably get Reagan to take her."

"What kind of thing?" I asked distractedly as she kept adding eggs. So far, I'd counted an even dozen.

"It's over at Nickle Ranch," Faith said. "She's practicing barrels with her club."

"Is it okay if I tag along?" I asked.

Faith smiled. "Of course. I think April would love it."

"You know, I wear this hat, but I'm not really a cowboy," I said.

"Don't worry," she said. "We won't tell anyone."

"I need to pick up Diva. I didn't tell Morty that I'd be gone all night,"

"Kind of strange, you taking up residence at the inn," she said. "Couldn't you find anywhere else?"

"Why?" I suddenly wondered if she had an issue with the two men I'd so easily become friends with.

"It's a hotel not an apartment," she said, looking at me like I'd grown a second head. "And yes, I know they're gay. And no, that wasn't my question."

I smiled. She'd caught me showing clear expectations about rural bias. "Morty and Denholm have a loft on the third floor they're renting to me. It's pretty epic. Makes me feel like Batman or something."

Faith pulled a griddle out and placed it on the stove. "Do you like bacon or sausage with your eggs?"

We'd had a big meal the night before, but I was starving again. My body was doing its best to rebuild after being abused over the weekend. "I have to choose?"

"Not really." She pulled out two packages and laid out bacon strips and sausage patties onto the griddle.

"Geez, how many people are you feeding?" I asked.

"This is a working ranch, Biggs," she said. "We have stalls to muck, sheep to feed, water buckets to clean, hay to move."

"Don't forget that fence I told you about on Saturday. I'd like to be able to let the horses out on that side tomorrow," Darlene Hudson said as she entered the kitchen in a puffy pink bathrobe. She walked around the end of the island to give me a hug, surprising me with her familiarity. I enjoyed the contact all the same. "Good morning, Biggs."

"Good morning, Mrs. Hudson," I said.

"Please, call me Darlene, dear," she said, looking at the clock. "Why is it that we're up so early? Tell me someone had the decency to start the coffee."

"I'm afraid that was me, Mrs. ... Darlene," I said. "I heard something outside. Turned out it was nothing, but I woke Faith."

"Bob was back, working on his velvet," Faith said. " I told him about Raff."

"Of course you did, dear," Darlene said, pouring cold coffee out of the carafe. "How do you take your coffee, Biggs?"

"In a cup," I said. "Temperature is negotiable."

She smiled and pushed the carafe back into the stainless-steel coffee maker and added grounds. "So, she tried to run you off and you stayed? I've wondered who *that man* would be. After meeting you, I can't say I'm surprised."

"Why's that, ma'am?" I asked.

"It's a mother's prerogative to think the best of her children," she said, switching the coffee maker on after adding water, "and recognize the areas where they need to make progress."

"Mom," Faith tried to interrupt.

Darlene ignored her and continued. "After Raff, Faith dated a few times, but there was always something wrong with those men. Too short. Too fat. Too skinny. Too annoying. Those she didn't flat out reject, she sent running. You're none of those things and you don't seem the type that runs."

"I've dated maybe four men since Raff," Faith said.

Darlene nodded, walked over to grab an electronic tablet from where it was charging at a nearby desk and came to sit on the bar stool next to me. "Six," Darlene said, swiping at the tablet. "Have you thought about how you'll talk with Raff after learning what you have? I can't imagine that was easy for you to hear."

"Boy, you guys don't pull any punches around here, do you?" I said.

"I'm sorry, Biggs," Faith said, flipping the bacon and coming over to give me a reassuring hug. "It's all coming out one way or another. Mom tends to be uncomfortably direct."

"How unvarnished do you want it?" I asked.

Darlene looked up and pushed the tablet back. "Now we're getting somewhere," she said, locking eyes with me. "I married a rancher who was a Marine first and forever. I know exactly what his answer would have been."

"Did your husband see action?" I asked.

Darlene nodded almost imperceptibly.

"Then you already know. If it were up to me, I'd put Raff in a hole," I said, breathing evenly.

"It's not up to you?" Darlene asked.

My mind spun with possibilities and I couldn't fathom why she was pushing me like this. "It is not," I said. "I only know the end of the story. I know that what he did hurt Faith, enough that she can't live with it unless the people around her help hold that pain. I'm also certain she doesn't need me stirring things up. I've seen a lot of really bad things, Mrs. Hudson. Things I can't talk about because that pain is still too much for me."

"Biggs, you don't have to," Faith whispered in my ear. I felt wetness on my neck.

"You're pretty self-aware for a vet," Darlene said, her voice almost a whisper.

"Honestly, I've wondered if I can have a relationship at all," I said. "Sure, I want one. But how do I live with someone who hasn't been through the shit? Do you know who never asks if you've killed someone?"

"Another vet," Darlene answered. "Bless you both, but you're in for a rough ride."

"Oh, Gawd! We're having *that conversation*, aren't we?" Lexi said, entering the kitchen. "Seriously, can we never move on from this?"

"Lexi," Darlene exclaimed, aghast.

"I'm serious! It's like Groundhog Day around here."

Faith kissed the top of my head. "And that's the other side of living in a house full of women," she said. "Don't make the mistake of taking yourself too seriously. I got eggs this morning, Lexi. Why don't you feed the sheep while I finish breakfast?"

"You're such a brat."

"How's the leg looking?" Darlene asked me, ignoring the ensuing squabble.

"It's fine," I said.

"You haven't looked," she said, exasperated. "Pants off."

I shook my head in defeat. It was a conversation I'd already lost once and I wasn't ready to go another round with her. I slid the sweatpants down and was pleased to discover that only a few smudges of blood had seeped through the bandage.

"That's an improvement," Darlene said. "Let me grab your jeans from the dryer. I'll give you a fresh dressing. You might actually heal if you stay off it for a few days."

"Yes, ma'am."

⸏⸏⸏

"Sorry about all that," Faith said as we pulled down the gravel drive and turned north toward Wood Creek. We'd decided to spend the day together since we both had it off.

"Your family is great," I said.

"You know what I'm talking about."

I grinned. I did and it didn't matter.

"Butte-4, do you read? This is Base. Over." My radio crackled to life with Hollie Wilder's voice.

I grabbed the microphone from its cradle. "Base, this is Butte-4, go ahead," I answered.

"Biggs, are you in a position to stop by the station? Over," Hollie said.

"Roger that, Base," I answered. "I can be there in twenty minutes, over."

"Copy that, Butte-4. Sooner is better. Base out," she answered.

"What's that about?" Faith asked as I hung up the microphone.

I accelerated and flipped the switch that would strobe my newly-installed grill and brake lights. "I have no idea."

Fifteen minutes later, we pulled into the parking lot behind the station.

"Do you want me to stay in the truck?" she asked.

"I don't think so," I said. "If it looks like I'm going to be tied up too long, you can take the Bronco back to the ranch."

"I've never gone in the back entrance before," she said as I keyed through the heavy steel door.

"That's probably a good thing," I said, leading her through our processing area and choosing the elevator that would drop us next to the temporary lockup on the second floor.

I was lost in thought, trying to figure out what we were walking into when Faith caught me off guard. As soon as the elevator door closed, she turned to me, kissing me passionately. I deepened the embrace, pinning her against the wall and returning the kiss. I was left wanting more when the chime dinged, announcing the second floor, and Faith pulled away.

"What was that about?" I asked.

"I don't want last night to be over yet," she said.

I smiled, straightening my hat. "Me either."

As I walked her past the cell where I'd spent my first night in Wood Creek, I was mildly surprised to discover that Bobby Quinn wasn't in there cooling his heels. The door between the station and the cell room was open and I walked through. Hollie was by herself and looked up as we entered.

"Thank you for coming in," Hollie said. "I can't raise Cal, and Gene is out with the new deputy."

"Who's that?" I asked, crossing the room to her desk. About halfway in, I'd noticed a man sitting on the bench on the opposite side of the glass partition that separated the station from the foyer and stairs. He must have been expecting me because he stood.

"Franklin Watts," Hollie said, just before the thickset, slump-shouldered man entered the room with a grimy baseball cap in his hands.

"Where's the sheriff?" Franklin Watts was a rough-looking man who reeked of alcohol and tobacco smoke.

"I'm Deputy Biggston," I said, stepping protectively between him and Hollie. "What can I help you with, Mr. Watts?"

"I heard the sheriff was looking for my girl on Saturday."

"That's right," I said. "We just want to talk with her."

"She didn't come home yesterday," he said. "I called the school. She didn't show up for first period."

"Is that unusual?"

"What's that supposed to mean?" he growled, taking a step toward me.

"Doesn't mean anything," I said. "I was in high school once. I didn't always make all my classes."

"Why was the sheriff looking for her? Is she in some sort of trouble?"

"No. Like I told you, we just need to ask her questions about something that happened at the game last Friday. I'm hoping she'll be able to help us with a case we're working on," I said. "How about you have a seat over here and you can tell me what's up?"

"My girl is missing and I think you know something about it," he said, pushing a big finger into my chest.

"Mr. Watts, you're upset," I said, grabbing his finger and twisting it back toward him. I could feel his muscles starting to bunch. "Don't do something you'll regret. We're looking for Zoey and if we work together, we have a much better chance of finding her."

Resignation filled his face and he pulled his hand back quickly. "I don't know anything. She doesn't spend much time at home."

"When's the last time you saw her?" I asked.

"Saturday. Around dinner time."

"What happened after that?"

"I told you, that's the last time I saw her," he said.

"Does she have her own car? Did she leave with someone? Was she dressed up?" I asked.

"She was all dolled up. Looks just like her mama," he said, his eyes drifting off at some memory. I wondered what a breathalyzer would show for his current blood alcohol content.

"Stay with me, Mr. Watts," I said. "Did she leave with someone?"

"That smug little Quinn bastard," he said. "I remember because he peeled out in that blue Camaro."

"Do you remember what time? You said dinner, but can you narrow it down any further?" I asked.

"It'd been dark a couple of hours. Maybe seven," he said.

"Do you have any idea where they were going?" I asked. "Any plans they might have made?"

"She doesn't tell me anything," he said. "You know how it is. I'm just the turd that pays the bills."

I pulled a generic business card from the drawer in my desk and wrote my cell phone number on it. "If you think of anything or hear from her, call me immediately. Do you understand me?"

He nodded. "She's in trouble, isn't she?"

"Why do you say that?"

He turned and started walking out of the station. "I can just feel it."

"Thank you, Biggs," Hollie said, once Watts had disappeared down the stairs. "He was really worked up when he got here. I didn't think he was going to leave."

"Will you let Cal know Mr. Watts stopped in?" I asked, stopping at her desk. I turned to smile at Faith who'd taken a seat across the room.

"Sure," she said then leaned forward, whispering. "Are you crazy?"

"Crazy?" I asked, leaning forward and keeping my voice low. "I don't follow."

From the opposite side of the room I heard Raff's unmistakable growl. "What the hell are you doing here?"

"That," Hollie said, surreptitiously pointing across the room.

I turned and located Raff, who'd entered the same way Faith and I had. I assumed he'd been asking me, but his eyes were trying to bore a hole in Faith. At the sight of Faith's stricken face, I knew I'd made a terrible mistake.

"I ... I ..." Faith fumbled with her words and then looked over to me. Gone was the woman who leapt over bar tops with a baseball bat. In her place stood a terrified girl. The incongruity of her fear momentarily froze me in place. It was hard for me to imagine she was afraid of this doughy, self-important asshat.

Raff's advance in her direction spurred me to action.

"Biggs, Raff, no!" Hollie uttered in horror as I closed the distance.

Raff, however, only had eyes for Faith. I saw her shrink back as he reached for her. Just before he made contact, I intercepted Raff's outstretched hand and violently spun him, sending him stumbling into one of the other desks.

"Back off," he growled, turning back toward Faith.

It felt like the next moments happened in slow motion as Raff's hand fell on his service weapon. The click of the holster's leather safety strap was followed by his shoulder bunching as he worked to draw his weapon. The phrase *slow on the draw* came to mind as he fumbled. I closed the distance between us and grabbed his wrist before the weapon left the holster.

"Settle," I warned as he struggled to free his hand. Raff brought his other arm around in an ineffective grapple or punch, I wasn't sure which. I stepped into his strike, my newfound leverage loosening his grip on the weapon. I pressed my advantage and turned him once again, this time not releasing his hand as I pushed him into the wall.

"Stay out of this, Biggston," he shouted, his voice high with distress. "This doesn't concern you."

I leaned into him and whispered in his ear. "Ever put another hand on Faith Hudson and I'll put you down. I don't care where we are, do you copy?"

"Get off." He struggled against me, but I just pinned him even tighter against the wall, pulling his arm up painfully.

"What the hell is going on in here?" Sheriff Leonard asked. "Biggs, let that man go."

"Do you copy?" I asked, pulling his arm even higher. I heard Leonard closing the distance, but I didn't care. This was between the two of us.

"I copy. Fuck!" Raff squealed.

I stepped back, holding my hands up to show I was complying with the sheriff's order.

"Biggs, what the hell was that about?" Leonard asked.

Raff glowered, his face bright red with anger. "He fucking went nuts," he sputtered. "I'm going to press charges."

Leonard slowly turned to look at Faith, who was now standing next to the front wall of the station, looking out the windows. He then turned back to me. "You got anything to say for yourself?"

"My mistake, Sheriff," I said. "There was a misunderstanding. I thought I saw Raff go for his weapon. Instincts kicked in."

Leonard raised his eyebrows as his eyes fell on Raff's service weapon, which was unbuckled and no longer well-seated in its holster.

"Well, hell. You boys need to get over this damn pissing contest. Raff, if you want to file a complaint, you know where the forms are. Same goes for you, Biggs," Leonard said. "Now, you want to tell me what you're doing here in the first place?"

"That's my doing, Sheriff," Hollie said, walking over to join the conversation. "Franklin Watts stopped by this morning. The school called and Zoey hadn't shown up. He was upset and I called Biggs after I couldn't reach anyone else. You could check your voicemail once in a while, you know."

Leonard nodded, taking the criticism. "What'd you get from Watts?"

"He last saw Zoey on Saturday night around seven," I said. "Watts smelled like he'd been drinking pretty hard this weekend, though. His timeline isn't reliable."

"Tough home," Leonard said. "I imagine Zoey's hiding out in a girlfriend's basement. We get a few cases like this every year."

"Like what?" I asked.

"Runaways," he said. "Home life is a wreck, they get into drugs and alcohol. She'll turn up in a couple of days. Most of the time it takes 'em a couple of tries at getting out of Butte County. Now, I order you to stand down and get that leg rested, you understand?"

"Yes, sir." I picked my hat up from the desk where I'd set it while talking to Franklin Watts and settled it on my head. Faith was still staring out the window and I suspected she'd need help getting through the room. She turned as I approached. "Want to get outta here?" I asked.

She nodded.

"Faith, I didn't mean anything," Raff called after us, just before we exited the station's main entrance. Straight ahead was the public elevator that sat in full view of everyone in the station. We took the hallway leading to the back, went down the stairs and finally out through the front of the building. I'd parked in the back lot but wanted both a quick exit and a chance to cool off.

"You didn't have to do that," Faith said, after we'd walked away from the station and around the corner. The distance between us felt like a mile and I knew I'd probably blown whatever chance I might have had with her. Leonard was right. Men carrying guns had no business in a pissing contest.

"I'm sorry I over-reacted," I said. "You didn't need that."

"Is that how you see it?" she asked, her hand coming to rest on my jacket.

"I know I blew it. I saw Raff coming for you. All I could think about was what we talked about this morning," I said. "I know it's not my fight."

"You made it your fight. Other than my family, I've never had anyone do that for me." She leaned in to give me a kiss.

The glint of sunlight off glass caught my attention. Instinctively, I threw myself into Faith, knocking her to the ground, just as a triple-round burst of automatic fire chewed into the building's granite façade behind us. Frantically, I searched for cover and found a parked pickup truck. Without explanation, I dragged a bewildered

Faith behind the truck's back wheel and pushed her down, stepping protectively in front of her.

"What's happening?" she asked, her voice as small as it had been when Raff had reached for her. I fumbled to draw out my .357 while staying crouched behind the truck.

"Stay down," I said. "Someone's shooting at us."

More shots didn't come, so I figured our cover was good. No doubt the shooter would reposition to finish the job. I poked my head up and glanced back to where the shots had come from. I saw a muzzle flash and ducked back as fresh bullets chewed into the building behind me.

A scream from the direction of the shooter warned of the situation escalating. I had to move. I crept forward. My thigh wound objected angrily but not enough to overcome the rush of adrenaline I was riding. Reaching the front of the truck, I popped up, ready to duck down again but it wasn't necessary. A figure carrying a rifle ran across the street about a block away. I returned fire, loosing two shots, both narrowly missing the shooter. Cognizant of possible collateral damage, I refrained from continuing to fire.

The gunman didn't break stride and I lost sight of him as he disappeared behind the building at the end of the block. I raced toward him and a couple seconds later I pulled up, slamming my back into the cold stone just shy of the corner. I had no idea what I'd see when I looked around the edge. I ducked and spun away from the building, ready to dive for cover if necessary. It wasn't. Twenty yards down the street, the sniper was just jumping into the passenger side of a white pickup truck. I looked for plates and found nothing. The truck roared off in a cloud of black exhaust. I ran into the middle of the street, settled into my stance and fired until the weapon clicked ineffectually.

"ARE YOU HURT?" I knelt in front of Faith who sat where I'd left her in a pile of slush. "Faith, I need you to talk to me."

"They were shooting at us," she said, her eyes wide with panic.

"What the hell's going on?" Raff Butler leaned around the corner of the building, gun drawn, his eyes scanning the street.

"Sniper," I said. "They've taken off. I need to get Faith inside."

"I got you covered," Raff said, running for the truck and planting his shoulder against the front quarter panel. He aimed in the direction the fire had come from.

"I heard gunfire," Leonard said, meeting us on the first floor of the station, his own .357 drawn. "What's the sitrep."

The door opened again as Raff joined us.

"Someone was shooting at Biggs and Faith," Raff said. "I saw muzzle flash from the window. They were standing right outside Engle's Gift Shop. Automatic bursts, I'd guess modified AR-15."

"White pickup headed east on Main," I said. "Driver and passenger. I think I winged the shooter. Can't be sure though."

"Raff, go. I'm right behind you," Leonard said.

"Faith, you okay?" I asked. My blood boiled with the excitement of the chase.

"Don't even think of it, Biggs. You're suspended," Leonard said. "You get back upstairs and tell Hollie what's going down. I don't want either of you leaving the station until you hear from me."

"Shit, Cal, I saw him," I said.

"Crappy old white pickup headed east. I got it," he said. "Limits it to about a hundred trucks in the county. Blood ought to help, though. Tell Hollie to get Gene and Fox back. I want them patrolling Wood Creek, just in case our shooter didn't do the smart thing and get out of town."

I looked to the back door, but Leonard cut me off. "Son, I'm giving you an order."

I felt a hand on my arm and once again became aware of Faith's presence. Even if I wanted to, I couldn't leave her. "Copy that," I said. Cal searched my face and must have decided I was serious about complying because he turned and jogged toward the back door.

"Are you hurt?" I asked, turning to give Faith my attention.

"No. I don't know," she said, placing a hand on her neck.

I ran my hands along her back, flicking crystalized snow from jeans that had been soaked through by the wet street. I turned her around and inspected her for damage. She had an oozing wound on her neck, from rock chips or glass, and her movements were wooden as if she were under anesthesia. I'd seen the signs often enough to recognize them as shock.

"Give me your coat," I said, sliding it off her back.

"What?" she asked. "My purse. I lost it."

"I'll get it," I said, taking my own coat off and wrapping it around her shoulders. I rubbed her arms, trying to get her to focus on something. She still wasn't making eye contact, but she did unexpectedly pull me into a hug.

"They were trying to kill us," she said.

"Me. Not us." I picked her coat up off the floor and led her to the elevator. "I'm sorry I put you in the middle of this. I must have stepped in the shit when I took Luca down."

The elevator dinged and I helped Faith inside. As the doors

closed, she wrapped her long arms around me. "You saved my life, Biggs. I just stood there. I didn't know what was happening until I was in the gutter. I was even mad at you for pushing me. I'm so sorry."

"You couldn't have known, Faith," I said.

"But you did."

"I wish I could say it was the first time someone's shot at me," I said ruefully. "Wasn't even the first time this week."

She pulled back and gave me a lopsided grin. "Luca shot you last week."

"Nice," I said, returning her grin. "We need to get you out of those wet pants. You're acting a little shocky."

The elevator dinged again, announcing our arrival on the second floor.

"Henry, Faith, are you okay?" Hollie asked, unlocking the door when she saw us exit the elevator. "Faith dear, you're bleeding."

"She took a ricochet," I said. "Could you stay with her a minute? I'll grab the first-aid kit."

"What's going on, Biggs?"

"Shooter on Main Street took a swing at Faith and me. Leonard and Raff are chasing a vintage white pickup headed east on Main. He wants you to call Gene and Deputy Fox back to patrol Wood Creek."

"Does he want me to call State Patrol?" she asked.

"He didn't say," I said. "There was only one shooter. He had an accomplice in the car. My best guess is they're long gone. We'll be lucky if Leonard and Raff can pick up their trail."

"Base, this is Butte-3. I've got nothing," Raff's voice came over the radio. "Did Butte-1 find anything? Over."

"Butte-3, this is Base," Hollie answered, picking up the microphone from her desk. "Butte-1 has not checked in yet. I'll advise on contact. Over."

"I'm turning north on Slim Butte Branch. I see gravel dust ahead. Butte-3, out," he said.

I guided Faith over to the visitor's bench and left her long enough to retrieve the first-aid kit. When I dabbed at her neck, she recoiled.

"Damn, sorry, Faith. We need to go to the hospital," I said, gently adhering a gauze pad to the wound. She had shrapnel in her neck and I had no idea how bad it was. "Hollie, I'm taking her to the hospital."

"Biggs. My purse," Faith insisted.

"On the way to the truck," I promised.

"I'll let them know you're coming," Hollie said.

I pulled out my .357 and spent a moment reloading, then slid the barrel into the back of my pants. It was a poor choice, but I wanted easy access. "You doing okay, Faith?"

"My neck hurts," she said, reaching for the bandage.

"I bet," I said. "We're going for a ride."

"I know. I heard," she said. "I need my purse. I need to call Reagan so she can take April to Nickles' Ranch after school."

"Safe to say you're feeling better," I said, handing her my cell phone. "Call Reagan. I'll grab your purse on the way out to the truck."

I decided to take Faith out the back. I'd have access to alley cameras and could make sure we weren't walking into a second ambush of the day. Fortunately, there was no one around and we made it out to the truck without incident.

———

"I ran out to the Quinn ranch. Bobby Quinn has an alibi for this morning. He was in Hemmingford looking for Zoey Watts. I don't think it was him." Leonard had found me in the hospital ER, waiting for the doctors to finish with Faith.

They'd removed a small shard of glass from her neck, given her two stitches and refused to let her leave without antibiotics and a tetanus shot. I'd stepped out of the room, preferring to let Faith fight that little battle.

"As much as I'd like to pin this on Bobby, it wasn't him. I've got some other leads to run down. In the meanwhile, I need you to stand down. I got a call from State Patrol. Somehow Cropsie got word about the shooting and is already up my ass."

"I didn't get a great look at the shooter, but I know I winged him," I said. "Give me a chance to find him. I just need to get a list of Bobby Quinn's known associates. I'd bet anything it's one of them."

"Son, I don't know how to say this any differently," Leonard said. "You need to back it down a notch. Killing Luca Quinn opened a can of worms that woulda been best left closed. Most folks around here see you as an outsider. The rest ... well, the list of folks that'd shoot you for what you did to Quinn is as long as my arm."

"You can't seriously be asking me to sit around while people are lining up to take shots at me?" I protested.

"According to you, that shooter had a scope," he said. "That right?"

"I'd guess a tactical sight," I said. "But sure, that or a scope."

"How far you say he was from you?"

"Fifty yards, give or take."

"This might be hard to hear, but I don't think he was shooting to kill," Leonard said. "Most folks around here who carry a rifle are hunters. Fifty yards with a scope is a gimme for any decent hunter, wouldn't you agree?"

"You're saying they intentionally missed?" I asked.

"We've seen it before," he said. "Not much different than shooting up a stop sign. They're just blowing off some steam."

"Except Faith and I aren't stop signs," I said. "That's attempted murder of a police officer."

"Tempers are running hot, Biggs," he said. "I need you to lay low for couple of weeks while your leg heals. Stay out of the public eye. In the meanwhile, let the rest of us do our jobs. We'll find who shot at you and put this whole nasty business to bed."

"What if they keep coming for me or, even worse, Faith?" I asked.

"Well that gets to the second thing I need to talk to you about. I'm asking you man-to-man to leave those Hudson girls alone. Especially Faith."

"I don't understand."

"Raff and Faith have a complicated relationship," he said. "You gettin' in the middle makes it even more complicated."

"I shouldn't have brought her to the station," I said, acknowledging my mistake.

"For one," Cal said. "You need to let her go, son. I'm not going to have that kind of trouble in my house. Do you understand what I'm saying?"

"Break it off with Faith Hudson or lose my job?"

He smiled wolfishly. "Never one to beat around the bush, are you? I feel like you've got a bright career ahead of you here in Butte County. And second, I need you to tell your friend that since we've wrapped up the Lynch and Shephard investigations, we won't be needing his services anymore."

"What about the broken GPS units?" I asked.

"I had Hollie look at them just this morning," he said. "Looks like the equipment is in good shape."

I nodded. There wasn't much I could do about it. "I'll call him after we get out of here."

"Don't forget what I said about those Hudson girls," Cal pushed.

"What about us?" Faith asked, from behind me. Leonard had to have seen her approaching, but I startled at her voice.

Leonard nodded his head and grabbed the brim of his hat, as if tipping it to her. "Ma'am." He turned and walked down the hall, his boots clopping noisily on the tile floor.

"Biggs?" Faith said. "Tell me."

I shook my head. "Not here. Are we too late to make April's practice?"

"Are you serious?"

I nodded. "Let's grab Diva on the way out of town. We have some talking to do."

She shook her head and looked downcast as she walked back into the cubicle to grab her purse from the bed. "He got to you, didn't he?"

"Do you need to let them know we're leaving?" I asked.

She shrugged. "I'm pretty sure they know how to find me."

I appreciated that Faith didn't push me for further explanations as we exited the hospital. In the Bronco, however, when I started driving toward my apartment, she stared out the window, refusing to look at me.

"What did you mean by 'he got to me'?" I asked.

"He told you to stay away from me because of Raff," she said. "You're all the same. You cover up for each other."

"Give me a second," I said, pulling out my cell phone and punching in Snert's phone number. Before leaving town, Snert had installed a stereo with a hands-free connection feature. My phone automatically connected to the system and piped the conversation through the speakers in the Bronco's cab.

On the third ring Snert picked up. I glanced at the clock, it was just after lunch and Snert was probably swamped with walk-in traffic. "Henry, I was hoping to hear from you," he said.

"Are you too busy to talk now?" I asked.

"We are busy, but Melinda's brother Cristian is now assisting," he said. "He has freed me up considerably. We look forward to our trip to Wood Creek this weekend."

"I've got some bad news about that," I said.

"Oh?"

"We need to postpone," I said.

"Does this have anything to do with an officer-involved shooting this weekend near Highway 71?" he asked.

I sighed. "You heard about that?"

"I read about it," he said. "I suspect Lester and Pearl have as well."

"I copy. Look, the sheriff wants to cancel your contract. He's wrapping up the investigation and doesn't see a need for having you look at the GPS units."

"I understand," he said. "I feel I should warn you that missing data is quite unusual, Henry. I believe it warrants further investigation."

"What do you mean?" I asked. "Have you looked at it? How did you get access?"

"I was in communication with Hollie Wilder," he said, answering the last question first. "I believe the problem with the GPS data is not in the sending units at all."

"How could you know that? You haven't even looked at them."

"I will send you my analysis. Do you still have that rugged note-book computer I gave you during the Richard Manning investigation?" he asked.

"Of course. How else do you think I watch movies?"

I could hear the smile in his voice. "I do not believe you watch movies, Henry. The email I am sending will have an application that you must install first. I was going to bring everything out with me so I could present my findings to your sheriff. The work is done, so feel free to do what you will with the data. Is there any other reason Mel and I should not visit this weekend?"

"There is," I said. "I don't think it's safe."

"I thought you said the investigation was wrapped up."

"Someone took a shot at a friend and me today. Before you ask, we're both okay. I just don't want you and Mel getting involved," I said.

"You need to come home, Henry," he said. "If you have resolved the matter that drew you to Butte County, there is no reason for you to remain in Wood Creek."

Faith had been staring out the window, still annoyed by Cal's directive at the hospital. Snert's simple request caught her attention and she turned toward me. I knew my answer had to address more than Snert's concerns.

"I've met someone, Snert," I said. "That's why I have you on speaker. Faith, meet my best friend, Alan Snerdly. Alan, Faith Hudson."

"Hi, Alan," she managed, working through a frown.

"Hi, Faith. Glad to meet you," Snert said.

"Sorry to cut it short, but we've had kind of a tough day," I said. "There was a random shooting outside the sheriff station this morn-ing. We've got some frayed nerves over here."

"Wait! Before you hang up, did you get the package I sent out? Sounds like it was late getting there."

"What package?"

"Shipper shows it was delivered yesterday afternoon," he said. "Signed off by Mortimer Cook at Sage and Rosemary."

"I haven't spent much time at the apartment," I said.

"Open it, Henry," he said and hung up.

"Did you mean it? That you've met ... someone? What about what Leonard said?" Faith asked.

"I know you don't know me very well, Faith," I said, pulling into the parking lot behind Sage and Rosemary. "And I really don't know what went down between you and Raff, beyond what you've told me."

"So, you believe whatever Cal told you?" she asked.

"That's not what I'm saying."

"That's it then?" she asked, reaching for the door handle to open the passenger door.

"Hold on. I don't argue well, but you're not understanding me. Give me two minutes. If you want to bail after that, I'll give you a ride home," I said.

She pulled the door partially closed. "Two minutes."

"Something's off around here," I said. "I can't exactly put my finger on it, but I can feel it. That's enough to keep me around. I realize that doesn't answer your question. I don't want to confuse the two issues, but you need to know finishing this job is important to me."

"Go on," she said, tepidly.

"I don't know if you've noticed, but I don't always say a lot. I don't see a reason to correct people when they get the wrong impression. Words are cheap, Faith. People like Sheriff Leonard know how to use words. I'm not like that."

She raised an eyebrow and I could tell I wasn't making progress.

"That doesn't mean I don't know things or can't do things. I watch people and I'm good in a tussle. "

"This isn't helping," she said.

"Faith, the only person I want to be clean with is you. Leonard showed his hand. There was nothing to say."

She rolled her eyes. "You didn't say anything because he's your boss and you want to keep your job. What's this got to do with you being good in a fight?"

"I'm still not explaining very well," I said, shaking my head. "I'm good in a fight because no matter what my opponent says, I watch their body. I watch how they move. I watch what they do, Faith."

"Talk is cheap," she said, releasing the door handle.

"That's what I'm saying," I leaned across the bench seat and placed a hand behind her neck. She resisted at first and then relented, leaning in to accept my kiss.

"You must think I'm a freak," she said, when we finally separated.

"How so?" I asked.

"One minute I'm melting down in the station and the next I'm accusing you of playing the good-old-boy game," she said. "I thought I was over cowering to Raff Butler. It was just his voice and how he raised his hand. I thought he was going to hit me."

"Were you having a flashback to when he beat you?"

"How did you know?"

"It's called PTSD. It isn't just soldiers who get it," I said. "It's also not hard for someone who has it to recognize the signs."

"You have flashbacks?"

"Sometimes," I said. "Mostly during thunderstorms or if I catch just the right smell. Sometimes it'll happen when I hear a loud noise and I'm not expecting it. I've gotten help with it. Have you?"

"I don't need a shrink."

I chuckled. "I don't think they're called that anymore. I talked to a counselor. It didn't fix anything, but it helped me understand and deal with it."

"What happens when Leonard finds out we're still together?"

My smile broadened. "That's the best part. I don't have to care."

"But he could fire you."

I shrugged and pushed my door open. "You have no idea how

many jobs I've had since leaving the service. Two weeks is actually pretty good for me."

"Leonard can't fire you after what you did to take down Luca Quinn," she called after me. "He'd look bad."

There was a bark from the back door and Diva raced to greet us. "Why would Leonard fire his knight errant?" Morty asked, grinning as he looked between us.

"Did she give you any trouble?" I asked. "I'm sorry for not making it back last night."

"No trouble at all, but I'm going to ask for joint custody. I'm afraid I've become a bit too fond of *Her Majesty* to consider allowing her to domicile elsewhere," he said. "Denholm has requested your presence in the parlor, if you please. He has a tray of sandwiches."

"I can wait in the truck," Faith said.

"The invitation is for the both of you, my dear," Morty said, his eyes riveted to the bandage on her neck. "Aren't you just a matched set."

Faith looked at me for a reaction and I nodded toward the door. "Morty, did I get a package yesterday?"

"Why, I believe you did," he said. "With all the excitement, I'd forgotten about it until this moment. Go find Denny and I'll bring it along."

Faith mouthed, 'Denny?' to me as we worked our way through the back hallway. I shook my head. *Denholm* had made it clear to me that only Morty was allowed to call him that – and only because he was tired of fighting him on it.

"Ahh, Ms. Hudson, Mr. Biggston," Denholm said as we entered the parlor. "The sheriff and the bar maiden – the start of every tragic western story ever told. I do hope you're able to break the mold of those who came before."

I smiled. It was early for Denholm to be drinking, but that wouldn't get in his way.

"Morty said you wanted to talk to us," I said.

"Sandwiches?" he asked, pushing a plastic-wrap-covered plate across the kitchen counter just as Morty entered carrying a box.

"Are we allowed to talk to the press?" Faith asked, half-jokingly, looking at me for confirmation.

Before I could answer, Denholm stepped in. "My dear, you are a citizen of this fine county and under no obligation to withhold information about things you may or may not have witnessed. Mortimer and I have become aware of a shooting not far from this establishment. We have drawn a more than reasonable conclusion that the two of you were involved." He pointed at Faith's bandaged neck.

I nodded to Faith and then opened Snert's box with my pocket knife. Faith recounted the events in detail. She hadn't seen me fire the last few rounds but filled the details in reasonably well. I wasn't surprised to find a heavy armored vest and three more armored t-shirts.

"Put this on," I said, handing one to Faith once she'd finished her tale. The shirts were extra-long men's mediums, as I preferred to wear them tight. They would fit Faith just fine.

"I don't think so," she said, inspecting the shirt's bulk and lack of any sort of fashionable detail.

"Is that what I think it is?" Morty asked, picking one of the shirts up and pulling out the manufacturer's tag. "Do you have any idea how expensive this shirt is?"

"Several hundred a piece," I said.

"Bullshit," Faith said. "It looks like it was made by drunk sailors."

I pulled my t-shirt off and replaced it with the armor. I'd wear the thicker vest if I was out in any official capacity, but for now, the lighter upgrade would work fine. "They're armored," I said. "Snert saved my life last year with one of these. I think he has a standing order with the manufacturer."

She shrugged and started pulling off the collared, western shirt she wore. While she had on a bra, I was surprised she'd disrobed that much in a room full of men. "Tell 'em about the data your buddy Snert sent. Or can they see that?"

"What data?" Denholm asked. The ultra-calm demeaner was a tell as to his level of interest. When Denholm really wanted some juicy piece of information, he stilled his body movements.

"I don't know yet. You'll need to treat whatever we see as off the record if you want me to look at it in here," I said. "The data belongs to Butte County."

"You are absolutely no fun at all," Mortimer complained. "Let's see it already. Cone of silence engaged and all that."

I retrieved Snert's tablet and opened the attachments in the email he'd sent. The app opened quickly and a map of Butte County displayed. A timeline of several months displayed at the bottom. I hit the triangular *play* icon in the center of the screen and a puck at the left of the timeline started moving slowly across, a day at a time.

"What is this?" Denholm asked.

"Butte County," Mortimer said.

A legend appeared on the right side of the screen. The words 'Butte-2', 'Butte-3', 'Butte-4' and 'Butte-5' appeared in a list, each in a different color. As the days progressed, colors that matched each of the different designations appeared on the map, overlaying the streets and highways.

"Patrol routes," I said.

"Where's Butte-1?" Denholm asked.

"Sheriff got a new truck a few months back," I said. "I don't think they've had time to install all the electronics yet."

"Go to August 19th," Mortimer said, his voice catching in his throat. "Can you select just Butte-2?"

I placed my finger on the puck and dragged it back to August 19th. I then poked Butte-2. With rapt attention, we all watched as Deputy Lynch's vehicle started out from his home in Hay Spring.

"As DRAMATIC AS THIS IS, the information isn't new," Morty said, after watching Lynch's final drive for the third time. "Leonard told us his GPS unit failed."

I nodded. Morty was right. The data collection failure was well known.

"Unusual that your friend included such a broad timeframe," Denholm said. "I'd like to know what he was thinking."

"That's not hard," I said, closing the app and selecting a video conferencing app. A few moments later, Snert's face showed on the screen.

"Hello, Henry," he said. "Is everything okay?"

"Hey, Snert. Yeah, we're great. I've got Morty and Denholm here with Faith and me. We're just looking at that data," I said.

"Mortimer Cook and Denholm Campbell? From Chicago?" Snert asked, his voice high with excitement. "It's such an honor to meet you."

"Very nice to meet you as well, Mr. Snert," Morty said.

"Alan," Denholm said, "His name is Alan. Don't be rude, Mortimer."

Morty gave Denholm a withering glare. "How would I know

that? Clearly, Biggs calls him Snert. I said *mister*, after all."

"Never much the investigator," Denholm said, pushing the shipping box to Morty with the shipping label in plain view.

"Ooh, so you can read," Morty said.

"Um, guys," I said, redirecting their attention. "Snert, we watched Lynch's route. It's pretty much what we expected. What are we missing?"

"Did you run the whole simulation?" he asked.

"Yes," I said. "Lots of patrol routes. I didn't really see anything odd."

"Run the whole sequence with just Butte-2 and Butte-3," he said.

"Whose vehicle is number three?" Denholm asked.

"The designation is for the deputy," I said. "Lynch was two, Raff is three."

"But nothing happened to Raff," Faith said.

"Hang on, Snert," I said. "I'm jumping to the other app."

"That's okay," Snert said. "Your tablet multitasks. I can still hear you."

I selected the two deputies and slid the timeline puck to the left so the simulation would start again. We watched as patrol routes popped onto the screen one day at a time instead of drawing the routes as they occurred. As the days progressed, the information Snert had seen became evident. There was a hole in the map. If you weren't looking for it, it would have easily been missed, but it was as if someone had taken the eraser at the end of a pencil and scrubbed out a small area.

"See it?" Snert asked, overhearing a murmur between Morty and Denholm.

"On Squaw Creek road?" I verified.

"That's right," Snert answered.

"Now add Butte-4 on August 29th," he said. "Pay attention to the time."

I restarted the simulation and gasped quietly as realization struck.

"Turn it off," Denholm demanded.

I nodded and closed the app. Snert's face reappeared on the screen. "I'm glad to see you're wearing the shirts I sent, Henry."

"Could you do one more thing for me?" I asked.

"Certainly, Henry," he said. "How can I help?"

"Pearl owns some land out here," I said. "Can you send me a map that shows the boundaries?"

"Do you think it is titled in her maiden name – Quinn or Ploughman?"

"Try both," I said. "I also want to see what's owned by Hannah Quinn."

"It will not be difficult," he said.

"Thanks, buddy. Talk to you soon." I closed the app.

"What's going on, Biggs?"

I ignored Faith for a moment and looked to Denholm. "You'll keep this to yourselves?" I asked. "At least until we have a chance to deal with it?"

"Of course," Denholm nodded.

I grabbed Snert's package and guided Faith out of the parlor. "I won't be able to come to April's practice, Faith," I said as we climbed the stairs.

"Biggs, tell me what's going on," she said.

I crossed the room, grabbed a box of .357 magnum ammo and started rummaging through a bag I'd brought from home. "The time-line, Faith," I said. "Char Shephard showed up in that black hole before Lynch was murdered."

"She probably went out to help Lynch," she said. "Don't cops do that?"

"That's not it. She went before his truck was found, Faith," I said. "Only reason I can think of is that she was part of it."

"You've got to tell someone," she said.

I pulled out the leather harness I still had. It wouldn't be perfect, but I'd be able to hold the .357 beneath my jacket. To answer Faith's question, I grabbed Snert's tablet and selected Shephard and Lynch and then chose August 19th.

We watched the unfolding animation as Lynch approached and entered the blackout zone without coming out the other side. Thirty minutes later, Shephard's vehicle entered the zone and then twenty minutes later exited at the same spot she'd entered. About an hour after that, Lynch's vehicle blinked into existence ten miles north and west of the black hole.

My email chimed as we were watching, the preview showing it was from Snert. I stabbed at the email and opened it. He'd located Pearl's property. If I hadn't just been staring at the map in Snert's app, I might have missed it, but the two properties he'd identified, Quinn Farm and Pearl's land, were centered in the blackout zone. It confirmed my growing suspicion.

"What now?" she asked.

"Now, I take you home and you don't say a word about this to anyone," I said. "Not Reagan, not your mom. You know too much. This thing is bigger than Luca Quinn."

"What are you going to do?" she asked.

"I'm not completely sure," I said. "I've got a couple of things to follow up on. I'm hoping to get some answers."

⌁

"Ranger White," Jasper White answered his cellphone. I'd gotten the number from Hollie and called him just as I pulled out of Faith's driveway.

"Jasper, this is Henry Biggston," I said.

"Deputy Biggston, what can Fish and Wildlife do for you today?" he asked. Wind caught the speaker of his phone and I imagined him outside, checking hunting licenses.

"I ran into something the other day on patrol and it's been bugging me. I wondered if you'd have time to meet me over at the top of Squaw Creek road where those hiking trails enter the forest," I said. "I could pick you up if that'd help."

"I'm just finishing up with something. Which way are you coming from?" he asked.

"I'm on 385, south of Wood Creek," I said. "Just about to get on Squaw Creek."

"I'm not that far from you. How about you meet me in that parking lot next to the trailheads. We can talk there," he said.

"Appreciate it," I said.

The area hadn't gotten any more snow but with trees lining the south side of the road, the sun hadn't had a chance to melt what had fallen. It was easy to get lost in thought while driving through the snow-covered forest and I almost missed the turn to take me up the big hill to the top of Squaw Creek.

"One minute," I told Diva as I slowed to a stop. The Bronco's four-wheel-drive required me to lock the hubs in and I couldn't imagine the road up to the trailheads was in any better shape than what we'd made it past already. The sound of an approaching truck got my attention and I waved as White pulled up in his dark green forest service vehicle.

"Deputy Biggston," White said, by way of greeting. He'd rolled down his passenger window.

"Thanks for coming out, Jasper," I said, opening his truck door and waiting while he moved a metal clipboard off the passenger seat.

"You said you had something you wanted me to see?" he asked.

I pulled out my phone and flipped back to the pictures I'd taken of the vehicle tracks that entered the forest. The tracks had been made during a freshly falling snow and wouldn't have been visible the next day.

"Where's this?" he grunted, tipping his glasses back to get a better look.

"Just up the top here," I said, pushing the zoomed-in picture over so he could get a look at the trailhead marker.

"Well that's not right," he said. "Nobody's supposed to be driving back there. I'm surprised someone didn't call this in. We have several avid hikers out here in the winter and they don't like it when folks tear things up. You got some warmer clothing with you?"

"What are you thinking?"

He nodded his head toward the bed of his truck. I followed his motion and noticed he was carrying a large snowmobile that hung out the back of his long truck bed. "Too much snow back there for a truck, but that snowmobile won't have any trouble. It's big enough for the both of us."

"Sure," I said. "I'll follow you up."

I jumped back in my Bronco and we drove the remainder of the distance to the trailhead. By the time I parked, Jasper already had his snowmobile offloaded.

"Hop on," he said, throwing his leg over the long bench seat. We probably only had three hours of sunlight left. "Dog gonna be okay in the truck?"

"Yup, she's fine," I said, climbing on behind him.

The noise of a snowmobile is such that once they're moving, you can't easily converse. White had lots of experience and we moved up the mountain at a good clip, gliding gracefully around trees and dropping into a valley on the other side of the hill. We'd been going for about twenty minutes when he slowed, allowing the snow to stop us completely.

"I thought it was probably hunters," he said. "Sometimes in the fall they'll scope out a new spot by bringing their Jeeps and the like back here. It's illegal, but it's hard to catch them unless we see tracks."

"Sounds like you don't think that's the case here," I said, walking around the sled. White had become interested in a pile of blue five-gallon plastic jugs partially hidden in a thicket. I joined him.

"I'll give you one guess at what they're bringing up with these jugs," he said, handing one to me.

I was about to say water when I sniffed the spout. It had an odor I didn't recognize, but it certainly wasn't water.

"Not sure," I said, handing it back to him.

"Liquid fertilizer," he said. "This was a grow spot."

"Marijuana?"

"There's a stream about a hundred yards down that slope," he said pointing west. "Those tracks were probably from the crew. They were pulling their equipment before the snow got too deep."

"Is that common out here?" I asked.

"Not at all," he said. "Sheriff Leonard seems to have a sixth sense about growers. I'm surprised he didn't find these guys. Not sure how he does it. I'll tell you this, though. They never do it twice. He's a real hard ass about it. Tell him about this spot and you guys can bust 'em next spring."

"Sorry for running you out here for nothing," I said. "I just didn't know what I was looking at."

"We've got more forest than my department can cover," he said. "I appreciate you keeping an eye out for me. I gotta say, I'm a little surprised to see you out and about. I thought I heard you got shot up by that Quinn fella."

"Grazed my leg. Nothing real big," I said.

"Glad that's the way it went down. Those Quinns are a tough bunch. We won't go on their land," he said. "Sheriff warned us off that a few years back. Said they're just as likely to take a shot at us as anything."

"And that's okay?" I asked.

"Nope. If we need access, we get Cal involved. He makes sure they're civil," he said.

"Do you get on their property much?" I asked.

"Only had to a couple of times. The land out there isn't good for much, but we'll get an odd antelope hunter whose kill strays onto Quinn property. Often as not, Quinn boys run 'em off and the hunters give us a call. Last time, we never did find the antelope." He seemed to remember something. "You know, I'm sorry. I forgot it was Luca Quinn you had to shoot last week. I didn't mean to bring that up."

"Is what it is," I said, shrugging.

"You want to look around? With the snow, there's nothing much left for us to do," he said. He'd taken pictures of the trash but made no effort to remove it.

"Sure, let's head back," I said.

———

"This is Sheriff Leonard," Leonard answered his cell phone.

"Cal, this is Biggs. Do you have a few minutes? I have a couple of things I need to run by you."

"Probably best we don't do that on the phone," he said.

"I'm just about back in town," I said. "Want to meet at the station?"

"To be honest, I was thinking of throwing on a couple of steaks and having a beer," he said. "You know, while we're on the subject, how about I get Raff to come along as well. We'll do a little team building. Maybe put this whole Faith thing in the rearview."

"It's about Shephard," I said.

"Not on the phone, son," he said. "We'll talk business at the house. Is it something Raff can't hear?"

"No, I suppose not," I said.

"Perfect," he said. "I'll send Rosita out for a couple boxes of barley pops. How about you come out around seven thirty? And leave that dog of yours at home. I've got new carpet."

I checked the time, I had a couple of hours to kill and knew just what I wanted to accomplish. "What can I bring?"

"Pearl raised a good one," he said, chuckling. "Don't bring a thing. We'll be eating bachelor style."

"How's that?" I asked.

"We'll cover the three main food groups. Beer, steak and potatoes. No need to mess up an otherwise perfect meal with green stuff," he said, chuckling. "Although a good bottle of whiskey wouldn't be frowned upon."

"Seven-thirty sounds good," I said. "See you then." I didn't love that Cal had hijacked my meeting, but unless Raff was involved, he'd need to know sooner or later.

I turned toward the hospital and a few minutes later pulled into the parking lot. I wasn't exactly sure what I was going to say, but I needed to look Char Shephard in the face. Unfortunately, when I got to her room, I found it had been cleared out.

"Can I help you?" a nurse asked.

"Char Shephard?" I asked.

"Went home a couple of days ago," the woman said.

"Oh? I thought she was headed to rehab," I said.

"I can't really say," the nurse said. "But I'm pretty sure she's at home."

I nodded and walked back out to the truck. I was about to call Hollie for her address when I realized I knew where Char lived. Gene had driven me past the home in an attempt to show me just how much I wouldn't miss living in one of the county-owned properties.

He was right, of course. The brick house was in poor repair. Through tattered curtains, I saw lights on inside as I walked up the cement walk.

"Who are you?" A kid had opened the front door, leaving the screen door closed between us.

"I'm Deputy Biggston," I said. "I kind of work with your mom."

"Who is it, Chad?" I caught a glimpse of Char in the dim light of her kitchen.

"Big man," Chad yelled back. "He says he's a policeman, but I don't see a badge."

"Let him in, Chad," Char called back, wheeling out far enough into the dining room that she could see across to the front door.

Chad opened the screen door and I followed him in. The place was a wreck. Dirty clothes and toys were everywhere. Chad looked and smelled like he hadn't had a bath in a week. I took my hat off and held it in my hand as I followed Chad over to where Char sat.

"I'm sorry to barge in on you, Ms. Shephard," I said.

"Call me Char," she said. "What do you want, Deputy?"

"Biggston. Call me Biggs. Please," I said. The smell of something burning caught my attention and I saw a small flame leap from the stove. I jumped around Shephard, almost running over Chad, to pull a cast-iron skillet from the stovetop. Whatever had been in the skillet was now unrecognizable.

"Back door," Shephard offered as I looked around frantically for somewhere to dump the flaming pan. I ran past her and Chad, struggled with the backdoor lock for a moment and finally made it through. I set the skillet on the cement stoop and left it to burn.

"Are you doing okay, Char?" I'd pictured the conversation going differently, but the squalid living conditions threw me completely off guard.

"We're okay," she said stoically, but there was a quiver in her lip that made me believe differently.

"I think you need some help," I said.

"Is that why you're here? To judge me?" she asked, her mood darkening quickly.

"No. I'm sorry. It's not my place."

"Darn right it's not," she said. "Maybe you should leave."

"I just have a couple of questions and I'll get out of here," I said.

"About what?"

"Maybe it'd be best if Chad watched TV or something," I said. Chad had taken up residence next to his mom and was leaning against the chair, still in his pajamas.

"Chad, go in the other room for a few minutes," she said.

"But I'm hungry," he whined. "I thought we were going to eat."

"Momma's going to have to start dinner again," Char said. "Let me and Deputy Biggs talk for a few minutes and then I'll make you something to eat."

"Mama," he whined.

"Chad. Go." She pushed and he walked away.

"You can cook while we talk," I said.

"Won't be much. I'm down to peanut butter," she said. "That hamburger was spoiled anyway."

The mental imagine I'd constructed of Char Shephard and the woman I saw in front of me were very different. In my mind, I imagined her as instrumental in Deputy Lynch's murder, maybe even pulling the trigger. At a minimum, she helped to clean up after it later.

"Why did you go out to the Quinn farm on August twenty-ninth?" I asked.

If I'd expected a big reaction, I didn't get one. "I wondered when you'd come. Are you here to kill me?"

"Kill you?" I asked. "What are you talking about?"

"George Lynch called me that day. He said he'd found something on the old Quinn ranch. He wanted to keep it quiet," she said.

"Why would he call you?"

"I suppose it doesn't really matter anymore," she said. "We'd had an affair, but mostly we were good friends. He knew he could trust me, so he called and I went out there. Probably best this way. Foster kids probably live better than this."

"I'm not here to hurt you, Char," I said. "What did you see at the Quinn Ranch?"

"They said if I told anyone what I saw, they'd kill Chad in front of me. They'd cut him into bits," she said. "Tell them I stayed quiet."

"I'm not part of whatever's going on," I said. "Help me stop them."

"You can't stop them," she said.

"I stopped Luca Quinn."

"I heard about the shooting downtown this morning," she said. "You're lucky to be alive. Take my advice, Biggston. Leave town tonight. Don't bother to get your stuff. Just get in your car and leave."

"I'm not doing that. Tell me what you saw."

She shook her head. "No. They already tried to kill me once."

"You'll never get away from these people."

"I told Cal," she said. "He said he'd protect me. Give me a place to live."

"He knows?"

"He talked to them. Made them leave me alone."

"Shit."

"Don't screw this up for me," she said. "Chad's all I've got."

SHERIFF LEONARD's home was a couple miles south of town on the edge of the national forest boundary. It was well past dark when I arrived and lights spilled out from every window of his massive log cabin home. Fifty yards from the house, the asphalt road split. The right branch led to a four-stall garage and the left turned into a brick-paved circle drive by the front entrance. I worried my Bronco might drip oil onto the bricks, so I pulled around and parked down the drive a bit.

Small pools of light illuminated the walk to a broad porch. The glimpses I got through the crystal sidelights surrounding the massive rough-hewn timber door made me feel like I might have under-dressed. A moment after ringing the bell, a Hispanic woman approached and swung the door open.

"Si?" She greeted me with a terse smile.

"Henry Biggston. Cal asked me to dinner," I said.

"Si, Mr. Biggston. Welcome," she said. "Welcome. Mr. Leonard is in the kitchen. May I take your coat?"

I wasn't used to being waited on and fumbled for a moment to remove my coat. The woman placed it on a hook in a small alcove next to the door and nodded for me to follow her.

The interior of the log cabin looked exactly like what I imagined a high-dollar mountain resort might be. In the center of the living room, melon-sized river stones were piled into a soaring floor-to-ceiling tower that disappeared through the arched beams twenty feet above our heads. A roaring fire crackled inside the huge, five-foot-tall double-sided fireplace built within the fall of rocks.

As I followed the woman, we walked to the right of the fireplace and I ran my hand along the side of the cool stones, no doubt gawking at the fantastic details of the magnificent home.

"Biggs. There you are," Leonard said, grinning broadly as he dropped the last of five fat steaks onto a grill built into the granite countertop of the island he stood behind. "Hope you like your steak rare, because that's the only way I grill 'em. Rosita, I won't be needing you anymore this evening."

She nodded. "Si, Mr. Leonard."

I set the scotch I'd brought on the island. It was hard not to feel a bit inadequate in the room. "This place is amazing," I said, my eyes falling on a back deck with a southern exposure. Moonlight and strategically placed floodlights illuminated the snowy field that separated Leonard's home from the forest several hundred feet away.

"Inherited it from my folks. Dad was a rancher turned banker. Made a killing in the eighties during the banking crisis. Bought up a bunch of land," he said, eyeing the scotch. "Glasses are in the cupboard next to the freezer. Three fingers on ice if you don't mind."

If I hadn't followed his eyes, I would never have been able to identify the freezer, which looked like every other piece of expensive cabinetry in the room. Even so, I made a few bad guesses before finding both glasses and the freezer. I wasn't really sure what three fingers might be, so I loaded his glass with ice and filled it with several inches of the amber liquid.

The sound of the doorbell broke the silence. "You've got your hands full. I'll get it," I said.

"That's probably Hannah," Cal said.

"Hannah Quinn?" I asked, icy tendrils filling my veins. Only a few days before, I'd killed her eldest son. "I should leave."

Leonard flipped the steaks and grabbed the scotch I'd poured for him. "Nonsense," he said. "I've already talked to her. Luca Quinn was a menace to everyone. She knows you did what needed doing. Go answer the door, you'll see."

"You can't be serious," I said.

Taking in my words and undoubtedly the look on my face, Leonard finally shrugged. "If this steak is burned, I'm blaming you," he said, giving me his best disappointed look. Nervously, I drained the small glass of scotch I'd poured for myself. I coughed involuntarily as I wasn't used to whiskey, but I felt no burn as my heart hammered in my chest.

An angry woman's voice joined Cal's at the front door. At that moment, the urge to run was greater than I'd ever known. It's one thing to shoot a man in self-defense. That's difficult to live with. I'd mourn Luca Quinn's passing in my own way, but I knew I'd done the right thing. Pushing Luca's death into his mother's face was cruelty beyond imagining.

The force of Hannah Quinn's entry was palpable. Like the gunner atop a HUMVEE, Hannah's torso rotated, searching until her eyes found me. She froze, her stare pinning me in place like twin fifty caliber machine guns.

"What the fuck is he doing here?" Spittle flew from her mouth as her face flushed bright red.

Cal stepped around her and in my peripheral vision, I noticed a third person still in the hallway. I found it impossible, however, to break eye contact with Hannah. Say what you wanted to about justification, but I'd wronged her by killing Luca and we both knew it.

"Don't stand there with your willy flapping in the wind, Biggs," Cal said. "Pour the woman a tall glass."

He returned my incredulous look with a head nod toward the bottle of scotch. As far as lifelines go, it wasn't much, but I took it and busied myself pouring Hannah a drink. When I turned back, I found that the shadowy figure from the hallway had come forward to join Hannah. It was Bobby Quinn, complete with fresh bruises and cuts over most of his face.

"I don't want your fucking whiskey, Leonard." Hannah hadn't moved from where she'd first entered the room. "I don't know what you're playing at here, but I'd rather shoot this fucker than look at him."

"Cal, this is a bad idea," I said.

"You're gonna pay for what you did to my brother," Bobby Quinn hissed.

We were all interrupted by the ringing of the doorbell.

"Shut up and go answer that door, would you?" Cal said. "Now, everybody, just settle down. We've all got to live in this county, so I say we get shit out on the table."

"Cal, it's too soon," I said as quietly as I could manage.

"Bobby, I'm not going to ask you twice," Cal's voice gained an edge I didn't expect from him. "That'll be Raff."

A timer beeped and Leonard turned as if nothing unusual was happening. Grabbing a hot pad, he removed a sheet of brown rolls from the oven and dumped them into a waiting bowl.

"What the hell, Cal?" Raff asked, walking carefully around the stationary Hannah.

"You're just in time, Raff," Leonard said, pulling steaks from his grill and stacking them onto a large platter. "Let's move into the dining room. Biggs, grab the rolls, would you?"

I wasn't loving the vibe in the kitchen, so I picked up my empty scotch glass and the wooden bowl of rolls and followed Leonard.

"Just set the rolls in the middle of the table," he continued, pointing. "I've got you on the end over there, across from Raff."

Along the south wall of the dining room, a bank of windows had the same view as the ones over the deck. Diamond-paned, leaded-glass windows gave the room a more formal look, which matched nicely with the fancy white cloth on a table long enough for ten or twelve people. At one end, there were five places already set.

Raff was next to enter the dining room. "Seriously, Cal, what's she doing here?" he asked.

"Eat first. I'm not letting good steak go to waste," Leonard said, sliding past the Quinns as they entered the dining room "Beer, anyone? Hannah, I got you and Bobby on the end there."

Hannah Quinn once again locked eyes with me as she entered the room. "We're not good, you and me," she said.

I nodded, barely aware of Bobby Quinn taking a seat next to me. "You're so screwed," he said, not so loudly that Leonard could hear him in the other room.

"You got a problem, Bobby?" Raff growled, warily eyeing both Hannah and Bobby.

"Yeah, I got a problem," Bobby said. "This bastard killed my brother. Then he came after me. If Leonard hadn't been there that night, he'd have taken me out."

"Bullshit," Raff answered. "Luca was dealing drugs. I'm surprised they didn't find any on you when they picked you up. How about you tell me where your girlfriend, Zoey Watts, is."

"Shut up, Butler," Hannah growled, still not sitting at the table.

Leonard came back into the room, carrying several glass beer bottles. "Hannah, sit the fuck down. Raff, drop it," he ordered. "We're going to have a nice meal and work this shit out. Everyone read me?"

Hannah Quinn clenched her jaw and reluctantly sat in the remaining seat next to Raff. "You're a light beer guy, right?" Leonard continued, handing me a bottle.

"Right," I said, accepting the bottle and placing it on the table in front of me. "What's going on, Cal?"

"How about this," he said. "Everybody drinks a beer. Everybody eats some steak. Then, I'll tell you how we're going to dig our little county out of the shit."

"You better not be wasting my time, Leonard," Hannah growled, taking a long drink of the beer he'd handed her.

Leonard nodded and held his beer out to Raff, asking for a toast. I couldn't think of anything less appropriate and was surprised when

Raff clinked his bottle with Leonard's. When Leonard pushed his bottle in my direction, I defensively picked mine up, mimed clinking the bottles and then took my own long pull. The beer was perfectly chilled and almost immediately, it worked to calm my jangled nerves.

Without any further talk, Leonard sliced into his thick steak and pulled off a bloody chunk. I watched as he took great pleasure in chewing it and then moved in for a second bite. Personally, I had no interest in eating. The whole scene was just too weird.

"So, Henry. I think you said you had something you wanted to talk to me about," Leonard said, his mouth full of steak.

To buy time, I took another long pull on my beer. All too soon, I'd swallowed and had no other way to delay. "I think I know where George Lynch was killed," I said.

"No shit," Raff said almost immediately, setting down his fork. "How?"

"I don't think this is the right time or place," I said, taking another long draw from my bottle. I prayed that the single beer would render me speechless because I was certain Leonard would compel me to continue.

"We're amongst friends," he said, gesturing with his knife to Bobby and then Hannah. "Quinns are your family after all. And before someone brings up that dumbass Luca, let's just remember how much trouble he's caused us all. Right, Hannah?"

"He was my son, Leonard," she growled, less angrily than I might have expected.

"He was your fuckup son," Cal answered unkindly. "State Patrol had him on their short list. Biggs here did us all a big favor on that one."

"Shit, Cal," Raff said. "What's that supposed to mean?"

"Go ahead, Biggs. Tell Raff," he said.

"Tell me what?" Raff asked.

"Lynch was shot on Quinn Ranch," I said. "He called Char Shephard for help, but someone stopped her. Ran her off."

"How the hell do you know that?" Raff asked.

"See what you can learn when you sit down for dinner, Hannah?" Leonard asked. "I bet you didn't know that Biggs here was about to figure out the whole thing."

"Cal, you're starting to scare me," Raff said, pushing back from the table.

From the corner of my eye, I saw a fist coming at me and I raised my arm to block. My response was sluggish, but I was still faster than Bobby. I pushed back and jumped to my feet, sliding the chair across the polished wood floor into the wall behind me. Bobby had also jumped to his feet and brought a second hand around. I dodged and grabbed for my steak knife on the table. I missed but managed to grab a plate.

"Boys, stop already," Leonard said, laughing. "You're going to make a mess."

I felt off, like I was just waking up. I barely managed to dodge Bobby's next blow and slammed the plate into the side of his head, knocking him to the floor.

"Cal, no!" Raff said.

"Stay put, pecker head," Hannah Quinn growled.

Like a wounded animal, I swung, trying to make sense of the conversation across the table. Twin leads from an electric shock device buried themselves in my armored t-shirt. I peered at Leonard, who held the other end of the device. He applied electricity, but nothing happened. My small victory was hollow. The effects of some type of drug worked through my system. I'd walked into a trap and had precious little time.

"Aww, shit," Leonard said, recognizing that his shock device didn't have the desired effect.

In a single smooth motion, I spun and grabbed my chair. I'd knocked Bobby over, but in my peripheral vision, I saw he was getting back up. Using the momentum of my spin, I threw the chair as hard as I could into the leaded glass of the window. The chair crashed through, leaving the small hole I was hoping for, barely missing Leonard.

Like a high school fullback, I rushed at the sheriff, my legs feeling like they were filling with sand. He crashed a big forearm into me as I drove us both into the broken window. For a crazy moment, everything went still as we sailed out of the house and fell fifteen feet to the ground below. If not for the drifted snow and a steep slope, one of us would have ended up much worse for the experience. Together, we tumbled twenty yards down the hill and slowed to a stop.

"Ohh, shit," Leonard complained from a few feet away.

I struggled to get to my feet and reached for the Walther I kept on my ankle. I managed to pull it out, but my fingers felt like they were the size of hotdog buns. I stumbled, trying to orient the gun on him. "Don't move," I mumbled, staggering side to side.

"My God, Biggs, you do not disappoint," he said, his cheerful voice returning.

"Shoot him," Bobby's distant voice called from the house. "He's got a gun."

Through blurry eyes I tried to make out Leonard as he moved toward me. "Kids these days," he lamented, his large hand wrapping around the gun and yanking it from my hand.

"What did you do to me?" I asked, fully expecting him to make good on Bobby's request. Instead, he hooked his arm under mine and walked me back toward the house.

"You can't believe what kind of crap we confiscate in this county," he said. "Stuff little jack-wagons use to drug their girlfriend's drinks so they can get their rocks off. Really, it's a story as old as time. Don't worry, no date rape for you. Although, you'll probably wish that's where this ended."

―――

The sound of whimpering woke me and I shivered against unbearable cold. I felt like I was coming out of a deep sleep and had no idea where I was.

"Is someone there?" I tried to ask the question, but discovered my mouth was bound with a gag. Nothing made sense and I concentrated on my breathing. The sound of whimpering continued. The fog slowly cleared from my brain and I realized my head was covered in a cloth bag. As feeling returned to my limbs, the pain came with it. I was hanging with my manacled wrists secure over my head.

Scuffling feet preceded the sound of a door opening and closing. The door wobbled and vibrated too much to be an interior door. It sounded more like an old warped and weathered door, like the one on Pappi's barn. The locking mechanism rattled against loose wooden planks. A light breeze stirred around me, followed by the heavy smell of marijuana.

A few minutes later, I heard the approaching footsteps of multiple people. They were heavy thuds like shoes on hard-packed dirt, their steps landing but not echoing as would be expected on cement. A scrape against gravel confirmed my suspicion that I was held in some sort of outbuilding. My arms and legs were numb from the cold and if my teeth could come together, they surely would have been chattering.

"Cut him down." Leonard's baritone was unmistakable.

"You sure?" Bobby Quinn asked. "He's dangerous."

"He's cuffed, Bobby," Leonard said. "And he's been hanging here all night like a slab of beef. Don't be such a baby."

I felt someone move behind me and suddenly my arms felt weightless as I crashed to the ground, my numb legs unable to handle the weight of my body. A moment later, strong arms wrapped around my chest and pulled me into a chair where the bag over my head was removed.

I blinked at the light streaming between barn boards. I was hypothermic and shivered uncontrollably. Somebody wrapped a thick blanket around me, but I wondered if my body had any further capacity to generate heat, given how cold I'd grown.

Roughly, Bobby Quinn removed the gag from around my mouth and my teeth chattered uncontrollably. I hadn't been this miserable since Ranger training.

"Damnit, Biggs, I wanted to have this conversation at dinner last night, but you jumped the gun on me a bit," he said.

"You drugged me," I managed, although I didn't recognize my own voice.

The tunnel vision I'd been fighting diminished enough that I could look around. The barn we were in was big but in poor repair. Not far from my position were drying racks filled with long marijuana stalks in various stages of readiness. Incongruous with the old rundown building, a modern laboratory had been constructed along the back wall. The large tanks and lab equipment looked expensive. On top of the overpowering weed smell, I could detect the odors of ammonia and spoiled fruit. Someone had been cooking meth in quantities large enough to supply thousands of addicts.

A heater kicked on and warm air wafted tantalizingly over my body. On the floor across from me sat an unconscious Raff and the body of Zoey Watts.

"How did you know?" I asked, my teeth chattering. The anemic heater was doing little to drive away the intense cold.

"Know what?" Leonard asked.

"That I had Lynch's murder scene?" I asked.

"I didn't, until Char called."

"Why dinner, then?" I'd visited Char after he'd invited me out for dinner.

He shrugged. "I really was looking to do some team building. I couldn't have you and Raff at each other's throats. Things took a bit of a turn after I heard from Char. I knew you were in too deep. I just have one question for you. How much of this did you tell Faith?"

I shook my head. "I didn't figure it out until after you told me to stop seeing her."

He rolled his eyes. "You'll excuse me if I don't completely buy that."

Bobby Quinn crossed the shed and held out a long black stick with electrodes on the end. I'd never seen a shock stick before, but it didn't take much imagination to recognize one. Without hesitation,

Leonard snatched the stick from Bobby and jabbed it into my neck. I jerked uncontrollably as it made contact and activated. The pain was unimaginable, like every nerve in my body had been lit up with fifty thousand volts – which I suppose they probably had.

"Get him back in the chair," Leonard growled as I fell to the ground and out of his range.

"Faith doesn't know anything," I said when I was finally able to talk again.

"Let me do it," Bobby said.

"Just a second," Leonard said. "Tell me. When did you get suspicious?"

"Of you?" I asked. He nodded, encouraging me to continue. "Never. Not of being involved anyway. Shephard just said you helped broker peace. She felt like you probably knew who did the shooting but couldn't prove it."

"Damn. Overplayed that one," he said. "Wish we'd talked before Char called."

"Who shot Lynch?" I asked.

Leonard handed the stick to Bobby who jabbed it into my side. For the first time, now that the blanket had fallen to the ground and the drugs were wearing off, I noticed I was shirtless. Someone had taken off my armored t-shirt and my chest was exposed, the blanket lying on the ground where I'd just been writhing in pain. I doubled over as my muscles spasmed and howled uncontrollably.

"Talk about something that never gets old," Bobby said, dragging me back into the chair.

"Bobby shot George," Cal said. "Not far from where we sit right now. Ironically on land your grandma Pearl still owns, if I remember correctly."

"From the loft?" I asked.

"How would you know that?" Leonard asked.

"The shots were from an elevated position. The truck traveled ten to twenty yards between shots. I estimated Lynch was going thirty miles an hour at the time of the first shot," I said.

"Well, hell, son, you're really gonna make me miss having you around. How'd you figure all that?" he asked.

"The geometry isn't that hard to work out," I said. "I'm guessing on some of it."

"If that truck was moving faster, the angles would have been different," Bobby said.

I shrugged. He was right. I'd worked the numbers around to fit several different scenarios, but the one I'd stated was the most plausible I could come up with. In the end, it didn't matter that much.

"Why Raff?" I asked. "He's not in this?"

Leonard kicked Raff, who grunted but refused to wake up. "Bringing him out here was a last-minute call," Leonard said. "After I heard you'd been over to Char Shephard's, I got the Quinns to join us for dinner. You can imagine they were receptive to the idea."

"Raff's not in this?" I asked again.

"Right?" Leonard asked, as if we shared a common understanding. "If I wasn't in the middle of all this, I'd have been pointing a finger at him too."

"Your body count is too high, Cal," I said. "State Patrol isn't going to miss all this."

"ISD is gonna close the other investigations, thanks to you and Luca Quinn. All we need is a good story when you show up dead. That's where Raff comes in. Turns out you and Raff are going to come to blows over the girl. I've got Hollie who saw the two of you scuffling back at the station. We've got Raff's complaint. Poor Raff was so jealous, what with you coming in out of nowhere and showing him up at work and with his girl. I think we'll be able to put this sorry tale behind us. That's why I need to know about Faith. If she knows too much, I think we'll go murder-suicide."

"Faith isn't in this," I said.

"So you say. I figure you're not exactly a reliable witness," he said. "If I do figure Faith to be clueless, or at least controllable, we'll just go O.K. Corral and have the two of you shoot it out. Hell, I bet I could convince Raff to do that on his own."

"What now?" I asked. "What about Zoey Watts? This is sloppy, Cal."

Bobby Quinn zapped me with the stick and I was on the floor again, writhing in pain. He dragged me back up into the chair and drove his fist into the side of my face, knocking out a tooth. I barely kept myself from sliding back onto the ground. "Don't talk about my girlfriend, dickweed," he yelled. "If not for you, we'd still be going out."

Leonard chuckled. "It's so wrong just how twisted these Quinns are. He's not upset that she's dead, just that he can't date her anymore. Now tell me about Faith, because I feel like Bobby-boy is just getting warmed up."

"Faith isn't part of this. I didn't know anything to tell her," I said, spitting the tooth, along with a mouthful of blood onto the ground.

"Gonna be a long day for you, Biggs," Leonard said. "Stay away from the body, Bobby. We'll give Raff a headshot. It'll cover up your fine work."

A SPLASH of cold water jerked me back to consciousness. The chain that held my manacles together had been hooked around the tines of a front-end loader. With the tractor's bucket raised, I hung painfully off the ground, slowly spinning. The tractor chugged and bucked as its operator shook the bucket, looking to get my attention. They had it.

From between swollen eyelids, I noticed I'd been moved outside. As I spun, I took in the scene. We were in the middle of a rolling, grassy field. The only building I could see was the dilapidated barn where I'd been tortured and beaten for the last couple of hours. I felt fortunate that Bobby wasn't a pro in the torture department. It turns out, hitting a man with your bare hands hurts, especially if you've done nothing to toughen yourself up. Clearly, Bobby didn't work the fast or heavy bags at the gym. It was small, but I'd take any favorable turn I could get.

The tractor chugged and rolled forward. I caught sight of Raff lying on a plastic tarp a few yards ahead. Somebody had hogtied him – which was pretty difficult to get yourself out of. He was on his stomach with loops of rope keeping his arms pinned to his sides and his feet cinched up in the air. He was alive. I could see him wriggling, but didn't think he'd get loose any time soon.

"Lower him a bit, Bobby. I wanna talk to him," Hannah Quinn shouted over the tractor's loud diesel huffs. As far as I could tell it was just the four of us in the field next to the barn.

Bobby lowered me slowly, careful to keep the bucket pointed up. Hannah slapped the side of my head as I came within reach. Fresh pain bloomed through my pulverized face like a nuclear cloud. From my breathing, I knew I had a broken nose. I suspected the damage to my face was substantially worse. I fought back a yowl of pain. Hannah reached through the rip in my jeans and grabbed my thigh, dragging her thumb through the ragged path of my bullet wound. At some point earlier in the day, Bobby had discovered the wound and gleefully removed the staples with rusty pliers.

"I got your attention, boy?" Hannah asked, grabbing my chin to force my head around.

"Lester will come for me," I mumbled through torn lips. My wrists ached from being strung up, but I ignored the pain and tried to pull against the chains. Somewhere along the line, I'd been warmed up, no doubt with the goal of keeping me conscious longer.

"My land. My rules. Let him come," she said.

"Not your land," I mumbled.

Hannah grabbed my leg again. I jerked back, rattling the chains above my head. In trying to get away, I realized my manacled wrists hung together and the chain between them was looped evenly over one of the bucket's tines. With my right hand, I reached up, causing the chain to slide to the left. Unfortunately, Hannah was digging her fingers into my thigh and I didn't move far enough away to break her grip. I swore as she had her way with me.

"Anyone tries to come and take it, I'll kill them too," she said. "That's the advantage of having one foot in the grave."

"He givin' you trouble, Momma?" The tractor shook as Bobby Quinn jumped off and came around. "I can tune him up a little for you."

Bobby's hands had been wrapped in athletic tape. I hoped they were torn to pieces from beating on my head.

"Inbred hillbillies." A last-ditch idea formed in my mind.

Anger flashed across Bobby's face and he charged at me like a bull. In reality, what came at me was a flabby, never-worked-a-day-in-his-life bully who'd gotten by on the legacy of his larger, meaner brother. The mistake Bobby made was an honest one. I looked like crap, I felt like crap and my face was so puffy that it was likely beyond recognition.

Grasping one of the chains, I pulled and brought my knees up. Timing was tricky and Bobby saw the danger a moment before I struck. He attempted to pull back but stumbled on the rough ground. I had intended to wrap my ankle chains around his neck, but his flailing ruined my plan. I adjusted to his new incoming trajectory and lashed out with both feet instead, bringing a manacled ankle across his jaw. He dropped like a sack of potatoes.

"No!" Hannah Quinn cried angrily and fumbled in her pocket, searching for a weapon.

I twisted out of control, losing sight of Hannah for a few seconds. Pulling with my shoulders and thrusting with my legs, I attempted to scoot the chain up and off the tine. The chain moved, but I couldn't get free.

A loud report was followed by the metallic ping of a bullet ricocheting off the bucket. Hannah had successfully drawn her weapon. I was the proverbial fish in a barrel and she would soon find her mark. Unexpectedly, while swinging, my foot had hit something solid on the tractor behind me.

Without thinking, I twisted my hips, forcing me to spin against the taut chain. My bare toes touched metal and I held on with everything I had. I looked up and pushed off, launching myself toward the top of the bucket. I forgot about my odds and how tired I was or how much pain I was in. Those weren't the sort of things that counted when your life was on the line.

A second shot rang out and the tractor's engine screamed, spinning metal grinding in on its stationary frame. As soon as there was a little give in the chain, I lifted and yanked with every bit of strength I had, popping the length up and over the tine. I fell, crashing to the ground just as the third shot rang out.

I didn't blame Hannah for missing. Hitting a moving target with a pistol was harder than it looked. I pushed my arms into the frozen dirt, rolled my body forward and sprang at my quarry. Hannah, shocked, swung her pistol just as my shoulder struck her midsection, doubling her over. I heard the sickening crack of her ribs as I drove her into the ground. She screamed in agony and I wrenched the pistol from her hand.

The report of a rifle shot and the spray of dirt next to my heel warned me of another shooter. "Call 'em off, Hannah," I growled, rolling away from her. I stayed low and scanned the horizon, not finding the shooter.

Bobby groaned, rolled on the ground, and made a clumsy attempt to get up. His chest exploded in a mass of blood and bone at the same moment I heard a second rifle shot. Bobby died instantly. My mind spun with data. With this second shot, I calculated the location of the shooter. Based on the damage to Bobby, he was using a high-powered round.

I dove behind the tractor. Unlike modern vehicles, old tractors were constructed using heavy-gauge steel. Even with heavier rounds, the sniper would have a hard time getting to me through the tractor, although it left me pinned down

Hannah Quinn groaned again, apparently unaware of her situation. Her eyes fell on Bobby as she attempted to stand. Confused at the sequence of events, she looked at me questioningly.

"Hannah, get down!" I yelled. A cloud of blood replaced her shoulder and upper chest seconds before her lifeless body tumbled forward.

We weren't that far from the barn. I could easily make the distance in a couple of seconds if my legs were free. The more pressing problem was that Raff was still lying in the open, trussed up like a pig for slaughter. I rose up and poked my head out looking in the direction of the shots. Reflection from the glass of a scope warned me of what I already knew was coming. I ducked back before the bullet whistled over my head like an angry bumblebee. I'd seen what I needed. Leonard was back. He had stopped along the road and was firing his rifle from a bipod resting on the truck's hood.

Mortally wounded by Hannah, the tractor chugged angrily, smoke billowing out from its engine. What I wouldn't have given for a lot more smoke to provide a screen against Leonard's shots. I ducked out from the front wheel and then back. A shot buried itself into the solid rim behind my back. I'd been wondering if Cal's rounds could pierce the thick metal and was grateful to learn they could not.

I used the time it would take for him to reset his shot to jump up into the tractor and slip the hand clutch back, pushing the tractor into gear. The engine was nearly dead, but I only needed a few yards to provide protection for Raff.

The metal tractor seat exploded, fragments tearing into my right hand as Leonard took aim at the only piece of me he could find. I'd just pulled even with Raff when a shot hit the engine, rocking the tractor and cutting off its coughing belches. I'd hoped to use the tractor to get to the barn, but that hope died as the motor sighed loudly and seized.

I was already off the tractor, shuffling as fast as I could. Leonard hit the tractor with a second shot, but I looped my good hand through the ropes holding Raff's legs and dragged him toward the barn. Leonard must not have expected me to save Raff because he missed the open shot. I found as much cover as I could around the corner of the barn and dropped low. Knowing we wouldn't have much time, I frantically worked on the knot that held Raff's hands to his feet. My right hand was damaged and had little feeling, but I managed.

"What the hell!" Raff coughed as he pulled the gag from his mouth once his arms were free.

"Cal's got a sniper position," I said. "We're pinned down."

"He shot Hannah and Bobby?"

"He's cleaning house," I said, searching for a way deeper into the barn.

The sound of a vehicle starting warned us of Cal's decision to change positions. I ran back to Bobby and searched his pockets, looking for anything that might help. My heart leapt as I pulled out a cell phone. Cal's beefy SUV bounced over the pasture land as he sped toward my position.

I dropped Bobby's phone and raised Hannah's pistol. It was a .38 special, not a lot of gun. My eyes were bleary from the beating and my vision doubled as I pulled the truck into view. I could just make out Cal's grinning face as he violently bounced toward me. The sick bastard was actually enjoying this life-or-death battle.

Fighting against blurry vision, I calmed my pulse. I'd get one shot. Even if my hit was lethal, with my legs still bound, Cal's truck would likely finish what he'd started. It didn't matter. Leonard had to be stopped. I waited, allowing my heart to slow. I would fire a single shot when he was at ten feet and then rapidly fire the remainder of the shots.

Mentally, I counted down. Three ... Two ...

The gun went off when I was struck from the side. Helplessly, I watched as the shot went wild and Cal flew past, bouncing wildly over the rutted pasture. I hit the ground hard and pushed into a roll, Raff's arms still around me. I fought to line up again on Cal's truck as he jammed on his brakes.

"Shit, Raff," I grunted, but Raff was already in motion. He yanked at me, trying to pull me back to my feet.

"We need cover," he said. "I hear sirens."

My hand fell on Hannah's .38 that had been knocked free and I allowed Raff to help me run toward the barn. He'd ruined my show-down with Leonard, but I didn't for a minute believe this fight was over. Just before we slid through the big wooden side door, I caught a glimpse of Leonard's white Yukon. He'd turned in our direction and was coming fast. Any other driver would probably have wrecked the vehicle on the rutted ground, but Leonard seemed invincible.

We'd no more than made it inside when the wall exploded and the Yukon skidded to a stop in the middle of the barn. Caught up in the flying debris, Raff and I were tossed aside like ragdolls. Stunned, I scrabbled in the rubble looking for a new escape strategy.

"That's what I call team-building, boys!" Leonard said. "Now, give up and we'll call it a good day of catching bad guys. All the good guys get to go home and we'll blame all this shit on the Quinns. Everybody's a hero."

"Fuck you, Leonard," Raff shot back.

I winced, Leonard had gone from sunny to dark and his eyes needed a moment to adjust. By talking, Raff had given his position away. The fast fire of an automatic assault rifle tore through the barn and Raff screamed as he was struck.

I stood up from the rubble and leveled Hannah's pistol. "Drop the weapon, Cal," The barrel of his rifle was pointed away from me by only a few degrees, but we both knew I had him dead to rights.

"Doesn't have to go down like this, Biggs," he said. "There's a lot of money to be made here in Butte County. I've got millions. I'll share it with you. Wouldn't take much to get a new lab rolling. State Patrol will love that we brought this one down."

"You killed innocents, Cal," I said.

"Not true at all." His tone was almost cajoling. "Bobby Quinn shot George Lynch. Him and his buddies ambushed Shephard before I could broker a truce. Hell, that sniper outside the station was even Hannah's call. I'm the good guy here, Biggs. These Quinns were animals. It's frontier justice, but it's still justice."

"What about Raff? You just shot him."

"Heat of the moment. Mistakes were made," he said. "Let me spin this. I'll cut you in for half. We'll give Raff a couple hundred thousand if he lives, but there's still a cool million in it for you. We'll find a new chemist and get back into production. This time I'll make sure it stays out of Butte County."

I sighed, which Leonard took as acceptance. Rustling from where Raff had fallen drew Leonard's attention and he raised his gun,

254 / JAMIE MCFARLANE

sighting in. "Sorry, Raff. I changed my mind. You're going to be too hard to explain," he said.

I fired without hesitation, my bullet plowing into Leonard's right shoulder, spinning him around. He had a look of surprise on his face as he fired uncontrolled into the barn wall. I stumbled through the clutter and closed the distance between us. Fighting through the pain, he attempted to track my progress but the weapon's recoil got the better of him.

Rounding the back of his truck, I caught a grimace on his face as he dropped the rifle and pawed at his holster. "Give it up, Cal. Your shoulder's ruined," I said.

"You're not taking me in, Biggs," he said, somehow managing to get his pistol into his hand. "You know what jail would do to a guy like me."

I launched myself at Cal, covering the last few feet with my arms outstretched and focused on his gun hand. With manacles on my wrists, it was a difficult fighting position but he dropped his pistol on impact, choosing instead to wrestle his way to freedom.

As real brawls tended to be, our fight was inelegant and brutal. Leonard bashed at my battered face with his left forearm. Blood sprayed across the small space between us as wavy explosions of light and pain clouded what vision I had left. In turn I jammed my hand into his wounded shoulder, twisting and grinding at the broken collar bone. Both of us howled in pain. Leonard was strong, but too many steak dinners and too much beer had softened him.

I twisted and flipped Cal over backwards, placing my knee on his neck as he tried to roll out from under my attack. Cal quickly recognized that his window for success was closing again and he bucked, tossing me to the side. He pushed to his knees and searched for his weapon. I took advantage of his shift in focus and moved around behind him, looping the manacle chains around his neck and pulling enough to get his attention.

"Give up, Cal," He continued to struggle forward, his fingers inching toward the gun he'd dropped. I snapped the chains and fell back onto the barn floor, pulling him on top of me.

Instinctively, he reached for the chain with his good hand, but I held tight, weathering his frantic thrashing movements.

"Never," he croaked, bringing his fist down onto my wounded thigh. I suppose I had Bobby Quinn to thank, but after being tortured for a long time, pain becomes relative. White-hot agony registered all the way up my spine, but the feeling just wasn't that new for me. I gave another tug on the chains around Leonard's throat and he started to go limp.

I loosened my grip on the chains, but only enough so that he could breathe. If he continued to fight, I'd just keep choking him out.

"Biggs?" Raff called from somewhere on the other side of the truck.

"Yup," I answered. "How bad are you hurt?"

"A couple of good hits," Raff answered. "I think I'll live, though. What's going on with Cal? You kill him?"

"No," I answered.

"I was wrong about you," he said.

For some reason, the statement just caught me as funny. I was in a ridiculous amount of pain but was riding a wave of adrenaline. I chuckled and found I couldn't stop.

"You're okay, too, Raff," I said.

"Are you really dating Faith?" he asked.

I lay there for a few seconds, thinking about Raff's question as Leonard started to regain consciousness and struggle against me. "You move, I'll choke you out again," I growled.

"I mean, it's okay and all," Raff continued. "I know she'll never have me again. And I just want you to know I think you'd be good for her."

Leonard, still stretched out on top of me, groaned. "Oh, for Pete's sake," he said, his voice hoarse.

"Thanks, Raff," I wasn't sure that getting permission from Faith's abusive ex was something I needed or wanted, but Raff was probably in the middle of some serious soul searching. Getting shot up will do that to a person.

The wind outside shifted, bringing with it the sound of sirens.

"You hear that?" Raff asked. "I think they're here. How do you suppose they knew where to come looking for us?"

I didn't answer. I lay back in the dirt, keeping my focus on Cal. A couple minutes later, I heard the familiar sound of clicking nails on wood. Diva's nose nudged against my head and a big pink tongue scraped painfully against my face.

"We have wounded in here," I heard a woman whose voice I didn't recognize shout. "Hey. Stop! You can't go in there. This is a crime scene."

"Stop me," Faith's voice answered. "Diva's over here. She must have found Biggs."

"Get Raff," I called out. "He's by the front door. He's been shot."

Faith stepped into view, her tall figure backlit by the afternoon sun that flooded through the blown-out side of the barn. She carefully picked her way through the debris. From beneath her cowboy hat, long sandy-blond hair lifted in waves as a breeze blew it over her shoulder. She looked back and forth, moving around the SUV until she stopped, catching sight of me still holding Leonard in place.

"Oh, damn," she said, taking in the situation. She turned and waved her long arms. "Detective Cropsie, we need help!"

The state patrol detective appeared a moment later next to Faith. "Officer Hardy," she called.

The much larger figure of Gigantus appeared next to the diminutive detective. He shook his head as we made eye contact. I got the feeling he had fully expected to find me at the bottom of the pile.

"Gigantus," I said. "There's a rifle above my head, a .357 pistol near my hip and a .38 Special – I think – under the truck. Leonard is conscious, but I got him for the moment."

His eyebrows lifted at my nickname. "Call me Otto," he said, stepping next to me. He removed two of the three guns that were in plain sight and handed them to Detective Cropsie. When he turned back, somehow Leonard had found the .38 special I'd dropped. Gigantus didn't even flinch. He simply leaned down, wrapped his meaty hand around Leonard's and forcefully removed the gun.

Two more state patrol officers arrived and at Cropsie's bidding, lifted Leonard off me, cuffed him, and led him outside.

Faith knelt down and wrapped her coat around my chest. I closed my eyes. The scent of her and the residual warmth in the leather enveloped me. It felt like Christmas morning and for a moment, the pain in my body was forgotten. Diva seized on that moment to wriggle in next to me, forgetting her cop duties completely.

"I'm not sure we have keys for those," Cropsie said, crouching and pointing at the manacles that held my wrists together.

"You should check out Norm Bobbins at Bard's Auto in Wood Creek," I said, trying to focus because I didn't want to forget the information I needed to give her.

"Oh?" Cropsie asked.

"Yeah, he does the maintenance and has access to the GPS systems in the cruisers," I said. "Plus, I think Diva got a hit on him when I bought gas the other day. Bring in a K-9, the drugs would probably be enough to get a search warrant so you could look into his online activities."

Cropsie smiled. "We'll probably do just that."

An EMT walked up behind Cropsie and Faith. "I'm going to need to get in there," he urged.

"Faith, help me up. I can walk," I said. "Did you find Raff?"

"I'm over here, Biggs," Raff called, his voice had a distinctly sing-songy sound to it. "They got me stuck with some IV and I'm feeling nooo pain."

"Are you sure?" Faith asked, as I leaned heavily on her in an attempt to gain my feet. Detective Cropsie took a quick step forward and Diva's hackles went up. Cropsie's eyebrows came down and she gave Diva a sharp *tsk*. Properly cowed, Diva twisted her head to the side and backed off. I didn't blame her. I was intimidated by Cropsie, too.

"Sir, you don't look so good. You should sit," the EMT said. "Let me get a gurney over here."

My head swam and I backed up so I could lean against Leonard's truck. I shook my head and pushed off. "You get Raff to the hospital," I said and took off through the rubble, firmly holding onto Faith.

"Are you sure, Biggs? You look really bad," Faith said.

"You did right, calling State Patrol," I said ignoring her question. I'd get to the hospital soon enough, but what I really wanted was a breath of fresh air.

"Wasn't me," Faith said. We stepped from the barn into the field that was quickly filling with emergency vehicles. "It was them." She pointed across to where Morty and Denholm leaned against the broad trunk of a vintage 1980's Oldsmobile.

I woke to the rhythmic beeping of a hospital monitor and slowly opened my eyes. I'd agreed to spend the night but had waived off the aggressive pain management the doctor recommended. As the room came into focus, I became aware of Faith lying next to me, her narrow body occupying a tiny portion of the already small bed. Her arm lay over my chest and I could feel the warmth of her against my side. I turned and gently kissed her forehead.

I heard movement across the room and I smiled as I discovered Pearl asleep in a recliner next to the window. I didn't have to look far to find Pappi, awake in the chair next to her. He nodded in acknowledgement.

"When did you get in?" I asked, my whisper sounding foreign to my own ears.

"Couple of hours ago," Pappi answered. "They really tuned you up, Henry. I'm sorry I put you into this. I never even thought it possible that Cal would be on the wrong side of it."

"Looks worse than it is," I said, trying to broaden my smile. I stopped because it hurt too badly. What I said was true – mostly. I had a long list of contusions, deep bruises and several loose teeth, but nothing was broken and I'd heal. The worst injury was my leg wound, which Bobby Quinn, his mom and Leonard had used to inflict pain. They had made a mess out of what was already going to be an ugly scar.

Pappi chuckled. "I doubt that."

"You should take Pearl over to the Sage and Rosemary Inn and get a good night's sleep," I said.

Faith stirred, my whispering causing her to wake. I stroked her hair and she snuggled into my side.

Pappi shook his head. "Only a few hours to daylight. See if you can catch a couple more hours. We'll be here when you wake up."

I scooted to the side and pulled Faith closer, giving her a better purchase on the bed. In the process, I ended up detaching a lead which caused an alarm to start warbling. Frantically, Pearl jumped in and worked to reattach the clip. She met with success only a moment before a nurse showed in the doorway.

"Everything okay in here?" she asked, frowning slightly at Faith's presence in the bed. To her credit she didn't push the matter.

"We're good," I said.

Sun was just peeking through the window when I woke to find Faith extracting herself from my arms and slipping from the bed.

"Don't go," I urged, already missing her company.

She pushed long sandy hair from her face and leaned over, searching my face for a safe place to kiss. She finally found a spot on my forehead.

"You have a visitor," she said.

Detective Roseland Cropsie from the State Patrol stood in the doorway.

"Detective Cropsie, what's going on?" I asked, knowing she wasn't at the hospital at seven thirty in the morning for a social call.

"We received a tip that I wanted to run past you. I'm afraid it's time sensitive," she said, looking apologetically at Pearl, who'd awakened and was looking around, somewhat confused.

"I'll be back in a few minutes," Faith said and brushed past Cropsie to leave the room.

"What's up?" I sat up and pulled at the leads on my chest, setting off the alarms again.

"Henry, you need to wait for the doctor to come by," Pearl admonished, but she walked over and flicked off the alarms all the same. We'd spent enough time in hospitals to know how to silence monitors.

Before Cropsie could talk, a nurse showed up at the door, her lips pursed into a frown. "Mr. Biggston, you need to lie back down."

"Give us a minute, would you?" Cropsie asked.

The nurse shook her head but left without further complaint. Her body language suggested she'd run into Cropsie before.

My hand shook as I carefully pulled the tape off the IV needle and slid it from my arm.

Cropsie pulled a small notepad from her purse and looked at it. "Yesterday, we received a tip about your shooter from the other day near the station. I wanted to run the information by you. I don't think I have enough for a warrant," she said, closing the door behind her.

"Oh?"

"State Police ran a radio spot saying we were looking for an older-model white pickup in connection to a shooting case. We got a call early this morning," she said. "The caller suggested that Rick Husenick's wife has been buying a lot of gauze and other large wound-treating materials. This person also believed her husband has a white, Chevy C-10. Is that the model?"

"It could be," I said. "I didn't get a good look at the front."

"The judge won't give us a warrant if you're not sure."

"You don't need a warrant," I said. "Butte County has two vehicles in Husenick's lot. Just say you need to look at them. Once you're in the lot you can look for that truck."

"Do you think Rick Husenick could be good for the shooting?" she asked.

"I don't know," I said. "Did he ever pass along to ISD that he found a second bullet hole in Deputy Lynch's vehicle? I told Leonard, but I imagine he didn't mention it."

"No," she said. "You're sure?"

"Yup." I slid off the bed and stood unsteadily. Pearl, seeing the potential for my doing a header, stepped in and gently grabbed my arm.

"What are you doing?" Cropsie asked.

"I'm going with you," I said, grabbing the fresh clothing Faith had picked up for me the night before.

"We don't need your help," she said as I crossed in front of her and headed into the bathroom. It was at this point I became aware of the fact that my hands had been traumatized enough that I was going to have trouble getting dressed.

"I'm coming anyway," I said.

Through the door I could hear a muted conversation between Cropsie and Pearl. A couple moments later, Faith's voice was added and then I heard a knock at the door.

"Biggs?" Faith called. "Can I come in?"

"Sure," I answered, holding the hospital gown in front of the underwear I'd just managed to pull on.

"What are you doing?" she asked, closing the door behind her. "That detective is all riled up."

"Help me?" I asked. Faith gave me a quizzical look. "I'm having trouble gripping things. Doc said I'd have that until the swelling went down."

"What do you need?" Faith asked.

"Help me put my clothing on," I said.

"Are you leaving?"

"Cropsie has a line on that sniper." Faith nodded and proceeded to help me with my clothing.

By the time we exited the bathroom, Pappi had returned, carrying several coffees.

"Hold on there, son. You're in no shape to be going anywhere," Pappi said. I could tell his words echoed the thoughts of both Cropsie and Pearl.

"I'm checking out," I said, not looking for an argument.

"I'm not going to stop you, but if you come, you're a civilian. Do you copy?" Cropsie said.

"Loud and clear, Detective."

Without another word, Cropsie left the room, pulling a phone from her belt.

"I can take you, Henry," Pappi said, recognizing that I wasn't about to change my mind.

"Why don't you and Pearl go over and get checked in at the Sage and Rosemary. Make sure to tell Morty who you are and they'll set you up with a nice room. I won't be far behind. State Patrol isn't going to let me get too close. I just want to see this through."

"Be careful," he said.

Pearl sucked in a breath and was about to object.

"I gotta go." Without giving her a chance to respond, I turned and exited into the hallway.

"I'm coming too," Faith said, catching up as I walked past the nurse's station.

"I was hoping you would. I don't think I have a car," I said.

Her truck was parked close by and while I wasn't sure I needed it, I was grateful for her help. She pulled from the parking lot and started driving without asking for instructions.

"We're going to Rick's Body Shop," I added unnecessarily, as a group of state patrol cruisers turned north in front of us with lights on but no sirens.

"I caught that," Faith said.

I grinned but didn't respond. A couple minutes later, we arrived in the parking lot in front of Rick's.

"Probably best if you stay with the truck."

"I'll be here." She leaned over and kissed my cheek.

I opened the truck door, grateful that my smile and grimace probably looked like the same thing.

Fresh air does a lot to revive a person. I limped over and caught up with Cropsie and five large troopers. "Rick runs this place with his wife. We're looking for an old white pickup truck with bullet holes in the cab. I'm pretty sure I tagged the passenger."

Rick's wife, Dawn, met us at the shop door before we could enter. "Rick's not here right now," she said. Her eyes were bloodshot with sleep-deprived bags beneath them.

"When will he be back?" Cropsie asked, pushing around the lead troopers.

"Out of town for a few days," she said.

"Dawn, we need to look at Shephard's car," I said, stepping around. "There are some details Detective Cropsie wanted to clear up." I couldn't help but notice she wouldn't make eye contact with me.

"I suppose that's okay," she said. "Just stay out of the rest of the yard. Rick doesn't like people walking around."

"Sure," I said, knowing full well that once we had access to the yard, there would be little she could do to stop us from wandering.

"I've got blood," a trooper announced. While we'd been talking, he'd opened a trash dumpster and pulled out a wad of bloody gauze.

"Get out of there," Dawn exclaimed. "Rick hurt himself a couple days ago. That's nothing. You need to leave."

Cropsie sucked air in through her teeth. "Mrs. Husenick, I'm detaining you to perform a probable cause search of your property for evidence of a recent shooting. I have it on good authority that the shooter who fled the scene in an attempted murder was wounded. If we find evidence to support this, you will be charged as an accessory after the fact unless you come clean, right now."

"You can't do that," Dawn protested.

Cropsie pulled handcuffs from her belt and grabbed Dawn's wrist, twisted her into submission, and cuffed her. "Search the house and the yard. The subject we're looking for is presumed armed and dangerous."

"No," Dawn cried. "Stop."

"She didn't know anything about it," Rick's voice called from within the building. "I'm coming out. I'm unarmed."

The state troopers moved quickly into action and after a few tense moments, had Rick in custody.

"Check his left arm," I said.

"Took a damn chunk out of me," he said.

"Quiet, Rick," Dawn ordered, turning on him. "You damn fool."

"They're gonna find the truck, Dawn," he said. "But I got info they need on Leonard. We'll come out all right."

Cropsie and I watched as Rick and Dawn were led away and placed into separate patrol vehicles. "You'll be glad to know the board cleared you on the shooting of Luca Quinn," Cropsie finally said. "You and the rest of the patrol staff will be on paid leave until I complete the investigation into Cal Leonard."

"When do you think that'll be?" I asked.

"Longer than you'd like, but shorter than it should be," she said evasively. "I understand you visited with Char Shephard. How deep is she in this?"

I shook my head. "I'm not sure," I said. "I think Leonard had her pretty messed up. She's already paid a heavy price for whatever her part of it was."

Cropsie nodded. "We trust juries to sort that out," she said. "It's a problem when officers decide to take on that role, too."

I sighed. "Copy that, Detective."

"I'll need you to come by tomorrow morning for an interview," she said. "There are some details I don't quite have nailed down."

I laughed. "You and me both," I said. "Leonard said he was sitting on a couple million in cash. Did you find it?"

"I don't believe that's the case. Calvin Leonard was eight months behind on his mortgage and deep in debt," Cropsie said. "Only reason his house wasn't foreclosed on is because the banker was an associate.

I opened five other investigations on the banker for similar issues. We're just at the start of this thing."

I shook my head. I'd genuinely liked Cal and was disappointed. "See you tomorrow?" I asked.

"Whenever you're up," she said. "I'll be in the office first thing."

I nodded and walked back to Faith's truck.

"Rick Husenick was the guy who shot at us? I went to school with him," Faith said as I climbed in. "I can't believe he'd try to kill me."

"Sounds like Leonard had something on him," I said.

———

"Pearl, when will you and Lester be headed back to Sutherland?" Denholm asked.

She sat next to him at the great table he and Morty had assembled in Sage and Rosemary's event room. A week had passed since the events at the Quinn ranch and Pappi and Pearl had been living on the Inn's second floor. She had arranged a dinner and invited Faith and her daughter April to join us, along with Morty and Denholm.

Pearl placed a hand over Denholm's and smiled warmly. "We've very much enjoyed your hospitality. Lester and I will be leaving tomorrow morning but will be back in a couple of weeks to take care of some unfinished business."

"Unfinished business? As in, the probate hearing for the Quinn farm?" Morty asked, suddenly interested. Lester shifted uneasily in his chair. He didn't like other people knowing his business and had a natural aversion to reporters.

If it bothered Pearl, it was impossible to tell. She smiled in response. "Hannah was my niece. My parents are long deceased, as are my sisters, Susie and Jane. I don't believe there are any other claims."

"The property you live on in Sutherland," Morty continued. "That was your father's farm, right? He bought it after ..."

Denholm must have noticed Pappi's face turning into a frown, because he cut the conversation off. "Morty, enough. We're enjoying a nice meal with friends."

"I'm just curious," Morty said, offering an unrepentant grin.

"There's no mystery," Pearl answered. "After my parent's divorce, Dad started over in Sutherland."

"Will you sell the Quinn property then?" Morty asked.

"We don't know," Pappi answered, irritation creeping into his voice.

"Between that farm and the ranch, it's a nice piece of land," I said, helping myself to more stuffing and gravy. "I think you'd get more if you sold them as one, especially the way the ranch side backs against the national forest."

Pearl smiled. "Well, dear, I imagine that all depends on what your plans are." I felt Faith's hand come to rest on my good thigh, under the table.

"Mine?" I asked incredulously. "What's that got to do with anything?"

"Now it gets good," Morty chuckled, clearly seeing a problem I didn't.

"You've accomplished what you came to Butte County for," she said. "Deputy Lynch's murder is solved and the criminals are in jail. What are you doing next?"

April reached over and grabbed my hand. Her cold, thin fingers gripped hard, demanding my attention. "Are you going back home? Are you going to leave us?" she asked innocently.

On my other side, I felt Faith squeeze my leg, reassuringly. "April, don't," she said quietly. "Biggs has been through a lot."

The table had grown quiet and I could feel everyone's eyes on me. I looked around the table at my family, both old and new. I reached under the table and brought Faith's hand up in my own for April to see.

"I'm not going anywhere, April," I said. "I made a commitment to Butte County. With Gene promoted to acting sheriff, I've been appointed first deputy. We're already short people. I couldn't leave even if I wanted to."

"Do you want to leave?" April asked, her voice small and carrying hurt. I found it surprising how much I cared what she thought and how her words cut straight to the heart of things. Faith shifted uncomfortably next to me and was about to admonish April again when I stopped her.

"You're right, April," I said. "I don't want to leave Butte County for other reasons. The two most important reasons are sitting on either side of me."

"I'll drink to that," Morty said enthusiastically, raising his glass.

I clinked my beer with Faith's wine glass.

"I'm sorry, Pearl, I know you were hoping I'd come back to Sutherland," I said.

"A young man needs to make his way. We've only ever wanted you to find your place in this world. I'll be honest, I never considered Butte County, but it makes a certain amount of sense," Pearl answered. Then she gave me a meaningful smile. "Lester and I could be making some changes of our own."

"What kind of changes?" I asked.

"We've been thinking of selling the farm, Henry," Lester said. "We were going to talk to you about it first, but it's part of the bigger conversation. We weren't sure how attached you were to it."

I shrugged. "It's the only home I've ever really known, but I suppose that's just because of you guys. Are you looking at places in town?"

"Haven't really decided," he said.

"Wait. Are you thinking about the Quinn properties?" I asked. I had yet to see the farmhouse up close but had heard unflattering descriptions of it. Hannah Quinn and her boys had apparently done little maintenance on the property.

Lester shook his head but it was Pearl who spoke up. "No, dear. If you plan to stay in Butte County, Lester and I would like to have you take over the Quinn properties," she said. "It'd be a lot of work, but you're young and strong."

"But if you sell your house, where would you live?" I asked.

"Wait a freaking minute," Morty said, setting his wine glass down hard enough to spill half its contents.

"Mortimer?" Denholm said. "What is it?"

"There's a rumor that the bank already has a contract on Leonard's mansion," Morty said. "They're just waiting to clear title after foreclosure."

"You're not serious!" Denholm grinned at Pearl, who looked like the proverbial cat who'd eaten the canary.

But of course, that's another story entirely.

ABOUT THE AUTHOR

Jamie McFarlane is happily married, the father of three and lives in Lincoln, Nebraska. He spends his days engaged in a hi-tech career and his nights and weekends writing works of fiction.

Word-of-mouth is crucial for any author to succeed. If you enjoyed this book, please consider leaving a review, even if it's only a line or two; it would make all the difference and would be very much appreciated.

FREE DOWNLOAD

If you'd like to receive automatic email when Jamie's next book is available, please visit http://fickledragon.com. Your email address will never be shared and you can unsubscribe at any time.

For more information
www.fickledragon.com
jamie@fickledragon.com

ACKNOWLEDGMENTS

To Diane Greenwood Muir for excellence in editing and fine word-smithery. My wife, Janet, for carefully and kindly pointing out my poor grammatical habits. I cannot imagine working through these projects without you both.

To my beta readers: Carol Greenwood, Barbara Simmons, Linda Baker, Matt Strbjak, Kelli Whyte and Nancy Higgins Quist for wonderful and thoughtful suggestions. It is a joy to work with this intelligent and considerate group of people. Also, to my advanced reading team, you're a zany, fun group of people who I look forward to bouncing ideas off.

Finally, to Elsa Mathern, cover artist extraordinaire.

4. On a Pale Ship

Witchy World

1. Wizard in a Witchy World

2. Wicked Folk: An Urban Wizard's Tale

3. Wizard Unleashed

Guardians of Gaeland

1. Lesser Prince

51382621R00154

Made in the USA
Columbia, SC
18 February 2019